T0165510

WATER SONGS

Seven Short Sagas

T K Wallace

ARCHWAY
PUBLISHING

Illustrations by C J Applegate

This is a work of fiction. All of the characters, names, incidents,
organizations, and dialogue in this novel are either the products
of the author's imagination or are used fictitiously.

Archway Publishing books may be ordered
through booksellers or by contacting:

Archway Publishing
1663 Liberty Drive
Bloomington, IN 47403
www.archwaypublishing.com
1 (888) 242-5904

Because of the dynamic nature of the Internet, any web addresses or
links contained in this book may have changed since publication and
may no longer be valid. The views expressed in this work are solely those
of the author and do not necessarily reflect the views of the publisher,
and the publisher hereby disclaims any responsibility for them.

Any people depicted in stock imagery provided by Getty Images are
models, and such images are being used for illustrative purposes only.
Certain stock imagery © Getty Images.

ISBN: 978-1-4808-6841-0 (sc)
ISBN: 978-1-4808-6842-7 (e)

Print information available on the last page.

Library of Congress Control Number: 2018910997

Archway Publishing rev. date: 10/08/2018

Contents

Water Songs 1

Swimming Crater Lakes

Something Wonderful

Swimming Crater Lakes

by

T K Wallace

Once I had a client who wanted to swim volcanic lakes. The island he wanted was Flores, which is a volcanic island, and there are three crater lakes.

Mr. Kent asked me to arrange passage, because that's what I do for him, and some others. I create travel and passenger 'arrangements' world-wide. This client is royalty. He requires me to travel with him in order to handle issues as they arise.

Traveling to Indonesia was a matter of getting to four airports on time. Kennedy International in New York City, Changi airport in Singapore, Won Pat Airport in Guam, and Jakarta's Hatta airport on Flores Island, Indonesia.

Despite what lord Kent wanted, this was not to be a short trip. Kennedy to Singapore can take twenty to forty hours depending how you book the flights. Singapore to Guam can take another twelve to twenty hours, Guam to Jakarta is another twelve to sixteen hours, and Jakarta to Ende airport is six to ten hours. This is a possible fifty to eighty six hours of travel.

When traveling long distances most people like to rest. While flying to Singapore you may get some sleep time on the plane. Once in Guam, you check-in to a hotel and wait for the Jakarta flight the next day. When you get to Jakarta, you need lodging to await the flight to the Regency. When you finally get to the Ende airstrip, you still have a hour drive to your destination. So, four to five days elapse in travel. The expenses of travel for Mr. Kent, his valet, his young passenger, and myself, with lodging, and food for a week, ground transport, and return flights, comes to about $30,000.00 USD, before they go swimming.

Our entourage is headed by Mr. Edward James George Oscar Kent, or the Lord of Kent. His small traveling companion is female. She also has a string of names before her preferred 'given' name of Harriet. She is a fit and lively young girl who speaks rather well for a teenage person. The valet, Herbert, is necessary to Lord Kent's wardrobe and whim.

I am expected and permitted to execute the plans I have initiated, approved, and arranged. I go by the name of Bruce.

Our destination is a dormant volcano, Mt. Kelimutu, which has three lakes. Lake 'Ala Polo', named, 'Bewitched or Enchanted' by the locals, is fed from the upwelling of volcanic waters. The water is most usually bright blue, but the steaming fumaroles, the 'upwelling waters' can change the color to a rich red.

To the east, lake 'Twui Kootainuamuri', is known as the lake of 'Men and Maidens'. It is only one hundred feet away, but about two hundred fifty feet lower, and the second largest. The color of the water is blue green and seems stagnant. The lake is fed from volcanic springs and cracks in the earth's crust.

Lake Ata Butu is the lowest and downstream a thousand feet away. This is the 'Old People's Lake'. It is closer to the villages and the crater sides are not as steep. This lake is filled from the run off for the upper lakes and the volcano. It has the darkest water of the three lakes. Laden with sediment, the water is also cooler. Fumaroles do change the water, but it's never a bright color.

I reserved rooms at the best lodging available. We agreed to meet for dinner, and then we all immediately slept for several hours. Travel takes its toll. But, the more you travel the easier it becomes. I was up and out before the others had found their slippers. I ordered afternoon trays of tea and cakes for the Royals. They were both appreciative. His lordship invited me to a working dinner.

That evening at dinner we sat for the first time as a group. Lord Kent sat at the head of the table with Harriett at his right hand. I sat across from her. Looking closely I realized she was a 'little person', and although young, not quite as young as I thought. When she spoke it was obvious that she was older than I had assumed.

After desert I spread out the aerial photos. "These are the crater lakes of Kelimutu."

"Yes, and there are hopes they have healing properties," said lord Kent.

Harriett looked at the maps and said, " Fascinating ."

I could only shrug and wait for more.

His lordship commented "The botanists say the Island is the place where things grow much larger than normal. 'Giant-ism', as they call it, is common here."

"How so?" I asked.

"There are gigantic examples all around you. Look at the flowers, the trees, and some of the native animals. They are huge. Did you know the Komodo dragon comes from here? Here on Flores Island, this lizard grows over twelve feet long,"

Lady Harriett smiled and said, "His Lordship is hopeful my size is a medical condition which may be cured. We'll see, I feel normal enough".

I upped her age to twenty five.

She continued, "Ok Eddie, we'll give it a try. I'll swim the lakes, but you must swim too."

The gov'ner blinks, "That wasn't part of the idea. It was just for you."

"See here, you're the one who wants me to grow larger." She looks at me, "Mr. Green, how old would you say I am?"

I scanned her closely, actually looking for the first time.

"I know I listed you as a child for travel purposes, but now that I look closely, I couldn't say . . . . ."

She applauded, "How prudent of you not to venture a guess. I am almost twenty three years old and still being regarded as if I'm still growing."

"Which you are." piped in Lord Kent.

"Yes I am, and I am getting used to being smaller than others. My future husband hopes I will grow larger. That is why I have decided that we will both swim the lakes, in the hope of growing together. Okay Eddie ?"

Lord Kent agreed. "Yes quite, Now Mr. Green, how do we go about this?"

I spread the photographs about the table. "As you can

tell, I've done the field work on this unusual idea. This lake is our first destination."

Lord Kent was excited, "It's quite beautiful isn't it my dear?"

She said, "The crater looks rather steep."

I confirmed, "Well, it is a challenge. And even more so, now that I hear two people want to swim. Is that right? The both of you wish to swim?"

Eddie nodded, "Apparently so. Yes, if that is my bride's wish, so be it. Can it be arranged ?"

"Well, yes, but a question first, just for clarity, You both wish to swim these lakes at the same time, umm, together ?"

"Yes, that is what I wish," says Harriett.

I ask, "Must you swim all three lakes on the same day? Because what I have in mind can't happen that quickly. But, you will be able to swim a new lake every second or third day, depending on the weather. In fact, the rest between may be better for you ?"

Eddie agrees, "A much better idea, It will give us every opportunity to judge the effect."

Harriett watches him and then blinks, smiles. "Oh Eddie, I do worry so."

"What worries you my dear?"

She pauses and then smiles as she answers, "We shall see what we shall see. I refuse to borrow trouble or be dismissive of other people's beliefs. I have seen too many miracles in my life."

"Last questions then, Do you actually want to swim

or do you just want to submerge your selves in the water of the lakes? Ah, pardon me m' Lord, I've never asked, can you swim?'

"Good questions, one and all. Easy to see why you're here Bruce, eh, my dear?"

Harriett answers for them both, "I swim quite well, and I to tend to float when not 'underway'. His Lordship closely resembles a retriever while he is paddling about."

Eddie objects, "It gets me where I'm going! At least my head is up, and I can see."

"Yes dear, Mr. Green, does that answer your question. Do you have any more?"

"No, not at this time. Please grant me leave to proceed with my tasks ?"

I excused myself from the table and walked away mumbling to myself. There were so many new ideas to consider my brain felt urgency from all sides. Then I realized that the urgency was not mine. So I took a deep breath and proceeded calmly, What's the first challenge?

They want to swim together in the lakes, privately, and then be extracted. Is the water safe? Asking locally about swimming was as good as it would get. If the local people swam there with no ill effect, it was safe for others to swim.

The bright fresh sunlight will require some protection. There must be an organic mix of Aloe and Coconut oils preferred by the locals.

Do they realize that crater lakes are usually surrounded by rather steep sides? Will they wish to walk down several hundred feet of pathways to the water? And then hike back out?

Considering universal access to swim the waters of three volcanic crater lakes brought the transportation aspects to a crescendo of cymbals in my mind.

We needed a helicopter capable of safely lowering two people down a length of steel cable. In this manner, the couple may swing from the helicopter onto the swim platform prepared and waiting for them. When finished they must be hoisted up and flown out.

Obviously we needed a fully covered luxury floating raft. While in the water, this sun protected enclave, must float with enough stability enabling a human to swim to and from, entering and exiting as they please. The raft should be a small water cottage with a swim platform and a few steps. It could be air dropped the day before, used for the day of swimming, and then relocated twice.

"Ah well, what's a little more work? Arrangements are my specialty . . ."

The royals were briefed and informed that we needed some time to pull together the various aspects of their request. They agreed to go sky hopping the commercial centers of Indonesia. So I created a shopping package which would take them a week to complete. They toured by plane and shopped by car and on foot while I worked.

I found a pilot with the proper heli-bird. She agreed to do the job if we outfitted her craft with a new heavy duty tracking arm and the extra winch for backup drops and picks. I agreed with cash, so we proceeded directly to a service contract. The captain was named Shely; short for Shellington.

Her bird, the Genevieve, was part of a search and rescue fleet which was always in need of additional funding. As you may imagine, search and rescue doesn't pay too well in this part of the world. Shely was chief pilot and the aircraft was her bird. She dictated and supervised the installations personally. Happily, I was always welcome for inspection and consultation.

"So, Bruce," Shely remarked one afternoon as she wiped her hands, "We're gonna play Dunk the Rich kids with these two?"

"Spot on, Shely. They want to go play in the water in their own way. And we will make it happen, safely I hope."

"What did you find for a swim platform ?"

"An offshore deluxe life raft. The kind used to outfit the big yacht. I can get one here in two days for us to inspect and rig to fly. It houses up to ten with all the bells and whistles."

"Ten? Why ten people?"

"Well, there's Lord Kent, Lady Harriett, Myself, and a lake diver."

"You and a diver?"

"I appropriated a crew member from the yacht to act as a diver. Tommy is coming with the raft."

"Sounds pretty cushy."

"Of course, You don't think 'the Gov'ner' and his Lady would actually know how to do anything do you? As for the boat boy / diver, if anything happens in the water, you surely don't think I'm the best one to assist."

"No, I suppose not, but it's probably a good thing to have you there. Are you going to handle the passengers and disconnect the line?"

"That was my plan, then reconnect it later so you can reel them up?"

"Ab-So Pos-So. So okay, We plotz the raft down way before we air lift the swimmers. You and the diver need to go with the raft earlier in the day right?"

"The yacht boy Tommy, will go with the raft and stay. I'll go down the cable before the Royals on the morning of each day. Someone up top will hook them in, and manage them for the drop. I'd like to use Herbert, they know him."

"As long as my crew is right behind yours to make sure he gets it right, I'm planning to rehearse the drop on dry land before we do the first one over water,"

I was relieved, "It's good to see eye to eye, we think alike on safety and procedure. But it is also good to also have an accord. Is it a deal then?"

Shely takes my hand and we seal the deal.

———⚬∽⚬⚭⚬∽⚬———

I get another Shely hand shake in the cockpit of the Genevieve as I prepare to drop. Tommy is already down and watching from the raft below. The breeze had dropped inside the crater which made for greater stability, but the noise was louder.

The hook was waiting for me to be clipped in. The jump chief says, "Okay, just like we rehearsed, I'm lifting you. Then you move outside to begin your descent. Tommy has the entire side and top open for you, Here we go."

I was lifted off the deck, the door slid back and the powerful new unit tracked out into space. The airman yelled, 'Clear', and the drop began at a slow rate. It accelerated down before it slowed right over the side of the raft and Tommy's grasp. He brought me in as I held the cable and knelt down to create extra slack. Tommy unclipped and yelled 'Clear' as the hook began to rise again.

"Genevieve to Raft 1, Genevieve to Raft 1, on Marine VHF ch 22, copy?"

"Copy", I squawked in return,

"How are you guys likin' that floating bordello?"

"Tommy's a great catcher. All is well here, we will make it work."

"I'm off then, see you in a couple of hours. We'll be on the hand held."

As Shell turned the craft to go, Tommy mused, "She's good, eh?"

"Aye, seems to be' and we began to unpack the raft for inspection.

I found the most amazing chandler's stock of fine foods, there was even a choice of wines. The other comforts were deluxe as well. There were extra fins and masks, towels,

Coco / Aloe, and even sunglasses. We waited in style while being impressed that even our satellite phones worked.

————— wooerooteoow —————

The Genevieve is parked at the airstrip with the Royals undergoing instruction. They face one another in their custom made harnesses. The hook descends between them and Herbert hooks them both. Shely gives a thumbs up and they rise from the floor, track out the arm and slowly drop to the tarmac.

Shely congratulates them, "That was most excellent. We do it once for intelligence and twice for experience, okay?"

The Genevieve heli-bird floats in the air as the Royals are being attached to the hook. The wind from the rotor pushes everything aside, even words, which is why they use hand signals. The thumbs up is given, the arm tracks out, and the royals drop three feet to the ground they have been hovering above.

————— wooerooteoow —————

The Genevieve called and 90 minutes later she prepared to drop the two passengers already in harnesses and ready to descend.

The Lord and Lady look at one another as they are joined at the hook, Lady Harriett smiles at Lord Kent and says,

"Easy does it Eddie, just like the Captain and Herbert

had us rehearse. Everything is according to plan. Why not enjoy the moment?"

As the line slows, the two drop onto the half open raft. They kneel in order to be released, and off the hook goes again.

"Genevieve is monitoring channel 22 VHF. Call us 15 minutes before you need us and we'll be on station. Mahalo". She lifted the bird away slowly causing as little air wash as possible.

Lord and Lady were wearing the mini jump suits Shely had crafted for them. The jump suit was a short legged standard one piece with a hoisting harness sewn all over the outside. They shed these to reveal their own swimming attire.

When asked if they wanted masks or fins they declined and crawled forward. At the side of the raft no one but each other existed. Their love and caring for one another was natural, easy, and precious to behold. They smiled at one another, turned hand in hand and slid over the side.

At this time of year, Tiwu Ala Polo, the lake of Bewitched Enchantment, has a bright Blue color. This is due to many geological aspects, but none of them compared with the blue of Harriett's eyes. Eddie noticed it just as they jumped. Her eyes matched the water.

Harriett's eyes were full of Eddie, making sure he could swim enough to stay afloat. But she heard my loud query of, ' MADAM !'. As she turned, I threw a large circular float which she promptly shared with Eddie.

Eddie allowed his curiosity. "How do you feel?" he said to her.

She smiled and replied, 'By using my hands', and then she sank.

Eddie floated along and then suddenly twisted in the water.

'Something's got me!', he yelled and jerked even more.

Harriett surfaced and shook her hair. She looked at Eddie and lifted his shorts from the water. As he reached for them, she threw them over my head into the raft and then proceeded to disrobe. One piece followed another as the two of them bared all to the water.

They swam and played around a bit as I readied their apparel along the edge. The raft and ring seemed to be a winning combination. She led him a fair distance away from the raft before he showed any discomfort. I took that as a good sign. They had a good time with her as tease, and then him as tease with a good bit of splashing and laughing.

When they approached the raft their attire was tossed to them. Lady Harriett accepted a towel from Tommy and I had one ready for Lord Kent. As they relaxed and became acclimated to the raft, I showed them where to nosh. They were decidedly happy and took turns providing tasty tid bits for one another.

After some time Lady Harriett wondered aloud, "Bruce, does the raft turn?"

"Turn, Madam ?"

"As in pivot. You see the sun is setting over there. May one swivel?"

"Ah well, yes it should, so You can, well, face the sun, yes?"

"Precisely, can it happen?"

"Tommy, there were spare paddles in the kit weren't we?"

"Yes Mr. Green we have two just back here," he begins to hunt.

Visualizing at the manual in my memory, I recalled that each of the 8 angled sides had a weight which hung below for stability. We should be able to rotate. Tommy came forth with paddles. I cleared a space at each side close to the edge.

"Okay, now with the paddle on our right side we will be pull the water back along the edge, moving us to the right. Let's try it smooth for three strokes. Are we in place? Ready, steady, and go, and go, and go, now let's wait and see."

"By Gum Bruce, that seems to be working. Continue as you please."

"By all means m'Lord. Tommy let's give her three more strokes, and Go, and Go, and Go, now let's see. Ah look, we're almost there. Let's do Two more and that should do it."

And it did, we stopped dead center to watch the sun descend.

—ⱳⱷⱺⱺⱺⱳ—

"Genevieve to Raft 1. Genevieve to Raft 1. Do you read me?"

I answered, "Genny baby this is Raft 1, now facing south.'

'How come? We did a north side drop, why aren't we staying with that?'

"The boss wanted to face the sun."

"Oh Well in that case, uh, did you guys turn that by yourselves?"

"Sure did, you'd be surprised what can be accomplished using both brains and brawn. You ready to get us out of here?" Tommy alerts the Royals to get ready.

"Well, we could be ready if it weren't for the south side pick up."

"Okay, tell me when you're ready and I'll alert the guy who pays the bills."

"That would be us ready as of now, or any time in the near future, as the sun is going to set behind that ridge in a few minutes." Lord Kent gives a thumbs up.

"His Nibs, says to send the hook down and they'll be ready, getting into the lift suits now."

Lord Kent and Lady Harriett both dress over their swimming attire and they help one another get adjusted as we stand by for correction and assistance. They kneel as the hook swings onboard the raft. Tommy grabs the hook as I say,

"Big Hug." They do as Tommy snaps the hook through both harnesses. I give the thumbs up and off they go into the sky. We wait until the royals are aboard

Genevieve before we hear, "Passengers aboard, we're away, thanks."

Shely would be back in about 90 minutes so Tommy gathered the trash and I repacked the chattels. Raft 1 would be moved and used the following day.

With one more lift from the raft, Tommy and I were flown back as the evening deepened into night. Shely offered to drop us on a hotel balcony. I said no thanks, but considered the possibility of trying it during daylight. I slept well.

—————ᴡᴏᴄᴇᴛᴏᴏᴋᴇᴏᴏᴡ—————

Early the next day I was happy to see the lovers lying out on a tanning deck. They looked radiant as they baked. I hailed them,

"Ahoy there, you intrepid swimmers. I was rather pleased with yesterday's operation, You?"

His Lordship un-blinded himself as he sat up. I noticed his skin was red and asked,

"How long have you been out here?"

"About a half hour, Eh Harriett?"

She lowers a sun bounce screen and we see she was red too. So I recommended,

"It's time to turn your bodies over so you take the sun more evenly."

She was pleased, "Oh quite, and many thanks to you Bruce. We enjoyed yesterday so much, we'd like to do it again tomorrow, is that possible?"

"Very much possible m'Lady, just not in the same place."

"So, where then? The next lake over? The lake of Men and Maidens?"

"Yes in fact the floating habitat is being moved to Lake Kelimutu today."

Lord Kent asks, "Can we be facing the sun this time, eh, Bruce?"

"Of course, m'Lord, my mistake. Well, then, I'm all for tanning too."

I began to relax and realized that I had not asked the big question.

"How Do You Feel? Have you noticed any difference?"

I failed to ask both questions, actually none of my business, I should keep my head in the job, just take the next step, and full steam ahead with my contract. Such questions are rarely permitted.

I stayed and made sure they turned over a few minutes later. I bribed the sauna attendant re-do their shoulders, And I watched as they moved in and out of the pool. They seemed to be agile and fit. She handed him into the water and said,

"You need to learn to swim. I know you can float, on your back then."

Delighted, I sat to watch. She floated him face up and then face down.

I sat at the edge, kicked back, dangled my bare feet in the water.

"So what was the water like? I mean in the lake? Do you mind if I ask?"

Harriett answered quickly, "It was interesting. It felt good. Seriously good, like almost enriching, wouldn't you say Eddie? Oh," She helped him stand, "I soaked myself and I wanted the mineral content all over my skin, completely covering my skin. So, ... I got naked."

Lord Kent added, "Actually you got me naked first, and then you joined in, eh?"

"Yes dear you were first. But, inquisitive Bruce, you wonder don't you?"

I admitted, "Uhm Yes, I must admit I do. uh, wish to inquire, um, any changes ?"

"None that we can tell, perhaps if we swim again tomorrow?"

"Yes Sir, Yes Mam, and to help make that happen, if I may be excused."

"Very good. Bravo, all the right answers, See you later then. Dinner, eh?"

I sent Shely a text, "It's a go," and asked her to join me for brunch.

———⚬⚭⚬⚭⚬———

At 11am I was sitting on a balcony overlooking the ocean with Shellington.

"We're set for tomoorrow. Tommy and the raft are off to the second lake, just a little off center."

Curious, I asked, "Why off center? Off center which way ?"

"Further away for a longer sunset. You said they liked the sun yesterday?"

"Yes thank you for remembering. They liked it enough to ask for more."

"And so we let them swim the lake of Men and Maidens, and a long sunset."

"Yeah, we can get out there about 11, and then be back by 12;30 or one."

"'It would be faster if I landed to pick them at the hotel. They might like it better than traveling to the airport You'd look rather brilliant if you 'arrange' it."

"Is there room to land Ginny?"

"I've used the tennis courts before, less dust flying about, it's screened in."

"Maybe, I think they'd like it. I'll get back to you."

―――∿∾◦◠◡◉◠◡◦∾∿―――

As they descended onto the raft I hear a conversation concerning the color of the lakes. Ala Polo had turned pink and today's lake, Twui Muri, was a bright blue.

"Why do you think it is? Bruce why are the lakes different colors?"

"I think it geothermic activity from below. Let's ask Tommy."

"You mean volcanic activity." asked the Lord

Tommy replied, "Technically yes, but of a very low volume, just enough to change the water color. The water should be like yesterday, maybe a little warmer."

"Heat rising from the volcano?"

"Right you are, Yesterday's lake Ala Polo is even warmer. It's changing too."

"Then let's go while the time is right," she stuck a toe in the water, "I'm in," and slid over side.

Eddie waited until she surfaced. "Well let's see if I learned anything," and slid in beside her.

She distanced herself from the raft and treaded water to stay in place.

"Can you swim to me?" She asked wistfully,

"What do I get if I do?" he enjoined.

"A kiss as a reward, and the joy of learning something new, if you dare."

She reached out. Eddie pushed away and began to swim toward her. As she caught him he got a kiss and I got a smile of thanks. I threw them the ring float.

They cavorted. I believe that is the proper word, Cavorted. They were naked and happier than ever. Lady Harriett was treading water and Lord Kent was learning through play time. She would make a splash on either side of him and he would dodge and splash back. They looked the same size in the water.

Upon their return I was congratulated by a dripping Eddie.

"Well, done Bruce, You got the Sun in the right place,"

Harriett chimes in, "I told you he was clever."

"We do our best, Sir. And while we're going on about that, I would like to make a change in our return."

"Our return?"

"Yes dear. He said, our return."

I continue, "M'Lord how far is it to the airfield from the hotel ?"

"Well I don't know, Herbert usually takes care of the driver, you see."

"The distance is about 5 miles dear. I've watched along the way."

I offered, "How would you like to return to the hotel by air?"

She enjoins, "How delightful, can we? Where is the landing pad?"

Lord Kent guesses, "Maybe the beach?"

Lady Harriett dismisses, "Oh no. The beach is out. We couldn't do that to the other guests. No one likes sand blowing about."

Tommy says, "True Dat. Abso – No - No den."

I suggested, "The tennis court then?" and called The Ginny on radio.

"Shely? Can you arrange a helicopter drop off on the tennis courts? Okay let me know." To the Royals I say, "She'll call me back."

The royals smile. Lord Kent commented, "Marvelous, well done."

I ask, "How was your swim today? I see you learned some new skills."

"A good day that's for sure. Eddie can float, tread water, and swim."

He agrees, "And, I feel confident while I'm in the water. Understand, a non swimmer can never be quite comfortable. And now, I do, now that I can swim."

Lady Harriett says, "He's a natural 'on top' of the water, and doing quite well for a beginner."

Eddie asks, "On top, what does that mean, on top."

"Swimming on the top of the water, comes first, then you learn to swim under the water. After all when you dive, you must then swim underwater."

"Dive? Who said Dive? And this underwater swimming? Which comes first?"

"Be brave my love. Diving comes first, underwater swimming comes easily compared to what you have already learned, ..but,... here is a bit of a bug-a boo. I think we should begin again."

"Bug-a-boo?" asked Lord Kent

"Begin what again?" I asked.

"It's like this, The next lake is to be the last of the three, right? And you, my dear, have just learned to swim. Wouldn't you prefer to swim all three lakes?"

"Yes, yes I believe I would, uh, would prefer what you suggest. Ah, Bruce?"

Staring off into space, I said, "Just re-estimating, m'Lord. You wish to add two trips to the schedule?"

"Uh, Is that what we wish Dear?"

"Yes Eddie, and thank you dear. And thank you Bruce, for being quick about the idea."

Eddie joshes, "Fun is where we find it, eh what, m'Lady?"

She asks, "Do you think your Captain will mind?"

I reply, "If she does, I have the wrong Captain." The radio squawks,

"Raft 1, This is Genevieve."

"Speaking of whom . . Go ahead Genny."

"The concierge has gone scurrying to get us permission to land. I called the grounds master too, he's on board, we'll get by."

"Excellent, keep us informed on that. Now, a new matter, got a minute?"

"What's up Pup?"

"I'll call you." He picks up his phone, steps outside the canopy, and dials.

Shely answers, "Wha's up wich you, dog?"

"Our loving couple would like to begin their adventure again now that his nibs can swim. So they would like to re-start so he can swim in all three places."

The radio transmits, "Is that a fact?"

"It is the fact, Shellington, we will need to extend your contract several days, hopefully at the current rate. Tomorrow's raft relocation goes back to the original starting point of Ala Polo, oddly, the Lake of Bewilderment."

"I can do that, I can do ALL of that, Mr. Green, happy to oblige his liege."

"Be True and mighty forces will support you. Phone off. On radio."

As he steps inside we hear the radio, "Raft 1 Raft 1, this is Genevieve."

"Go ahead Genny."

"Hotel manager sends word. The court is in use but will be free in an hour."

"Thanks let me check. m'Lord, m'Lady, the Hotel manager, Mr Giest, has given us permission. We may use the tennis court for landing one hour from now."

"Brilliant, Bruce, well done, our regards and compliments to all, yes?."

"Of course sire. Now, can we be ready for pick up in 45 minutes?"

"Definitely, Harriett m'dear, that leaves us time for one more dip."

"Yes dear, Bruce, please give our compliments and proceed on schedule."

"Very good, Mam. Raft 1 to Genevieve, Come in."

"Raft 1 this is Genevieve, How now browning cow?"

"Our Guests will be ready for pick up in 45 minutes, Roger?"

"On my way. Genevieve Out."

To the Royals I say, "You're going back to the hotel; no airport drive."

Lord Kent muses, "I think, I will go straight into the pool."

Lady H. asks, "The indoor or the outdoor pool?"

"Let's start at outdoors and then work our way forward."

"Yes, in that case, I think I shall go into the Ocean first, just to feel the sand in my toes, Then on to the pools."

'Oooh that sounds much better. Sand, and Salt Water, and then a rinse off.'

'Maybe a cocktail at the indoor pool?'

'Definitely.' They stand musing and Lady Harriett says, 'Eddie?'

'Yes m'dear?'

She pushes him overboard and says, 'You're all wet.'

———ᴡᴏᴏᴇᴛᴏᴏᴛᴇᴏᴏᴡᴡ———

Later, on the pool deck Lady Harriett turned to me and commented,

"Bruce, were I to have one souvenir from this trip, it would be this suit."

"Yes m'Lady? Why is that?"

"Because it was custom made for me. I have an unusual body . . rah-thuh"

"Ah, of course, the suit is yours and yours alone. As is his lordship's suit. They are one of a kind, handmade for you, and yours to take as a memento."

"When I find something that fits, I buy several in different colors."

I had to laugh at the wisdom and personal maturity,

"Good one Madam, I'll pass that on. . . . . and shall I order them for you?"

"Yes please, I'll have four, and Eddie will want four as well, as a surprise."

"I'll speak with the manufacturer today."

Noticing Eddie is away, she asks, "Is the lake swimming re-arranged?"

"Underway as we speak, It will be ready for you tomorrow."

She smiled and winked at me. I stepped away as Eddie returned.

"Eddie, Bruce tells me that we're all set to start at Ala Polo again."

"Ah, that's good. Did, uh you speak with him about the jumpsuits?"

"Yes Dear, he said they were ours to keep. Eddie, we are starting again tomorrow."

"Yes, and swimming with you from the beginning."

"Beginning with safe simple ways of learning."

"My dear, let's linger in the outside pool, to you know, to practice?'

My phone rings and I glance to see Shely's name on the screen. "Excuse me while I take this." I listen to Shelly but watch the couple. Lady Harriett pinches Eddie's chin, whispers in his ear, then they smile, and then I interrupt.

"Our captain has agreed to extend the contract by four extra days." They nod and smile.

"Okay, then we're going to get wet." And they dash for the surf.

I went back to my ear piece and answered. "Aye Shely, we need to talk."

———~∾⊶⊶⊙⊷⊷∽———

I smile again as Shely and I overlook the tennis courts.

She offers a toast "Aye Aye, here's to the crafty rafty Captain."

'It's Captain now is it? Better call me Purser. I have orders for 8 more jumpsuits."

"Really, they liked them that much? You're a hell of a salesman, Mr Purser."

"Yes, His four in navy blue with the royal crest. The other four are probably two khaki and two white. Yes? Soft snaps and straps for her if you please."

"That would make them fit better,"

Her smile is inspiring. I smile in return and then go for it.

"I wonder, would we, fit ?'"

She seems to hesitate, and then says, "I've wondered the same thing."

"Good, then we'll see, take it slow, okay?"

She raises her glass, " I'll drink to that. To Us ? " We toast. " To Us ."

"So, nobody gave you any problems? Not even the grounds master?"

"Especially not him. He allows me to blow the court free of debris with my rotor wash. Claims he can never get it that clean."

"Most excellent, the hotel likes having royalty around eh?"

"That's the word, it will be used in some way, private referrals, low key exploitation I'm sure."

"Thanks for the accepting the extension, have you done the numbers?"

"A man after my own heart, yeh, is always good for my balance."

She rubs her fingers together in the universal sign of income.

I remind her, "I like to pay as we go, you know that."

"Counting on it."

Shely looks at him, slips her hand into a pocket, and pulls out 3 envelopes.

"Done, done, and done, three times. # 1 is the current fees. # 2 for the extension, and # 3 is for the new suits, she texted me."

I take them and put them in my valise.

"Aren't you going to look at them?"

"Oh I will, and most carefully, at my portable desk, as it is these days. If there are any questions, I will call and you can explain them to me, alright?"

"FBM. Cheers." She toasts. "Actually, there are a couple of things I'd like to discuss."

I extract the envelopes, "What's on your mind?"

"First of all, we contracted for two weeks. I'd like to be paid, that's envelope # 1."

I separate the envelope, "I'm sure you would, please continue,"

"The new contract began as of yesterday when the change order happened."

"And what will that cost his Lordship?"

"Envelope 2. An extra weeks pay."

"I estimated that, well, actually I estimated 14 days pay at five days a week. But I decided to throw in an extra day for luck."

"Good, once again we see Eye to Eye. So; about payment?"

"Yes, I anticipated that as well. I have a bit of a disappointment for you."

"Really, you haven't done so yet, Don't tell me well has gone dry."

"In local cash, yes. Gold is all I have until we get to a larger bank."

"I do gold. What denominations?"

"Ounces and half ounces. What's the rate today?"

They both pull out pocket links.

She says, "1,250 an ounce."

I say, "That makes it easy, let's go for a walk."

We walk through the hotel until I stop by the indoor pool.

"I'll just be a moment', I must access safe deposit."

I leave her and go see the manager.

For some reason, hotel managers tend to give better service when you advance a large sum of money to hold for you. They eagerly understand that we will require access to the funds for payment of expenses as they occur. When traveling abroad, I usually keep some cash but mostly gold, and then convert to local currency as we go. I withdrew twelve ounces in heavy gold coins.

As I emerged I found Shely watching the royals play in the pool. She turned as I approached,

"Here you are, 10 Ounces in African Kugerands, let's call it $12.5. That is Ten K for services rendered thus far, and another two and a half in advance."

"Many thanks, Mr. Green, a pleasure doing business

with you, and the lovely couple. The business is most welcome. But look there,"

"Alright, and, I would be looking at what . . . . other than your blue eyes."

"Bruce, focus. The Royals. They have been getting a bit of exercise. I mean, I suppose it's more than they usually get, right?"

"I suppose, they are normally quite active, why do you ask?"

Eddie swarms out of the pool and asks, " Bruce, do you have something we can dive for ?"

I give him a Krugerrand. He pitches it to Harriett and then jumps in.

Shely says, "Well, while watching them again, mind you, I was wearing my designer hat for the extra suits, I looked at them again and noticed a difference."

"In what way?"

"Well, they've both lost some weight."

"Have they?" I look again at the frolicking couple.

Shely says, "They have, I'd like to speak with them and arrange a new fitting, okay?"

"I don't see any problem there. They know you're the designer."

We watch the pool play include jumping and diving for the golden coin.

Shely muses. "You know she's right, don't you?"

I ask, "About what ?"

"About wanting to start over? To start over now that he can swim?"

"Yes, I suppose, but it wouldn't be an option I would be likely to present.'

Shely says 'You know she's smarter than he appears to be'

"Don't you mean, she's smarter than she -"

'I spoke most precisely. You'll see " She addresses the couple,

"M'Lord; M'Lady, a moment if I may?"

Shely goes toward them with her arms extended in welcome.

"I've just finalized business with Mr. Green and I am pleased with the decision of starting again with your lake adventures. You are swimming, and now I see you are diving."

Lord Kent splashes and says, "Harriett has taught me a diving song."

Lady Harriett blushes, "Now Eddie. .," but he can only sing,

"I Love to go swimmin' with bow legged women, and dive between their legs." He does so as Lady Harriett squeals and splashes, then adds,

"Captain Stewart, We do hope there was no inconvenience in the addition we requested."

"On the contrary, m'lady, as a client, I hated to see you go."

"So tomorrow we start again?"

"Tomorrow we start again."

"Shellington, watch me dive under again, eh?" Lord Kent dives, swims, and surfaces.

I could only say, "Well, done. I think you're ready."

Lady Harriett says, "It's been quite fun actually."

As they climb from the water Shely says.

"Remind me tomorrow to take new fitting measurements, okay?"

Lord Kent yells, "Captain, are you leaving so soon?"

"Yes m'Lord, work to be done? Ta Ta,"

I watch Shely as she exits and can only smile. I am attracted to her. She is a good person. It feels as if she is growing toward her potential. I like that about people. We have the ability to envision change, and sometimes, we even have the courage to make things happen.

This evening I must begin travel arrangements for our return. I also have to track down an underwater camera for his Lordship. I did not to point out that the lake water has so much sediment that he won't be able to see anything.

Herbert and I still met the Genevieve at the airport. One hotel pick up and drop off a day was enough. And, as it developed, the hotel was not enamored with the fact that these pick up / drop off arrangements needed to be extended, to twice a day, for three more days.

It was resolved by a personal visit from the royals to the management. First of all they thanked him for his courtesy and consideration. They thanked him for recently acting as banker for gold and currency exchange. Then they requested the tennis court. It's such fun to use formal titles and throw money at people, and then watching them go all funny or weird. They call it, The Royal Schmooze.'

All that got us the tennis court / heli-pad twice a day, with advance notice. Shely and the grounds keeper took care of the whole thing. The hotel even had a sign made declaring the area to be of alternative use at certain posted times.

———∿∿⋯⟡⟡⋯∿∿———

The first day of the second run found us boarding a smaller bird with the same winch system. I asked what was up, Shely said she was taking it for a test drive. We were lowered with more care. Tommy went first and then I came next.

"Hawk 1, Hawk 1, this Raft 2. We are aboard. You are good to go."

"Raft 2, we're away. First is the airport to change aircraft. Also, we are requesting a landing time from the hotel."

"Roger, does that mean you are not picking up the Royals in the new bird"

"Rodger dodger, you old codger. They get big bird Genevieve, and yes I'll fly 'em. Only the best for our customers."

"How long is the round trip now?"

"30 minutes, See ya then. Hawk 1, cruisin." She swoops away.

Some moments later as I am unhooking the Royals, I notice an unspoken feeling of goodwill aboard. Such positive vibrations are hard to refuse or ignore, after all, we had accomplished this feat before. We helped them disrobe down to swimming clothes. This time I preceded, by throwing the floating ring first.

"Have Fun, Call when you want the camera."

"Don't be silly Bruce, the camera is for the pool at the Hotel."

They dove together and swam to the float. That's when they went native.

And that's what made me realize that some things are too good to pass up.

When the Royals came up the swim ladder, we wrapped them in large fluffy towels and sat them in the sunset. Each lounge had a drink on the table. There was plenty of coconut / aloe butter to prep the skin, even their English skin.

As they watched the sun, Lady Harriett stretched and yawned into speech,

"The water felt great today. Eh Eddie? Better than the first day, yeah?"

"Remarkably so, it helps me reflect on how much better it feels to have some control in the water. That alone makes it better for me. As for the water, I did not notice."

"Well I noticed you, my aqua man, you swim with delight and enjoyment."

"Bruce, did you know that I can dive off the raft and swim up under the center of your floating ring?"

Joining the conversation, "I am delighted you are having a good time. We have two more to go. That call was from Captain Shely, she is approaching now."

"Most excellent, Bruce. By the way, have you begun

return arrangements? Can we return home any faster than we arrived?"

The radio squawks, "Raft 2, Genny approaching for pick up."

"Standby, Capt. They're suiting up now." Bruce turns to Lord Kent,

"I was un aware that you were dissatisfied with that bit of travel."

Lady Harriett rolls her eyes and assists with the hook up. As they begin to rise toward the Genevieve he said,

"Not at all, It's just that I have been so impressed with your prowess in travel lately, I began to wonder if we could do any better on our return."

As the couple rose, I turned, shook my head, and said to myself,

"No good deed goes unpunished."

He called down, "Eh? what was that?"

"Just an old saying sir,', I wave as as they fly away,

"The Green family moto, Arguere primum duplices,", and as they pass out of range I say, 'Bill them double."

"Raft 2 this is Genevieve, our passengers are aboard, we are away."

"Copy Genny, come back for us in an hour."

"An Hour ? Flight time is 10 minutes."

"Come back any time you please, but be ready to pick us up in an hour. We're going swimming."

"Roger, that's a big woo hoo, I will be returning, as crew, in 10 minutes."

"We'll be the ones in the water."

When the Genny returned she came in lower than ever. The Heli hovered in a quick stop about ten meters above the water, and then we saw Shellington. She was poised outside the starboard door on the pontoon, with no harness. She executed a graceful swan dive which slightly pushed the Genny aside.

Herbert hesitated and then jumped to follow her down. By the time she surfaced, Shely was getting naked. Herbert however, had gone in fully clothed and began to suffer for it. We all took pity and quickly stripped him.

After swimming we were all in great spirits as we climbed aboard the Raft.

"Who's Flying?" I asked

"Jeremiah', my co-pilot," she answered.

"Who's lowering the hook?"

"Angelina, our steward. You met last week, she's also my best welder."

"Ah, the big blonde behind the helmet. Good way to check her work,"

"She's double tested and all done. She'll be along from now on. The Hawk is ready to go. There's the hook. You and Tommy first. Send your harnesses back down eh, last time we had to climb the cable."

As we ascend I look at the crater lake and say to myself,

"Just another day in paradise."

When we returned to hotel there were so many texts, v-mails, e-mails, and direct calls to return it keep me busy for the day. At my breaking point, I walked through the lovely lobby. From the indoor pool I heard,

"Bruce !"

I stopped to pretend I didn't know where it was coming from. I had to . . . .

"Ah Yes? Oh, Lord Kent, How is your evening? And her Ladyship...?"

"She is in the loo for a quarter hour now. Are you just getting in?"

"No sir, Tommy and I stayed a bit to see more of the operation. But then my desk demanded my attention. Departure plans and all that, you know."

We hear and robust female yell, 'CANNON BALL', and see Lady Harriett bounding through to jump, curl up and grab her knees. She hit the water swamping the pool. Lord Kent attempted to get a photo of her in flight.

When she surfaces, she asks, "Did I get anybody wet?"

The others in the pool all confirm with a wave and a smile.

"Eddie, did you get it?"

"Let's see, Bruce taught me to review all the shots in the camera."

"Well it is a new. I've noticed nothing has become simpler these days."

"Ah here we are, Oh yes, looks like I have you very nicely, just before you splashed us. Here take a look." He hands her the camera.

"Oh dear I'm making that face again, see? Eyes tight shut, cheeks filled.."

I ask, "By the way, are you attending the Dinner and Dance tomorrow tonight?"

"Dance, what Dance?"

I expand the proposition, "The one the Hotel is hosting, It's more like an open house with live music, of course, in hopes you will attend."

"Of course, for a short time then. Nobles oblige m'dear?"

Lady Harriett confirms, "Quite."

"M'Lady, our Ms. Shellington would like a word with you. It's concerning your suits I believe."

Harriett says, "Of course, would she like a drink? Send Captain Shely and the drink both to the hot tub."

"She is on her way here as we speak. Shall I provide for you as well?"

"Yes, but afterward at the table, pool side so I can watch Eddie,"

I confirm, "It shall be so, your usual or something new?"

"What haven't I tried?"

"Any number of combinations m'Lady. Should we start with what his Lordship drinks?"

She laughs "That's easy, a Coconut Pineapple Daiquiri with a long straw."

"Correct, and for you?"

"Nothing thanks, I'm good for now", and as I walk away, she says,

"Let the evening's game begin."

———ᵐⁿᵒᵉᵗᵒᵒᵗᵉᵒᵒⁿⁿ———

Shely arrived prepared for a swim. She stripped down and climbed in. The waiter delivered an ice cold dark rum and lime.

Harriett took advantage and said,

"I'll have what she's having."

His lordship laughs and declares,

"I have arrived in Heaven. Here I am in an Indonesian hot tub with two gorgeous, beautiful, women."

Shely stands and sips her drink. She takes a full taste and continues the toast,

"You are the luckiest of men."

"I'll drink to that, Salute."

"Salute." They all drink. Harriett stands and moves to a chair and table.

"Now Dearest, I intend to speak with Shellington concerning our extra flight suits, Do you wish to be a part of the conversation?"

"Not really, probably just confuse things. I'm off to the showers."

"Good idea, save me some hot water." She turns and speaks to Shely.

"Are you married?" She watches Shely blink as she continues,

"I am almost married. And, I am trying to show Eddie the pleasure of having someone about that, while getting to know him, cares for him."

"I understand, it's not my lot in life, right now anyway, but I understand."

"I can only wonder if it's working. Anyway, what were we going to talk about?"

Shely is direct, "Apparently you and Eddie, if I may ask, has he proposed?"

"No, no, not yet, he hints around, but hasn't come through, it's maddening."

"He takes you on trips, takes you on adventures, buys you clothes."

"Ah well, yes, not your burden; you know, thanks for listening. We were going to talk about jumpsuits. Did Bruce give you the colors?"

I interrupt, "I did give her the colors as we discussed."

Lady Harriett jumps in fright.

"Oh my, I must say, I thought you were gone, I mean I thought we were alone. Bruce, this talk of marriage was not for his Lordship, uh, it was just . ."

"Among us girls."says Shely, 'Private you might say.

I ask, "Do you mind if I stay? I may be of some help."

M'lady hesitates, "I don't know about that ….. however, be that as it may."

"Lady Harriett, you should know that after watching the two of you, the staff is convinced that you are getting more from the water than good clean fun."

She is amazed, "Why Yes, we are. Well said, that may be. What are you saying ….?"

I interject, "The staff wants to know if you and his Lordship would object if we used the pool after you retired for the day."

She is amused, "Why ask me, that's a question for

Eddie, not me. And why do I suspect you have not yet asked him?"

"You suspect because you are an intuitive person. You also know the value of having asked the opinions of others who may be related to the decision."

Shely entered the conversation, "And no, we haven't asked. To me we don't have to ask, we just do it. To Bruce, it's a different matter."

Lady H. says, "I feel the same. While you're there, why not take a swim?"

"Thank you, and how was your swim today? Did the water feel the same?"

"The water felt stronger, heavier. It felt good and satisfying as always.'

Shely says, "Satisfying' is an unusual word when describing swimming.'

'That's the way his lordship puts it, satisfying."

"Well it certainly looks good on you. I insisted on measuring you this morning because I was watching you yesterday. I think you both have lost some weight since we began."

"Could be, a good span of exercise lately. I've noticed Eddie's weight has been changing, I thought it was the swimming."

Shely re-assures, "We'll measure you again tomorrow before we begin sewing the first two."

"Delightful. After the sewing, could we 'Try On' the first two. I feel we are creating a new type of sports wear. Why not get what we want?"

"Of course, once we have the correct fit, the seamstress can produce several more in each size in a few days."

Lady Harriett clasps Shely, "I predict that we will love the extras, and have them mailed to Bruce."

"It will be as you wish. I will be happy to ship them wherever you like."

"Is that all? I'm off to join Eddie in the shower. Until tomorrow then."

———∿∿⊶⊙⊷∿∿———

Day Two of the second run was Lake Twui, ' Men and Maidens'. The day is partially overcast. The water was a deep blue green until a shaft of light illuminated the surface and below, and the water turned a lighter Blue.

The royals were having a float contest. They were face up in the water. Lady Harriett seemed to float a bit higher than lord Kent in the water. He could rise and float as high, but he had to have lungs freshly filled with air. So, I gave him a float belt and that leveled them out.

They did tarry a bit longer and both moved at a more leisurely pace. While they were floating on their backs, the sky went dark, then the clouds parted, the light shown through stronger than ever. It illuminated the floating royals, the light flashed and was gone. The sun returned shortly afterward.

The chatter was shorter as less direction was necessary for Eddie's tending. The raft controls read the water was 5 degrees cooler than previous days. So they did not swim naked, but they did stay and play in the lake water longer.

As we watched the sunset, his Lordship asked, "Bruce, I understand that you would like to treat the staff to a swim?"

"That is true, and we would like to have your permission to share ...."

"Please be our guests, we are happy to share, well, after we finish, yes?"

"Very good Sir, We shall follow your lead. Do you have all you require for the dinner and dancing this evening?"

"I don't know, Harriett, do we take anything to the gala this evening. I mean are we expected to arrive with gifts of any kind?"

Harriett muses, "No Dear, it is being held in our honor. The others may have gifts for us."

"Well that would be pleasant for a chage. Black Tie is it?"

I assure, "Actually no, the invitation stated 'Island Attire', with footwear optional."

"Delightful. No dressing for dinner? I think I'll enter from the pool."

Lady H. asks, "The indoor pool?"

"Yes in fact we can start the reception there, and then proceed to the Gala."

The water today felt as if it were full of promise. We had stopped trying to fit as a unit and hummed along as a finely tuned machine. I felt full of affection for life and the others around me. I felt the urge to tell the crew how much I appreciated each and every one of them.

Shell had us all dropped off at the hotel to save time and waste money. We went for a dunk in the surf and then into went to change. As I started the shower, Shely asked if I wanted some help. I turned to her and offered my embrace, and as she became comfortable and relaxed, I asked what she was thinking. She smiled and pushed me into the shower where she fulfilled the spirit of her offer.

———⁓⁓⊙⊙⊙⊙⊙⁓⁓———

Dancing that night was a pleasurable must. For those who had nothing else to do, and that was us, we started dancing to the indoor pool music one hour prior to the start time. The party began to catch up about the time the band started. We took over the dance floor and created havoc until dinner was served. We prayed aloud for one another and our own mother earth.

Our entire table finally met at dinner. Gathered together were Harriett, Eddie, Shely, and I. There also were Herbert, Angelina, and Tommy, all with dates. We made a twelve person table seem small. We danced between every course until just before desert. We feared desert would be massive and we would never be able to move. Instead we were served a Mango flan. It was light and tart with the Mango puree at the bottom instead of browned sugar.

We had two more rounds before the band quit. When we got back to the indoor pool deck, we found it shut down for the evening with protective chains erected as a barrier. The door to the outer pool deck was unlocked, but closed as the cool breeze was coming in from the ocean.

Accepting the disappointment I said, "Looks like the party's over. is over. Who's got to work tomorrow, hands, right oh' me too. Let's all to bed."

"Good times all," called Shely as she watched me. I smiled and extended my arms, she smiled and stepped over to me. I put an arm around her shoulder, asked her to come home with me, and she said yes.

During the wee hours of the morning there was a sound at the door.

Tap Tap . . . Tap . . . Tap.

Shely heard it first. "Bruce, shhhh, Bruce, you hear that ?"

"Mmph, ' what a dream . . . wha's this, uh up with uh. . . ?"

"Shhhh hear that tapping?"

"Ah . . . . . . nope," I tried to hear a sound, to no avail.

"Ok, puss boy, I'll go look." She starts for the door and hears tapping again

I heard it too, and sit up, "Wha's that? At the door?"

Shellington opens the door and a sliver of light slices into the dark. Outside, barely standing, Lady Harriett was leaning over to knock, only there no door this time. She misses the knock and falls inward smothering Shel.

I brought up the light as they go down. What I found at my feet was a drunken and bewildered tangle of two females. I pulled a pissed Harriett off of a pissed off Shely.

"Ahhh, you drunk bitch, don't you throw up on me!"

The lady says, "Ahh, ammm So Sorry, I miss the door that time,"

"She's hammered Bruce." I let Harriett drop to pick up Shely. I think Shely nudged Harriett on the way by, because she rolled over, face up.

"What's she on about? Where's Eddie?"

The corpse begins to laugh, "He's drunker, a'ready passed out."

"So, what are you doing here, m'Lady?'"

"Had ta ask Bruce a question," He lifts her into a sitting position.

"Okay, I'm right here, what can I do for you?"

"Can you-," a loud belch, "Ahhh, uh put me in touch with Sellingston?"

"Yes m'lady, I can." I say to Shely, "Let's move her to a chair."

"Let's use the table, three chairs. Dump her in the big one, there we go."

After some loud snorts and a few minutes later, Lady Harriett comes around.

She asks while trying to focus, "Bruce? Is that you?"

"No m'Lady. Bruce called me to see you, why?"

"How clever of him, I was 'specting a phone number. Good evening dear?"

"May I ask, how often do you call to Bruce in the night?"

"Well, I, don' axually. t'night'd be a first, uh time. Why?"

Shely is testy, "Because, dear, that seat has been taken. I stayed the evening to be with him and you are interrupting, that's why."

"OOohh, for that I apol'gize, I did not assume, that you, ah, would be here."

I try to assure, "It's true, she has never been here before, for any reason."

"Good to know, as least she's not fucking the help."

"I want Eddie!" came out like a blast, a torrent, a squall crossing the room.

"Shit," said Shely, "She's in Love. I know what this is, what she needs to-"

I bail, "Oh God It that the time? Ah, I'm due, at the beach; uh, pool."

The story, as it came out of Shely later, went like this. The lady was distraught. Shely was the only other informed / involved female around, so she got the load of questions.

"Doesn't he love me ?"

"Why hasn't he proposed ?"

"What if he doesn't?"

"What if this was a waste of time and there was no change in her body ?"

"What if all that happens, is that he learned to swim?"

All of these took some time to answer while consoling a drunken lady. Shely gave me the short version. Later, she shared the load like a fire hose.

"So I said, yes, I was sure that he cared for her, and then 'cared for her' made her cry. As to why he has not proposed, I guessed that was probably some man thing, like waiting for a special moment or some dumb man shit like that."

I could only think, blink, smile, and nod in agreement. She continued,

"As for the body changes. They are changing just because of the exercise they get every day now. But I told her I thought she was not only slimmer but seemed a little taller as well. They'll get measured again today."

"Wo hoa there, what did she say to that?" I exclaimed

"She cried at that too. More like tears of joy, she had noticed a slight change and been hoping it was true. She wanted it to be noticed, but is afraid that it may not be permanent.......And then she really started to bawl."

"Sorry about that."

"So I had to resort to the truth."

That thought took a bit of getting used to. "What did you say?"

"Well, she's drunk right? I used the KISS rule, ya know, 'Keep It Simple Stupid,' and I told her if he didn't love her for who she is, no matter what she is, he's probably not the right guy."

I exclaimed, "Wow, the big girl panties, eh? What did she say ?"

"Not much, she pretty much passed out then. She needed to think I guess."

"Wanna come use the spa? Long day ahead." I said with hope.

She nodded and disrobed, "Next to last day here, yeh?" and entered.

As she reached for me, I wondered if there could ever be another woman so attractive. We soaked as we discussed having Harriett retrieved, if so by whom? Maybe it was better to 'think' about it in the shower. We washed each other, and we shared dirty minds. Hmmm, perhaps Room Service could take her home.

——————————

And because some minds do think alike, when we returned from the spa we found breakfast laid out with covers over all. Lady Harriett was gone but she had signed the tab and taken a cuppa herself. The beautiful feast, warming ourselves in the morning sunshine, answering many texts, and returning a few calls, got the day moving.

The last of the messages, was from Lord Kent. I was requested to meet him at the front desk. He was perplexed.

"Bruce, why can't I get a simple delivery from Belgium?"

"I don't know. What are you expecting, why didn't you ask me before now?"

"To be honest, I had you doing so many other things, and this item was rather personal. I thought there was plenty of time to do it myself."

"I see. Or at least partially, what are you waiting on?"

"A Ring, damn it, The Ring, I fear I lost the thing in transit, So I ordered another one from Antwerp….., they assured me that it could be here in time."

"In time for what?"

"To celebrate our marvelous adventure together. I wish to propose."

I could only smile,

"You still can m'Lord. You may propose at any time, and the ring comes when it comes. It's the question, the proposal that matters most."

"Really, I thought they wanted a special day or some such. Are you sure?"

"As sure as I can be. Take my advice, if the ring is not here by sundown, propose anyway."

"Really? Anyway?"

"Yes. Now, tell me about how the first one went missing? Have you spoken with the Police? Or filed an insurance claim? You should do both immediately."

"I first noticed it was missing when I attempted to put it in the hotel safe"

I listened and responded, "Ah, and it wasn't where you expected?"

"No it wasn't, and I searched for two days before I ordered another from the diamond cutters."

"Good thinking, now let's go over the facts again and make a report."

———— ∿∿⌒⊙⊙⌒∿∿ ————

It turns out that the ring was worth a little over $100,000, and I had to get that figure from Antwerp. Eddie had insured it for twice that because of sentimental value. The jeweler had priority express mailed the package four days ago, with proper insurance.

Lord Kent had a standing date with Lady Harriett on the outdoor pool deck. They usually tried new and hopefully interesting seafood. Word of their curiosity had been mentioned to the head Chef and he labored to satisfy. Between the courses the royal couple amused themselves in salt water and fresh water bathing.

My day had grown with additional details concerning a possible robbery and reports, the morning and afternoon were more crowded than I thought.

As the royals met for lunch I had Herbert go through Lord Kent's things searching for receipts, delivery notices. Thankfully, he was good about keeping them all. Herbert assembled a pile of such on the desk in the study. Lord Kent had been his natural self while on vacation. He enjoyed having fun with money. There were receipts for everything from flowers to horse drawn cabs.

Thank God I paid for everything else or we may never account for all the purchases necessary on a trip like this. Once again I had to realize that he never really thought of the costs, he was only concerned with the convenience, or the time it took for things to happen for him.

While working in Lord Kent's behalf I became distinctly aware and amused that we would never think alike. But, I was forced to guess as to what he would do in a certain moment. For example, if he had to decide what to do, in a specific circumstance, what would he most likely decide to do?

Like with obtaining a replacement ring, he would probably be asked a lot of questions, 'What type of stone, what type setting? What size?'. He handled all those details before, so I decided that he probably would have told them,

"Exactly as I ordered previously. You do keep files don't you?"

However, they would not be able to ship as ordered. He's in fucking Indonesia now isn't he? He could rely on the diamond cutter and jeweler to insure it and ship it ASAP. To whom? To him. Does he remember that he requested for the duration of this excursion, all his mail goes through me? When the mail is examined and cleared, by me, then it's delivered to him.

Could a ring of incredible value arrive by normal mail?

After perusing the mail room collection and lifting several letters to look closer, I saw no express package nor any ring sized mailer at all. I went to the front desk and asked for any other incoming mail. The clerk led me to a sack waiting on a table just behind, and I tipped him for the privilege of inspection. Inside, there was one the size I was looking for and displayed foreign markings.

"Excuse me, Cedric, is it? Sorry to bother you, but this parcel is obviously for lord Kent. We will need the receipt you signed for his Lordship's copy?"

Cedric nodded, produced a receipt, and allowed me to keep the parcel. It was labeled as coming from Antwerp. I smiled as I picked up the parcel, Eddie really was one lucky guy. I wrote him a quick note and asked the bellman do deliver it to the man at the luncheon table beside the pool.

The note read, "Got a line on your parcel, found it stuck in transit. As a personal favor, Shely is flying to retrieve."

I called Shely and asked her not to answer her link for at least three hours, as she normally did during work. I requested her to meet us for dinner at 8pm. I scanned the pool deck and watched Lord Kent twitch as he read my note. I was reminded of a beggar who opened a door for a client of mine. I gave him a twenty and watched him blink back to life, enough to think.

I stored the parcel in the vault and began to wonder. I called and asked Herbert to search all luggage, clothing, and other travel items the Lord had brought along. As I arrived I found Herbert with every piece of clothing out and spread about the furniture for repacking.

"All present and accounted for Mr. Green. No extras in any of the bags. Good to get them sorted and ready though, we'll be traveling day after tomorrow won't we?"

"We will indeed, if I can get the royals to approve the itinerary I prepared."

———∽∿⌘⌘∿∽———

Later that day Shely checked in and gave me the update on the raft relocation, and said she would meet us before dinner. Lady Harriett checked in and asked that Shely call her as soon as possible, and Lord Kent checked in with me three times to prove how nervous he was.

I took a clue from Herbert and did my packing early. Actually it was repacking stuff I had already used on my way to the island and not since, But, I knew I would need them soon enough, so out they came to get repacked on top.

Guess who I brought to dinner? Miss Shellington Anne Stewart, a little known but very important person in her part of the world was my date. She was delivered in the only stretch limo on the island and treated with respect by the locals. Sitting with royals is such a norm for me, sometimes I miss that other people are famous. Shely is not only gorgeous, and wealthy, she is good company.

I asked Shely to present the missing ring as the result of her 'errand'. It put her on the 'preferred list' rather than a 'welcome guest'. She passed the ring to Lord Kent during cocktails. He took it aside for inspection. Shely continued to be the witty and charming gad fly. And then Eddie emerged,

"M'Lady Harriett? There you are, I would speak with you if you please."

Lady Harriett crosses to meet him.. "You would like to speak with me sir?"

"In deed I would," He holds up a ring. "Do you know what this is?"

"Oh Yes, Yes I know, I hope, Eddie are you asking ?"

"Harriett will you please gift me with-" and they both say, "Marriage?"

She looks him in the eye and quietly says,

"Ask again so all can hear."

He nearly shouts, "Will you marry me? Will you be my love ? Please marry me." he rings her finger.

She beams, "Yes, yes, I will accept, in front of all of these people, I will marry you, dear Edward."

They spun one another around in circles laughing and

accepting congratulations. Shely and I sat amazed and amused at their mutual excitement.

I broke the silence, "Tomorrow, we do the last lake ."

"I'm glad he proposed tonight. It was making her crazy."

"Was she? Him too. I told him to do it without the ring, just do it?"

"Right, Get 'er. Go get 'er boy. Get 'er done."

"Get 'er done. Right then, uh, Shely?" She looks at him.

"Will you marry me?'

She looks at me hard.

It was commonly known that when the Heli-Birds flew, money flowed too. The appearance of Heli -Birds, and the floating raft drew enough of a crowd that Shely and I decided to leave Tommy aboard overnight.

We see Shely with the same hard look as she estimates the sides of the crater. The hook descends lowering the royals to the raft. Day Three of the second run started with a challenge. Lake Ata Butu was hardest to navigate from the air.

It was the easiest to get to by foot. One of the reasons that it was called the Lake of Old People is because it has a climbable passage of less than an hour. The older people can go for a hike, go swimming, and return home in a few hours.

From the air it was tight, it was do-able, but tight.

This lake was the lowest elevation and was the final run off lake from Kelimutu. Ata Butu was about a half mile from the two other lakes and usually deep blue in color. In overcast skies she appears to have dark water.

The royals were dropped into the raft as dozens of people watched from the craters' edge. It seems the royals were a bit of a show for the locals. The tribes had certainly heard of them, the townspeople had felt their buying power.

Tommy and I were waiting on feet, royal feet encased in water shoes, and down they came followed by exclamations,

"Bruce Tommy, how good of you to receive us, I say there, have you met my future wife, the lady Harriett?"

"No fanfares if you please gentlemen. Just get us unhooked and then you may congratulate us."

We unhooked them and then we did as she suggested. As we stood before them, hugging and kissing them, I saw the size difference for the first time. She was a little taller and he was a little smaller. Not much, not a lot really, he was still taller of the two, just not quite as much so.

After they dove into the water, I called Shely on her mobile.

"Did you see it?"

She answered, "Maybe, what did you see?"

"She's taller and, he's smaller."

Shelly confirms, "Yeah, I think I saw that too, I took their measurements again today?"

"What do the numbers say?"

"It seems they have traded almost two inches in height. And about 10 pounds in weight. She grew, and he shrank, in both cases."

I was amused, "I wondered if they noticed? I'm sure they have."

"They had to notice, they swim together. They sleep together."

I chuckle, "And that's not all. They are engaged."

"They gotta know."

"Yeah, so, Ms. Stewart, what do you say, eh ?"

"What do you mean?"

"What about me and you, any new thoughts, I can re-assure you against?"

"Bruce, big bad Bruce, you make my head spin, I don't know, I gotta think."

"Take your time sweetie."

"But you're leaving tomorrow."

"You don't need that long do you?"

"Bruce…."

"Signing off, call ya when they're ready."

"Bruce,"

"Yeah babe?"

"Oh, hell. I'll call, I'll be on station waiting to hear from you. Bye."

When the royals came aboard they were shivering. A dense dark cloud had covered the lake and hills. Most of the native on lookers were gone.

Lord Kent said, "Looks like rain Bruce, should we call Shely to come quick."

Tommy says, "I don't think she can get here that quick. Watch, its moving pretty fast. But its not very big. It'll be a short one."

"How do you know?"

"You see the sunlight following it?"

I say, "Tommy, radio Shely. It's coming from over by the airstrip. She if can tell us anything."

"It's getting darker, it is definitely coming this way. What should we do?"

"Let's zip up the sides of the raft and open all the screened air vents. There now good, Now here's the important part."

"What's that,"

"Champagne, the raft came with four bottles. We have to drink at least one. Or maybe more if the storm lasts."

Tommy says, "I have the Captain on the line." The radio blasts.

"Hey Bruce buddy, Genie to Raft 2, We got rained on about 10 minutes ago. Tommy tells me you're about to get wet."

"Looks like it Shell. How long did yours last?"

"Maybe ten, maybe less,"

"Gee that's tough. Did you have any champagne to make it through."

"Oh yeah, you're toughing it out. Listen bub, I'm coming swimming later and there had better be some left for me, well, for us, you know, to have."

"Okay. Listen follow the tail of that shower and get the royals out quick."

"Leaving now. See ya then."

He turns to be handed a glass which he uses to toast.

"Well now, let's toast ah, m'Lord and Lady, a toast to your glorious plans."

"Thanks you Bruce. I'm sure we will have need of your services. Toast."

"I will see If my wife allows me to work. You see I've proposed to Shely."

"Bruce, you do know she's royalty, I mean locally, here in Indonesia?"

Lord Kent says, "As you could be, just as are you. You could be a Laird in her keep."

"Well that's a horse of a different color. She'll have to ask me then, right?"

"Steady on there mate, don't take her that far, it might be a reach for her."

"Nope, don't see it that way. If I'm worth marrying, I'm worth asking for."

Lady Harriett exclaims, "Hear Hear. More Champagne, more toasts!"

Tommy passes one forward, "Open another bottle, here comes the rain."

The pick up happened 20 minutes later and the two royals were literally hauled up in the net. They were both drunk to the funny bone and could not stop laughing at anything, let alone everything.

Shely promised to get them home and then return for

another swim. Once again the Heli-Bird descends low enough to be a dive platform. Shely pushes off once again, enters the water like a seal, and emerges close to Bruce and the raft.

"This is a first." She declared

"Definitely for me. Why for you?"

"I've never swam ? Swum? This lake before. The others, Yes, but not here."

"Why the others, and how?"

"I happen to own a helicopter, dummy."

"My bad, you're right, you go anywhere do anything, Search and Rescue!"

She looked at me and said, "Let's just go swimming," and sinks away.

"She'll never marry me," I said to no one, and sank down after her.

———⁓⁓◦◦⊙⊙⊙◦◦⁓⁓———

Because of the time differences, my job enabled me to stay up most of the night fusing over travel details. So, at dawn the next day, I did not feel and look my best to go traveling for the next 5 days.

Lady Harriett noticed, "Pardon my saying so Bruce, but you look a little worn, sort of pale."

"Thank you m'Lady, how kind of you to notice. All of your things are ready and at the transport. We're taking Shely's car service back to the airport."

She attempts to console, "Oh dear, that's it isn't it, She turned you down."

"Yes that's true. Thank you m'Lady, how intuitive of

you. If you will pardon me, I still have several details to attend. I'll be back in about an hour."

I fled back to my rooms in the hopes that no one else would see me in such a state. I slammed the door behind me and looked at myself in the mirror. I was a wreck. It's not often that I talk to myself, but today I was right there in the mirror.

"Let's see, what to do first? Get over Shely, Next, take a shower, and get over Shely, have a close refreshing shave, have a short restful nap, and do not dream of Ms. Shellington Stewart."

The long hot shower was a relief as I had not bathed the night before. The shave was certainly necessary, but hardly refreshing. The short sleep was full of the wedding images. Shely looked so beautiful in wedding white, the vision deepened my breathing as I slept. But, it was no use, my dreams re-lived her refusal in black and white silhouettes. She stood on tip toes and kissed me goodbye.

And then I slept soundly, ….. good thing I was already packed, …. and then awoke with a thought . . . . . all packed except for his Lordship's top coat.

We had been confusing our coats most of the trip since we left home. They were always in the way and forever being confused as to whose was whose. I found his Lordship's as I was un packing, and then again while re-packing. I had laid it aside intending to exchange for my own. I dressed for travel and slung the top coat over the rolling luggage.

———❧❧❧———

There is a tradition in most safari expeditions wherein the purchased chattels leftover are dispersed among the staff. The give away gathering was underway with his Lordship presiding. By the time I arrived the last two items were being presented.

"And to the Hotel Mariposa, we give the right to display our family crest." Lord Kent presents a family crest of the Kents, "This may be displayed signifying superior services and a damn fine place to stay. Please add this to the collection."

"Now as to that Raft. I would ask that the Shellington corporation dispose of this particular item. First of all, you'll never get it back in the cannister. Second of all it was released, or born here on the island, and should stay here on the island, as I have heard it said by so many natives and locals, if you please."

Angelina stood up to receive the gift and to shake his Lordships hand. And that was that, the ceremony was over and we were about to leave. I breathed a small sigh of relief that we would all be continuing with what we did best.

———∿∾◦◦✕◦∾∿———

The happy couple walked toward me expecting all to be ready. Lady Harriett commented that I looked well rested for having worked all night in their behalf. His lordship looked closely for the first time and nodded approval,

"Bruce, your services are greatly appreciated by Lady Kent and I. We shall discuss a bonus for that." He noticed his top coat slung across by bag "You will be traveling with us?"

"Yes, he will Eddie. After all, someone must keep your top coats straight."

I picked up his top coat. With a flourish I draped the coat around his shoulders and said, "Yes indeed, I think this is yours m'lord."

Lord Kent looked and laughed. "It's a too long for me now, isn't it my dear?'

"Yes it is. It does look good on Bruce. We'll find you another that fits."

"Quite." He removed the coat and handed it to me. "Time for change eh? Bruce? Please keep the coat, with my thanks."

I bowed in thanks while removing my hat. The royals walked past and I felt a happy lump in my heart.

I heard, "Nice meetin' ya." I turned to see Angelina's appraising look. She took out a note, handed it over, and walked away. It was addressed to me, but I didn't want to read it before leaving. I put the envelope in the pocket of my new traveling coat.

———∽∿∞∾∿∞∾∿———

We flew the reverse route to Jakarta and stayed over. We flew to Guam the next day and stayed over another night. As we flew to Singapore I did some internet magic and transferred our bookings to another Airline. We flew overnight and slept most of the way back to New York. It still took over three days to get home.

It wasn't until I heard the weather announcement from the pilot that I thought of using the coat I had dragged across the planet and back. I allowed myself to think of the goodbye note from Shely. I had been avoiding it for days. Maybe I had done it on purpose in order to wait read it when I got home.

In the breast pocket of the coat I found her note, and a small ornate box.

I opened the box to find the lost engagement ring.

I snapped the box shut. Then I opened it again to make sure.

Yep. Snap.

And then I heard the voice in my head say, "Read the bloody note."

I opened the envelope and perhaps imagined a faint whiff of her fragrance.

Big Boy Bruce,
Thanks for the really good time and all the lovely gifts that came along with the raft.
I hope to save some Champagne for your return visit.
Please return someday soon. I could use a man who can make something from nothing.
Shely

What could I do but smile?

What could I say? Nothing.

I could do nothing but wonder.

I could only wonder when I would make it back.

Something Wonderful

by

T K Wallace

There is something wonderful within all of us. Something that needs to be released in order to help us be more than we ever dreamed we could become. I'm not sure how to describe the belief of such potential. Sometimes I feel the impetus is just beyond reach, the scent of possibility teasing my senses, gently edging my thoughts toward unexpected results. This feeling is real, the pull is there, within the collective rhythm of our hearts.

This recognition from another person is what made me stop and turn as we passed on the beach. I took another look. I'm also sure this recognition is what made her turn and take another look at me too. I smiled. She smiled. I raised a hand to speak, when she spoke first.

"Hello, have we met ?"

"Yes we have, just now."

"Well, okay then," She walks toward me with a hand extended.

I close the distance, took her hand, and knelt in the sand. Looking up into her eyes I said,

"I, Theodore, name thee, uh-"

"Janet."

"Thank you Janet, I name thee, Goddess of Negril ."

"My thanks, Sir Theodore, you may rise ."

I kissed the back of her hand and stood with her hand in mine. I looked into her aquamarine eyes twinkling in mirth and stammered,

"What time did you arrive ?"

"Earlier today, how did you know ?"

"Because I have walked this beach every day for the past week and could never have missed you. I surmised you had arrived."

"Then you shall be known as, Sir Theodore; the Perceptive ."

"It is my honor to be thought of as perceptive by such as you ."

I bowed when she asked" Where are you staying ?"

"And she reads minds as well. You took the question from my tongue ."

She rolls her eyes at me as in, 'as if', and then she asks,

"Will you wade with me? I love the water but I'm not sure of the sea rays."

I took her hand and led into Caribbean water the color of her eyes.

"I will protect you. It's an easy opportunity to appear brave. The rays are as afraid of you, as you are of them. Just watch as we wade, don't step on any. And stay close in case I need to comfort you."

She smiled, and took my arm as we walked through the surf and further into the water. I pointed a finger.

"There's a leopard ray just to the right ." She drew closer tucking under my arm. I stepped toward the Ray. The wings flexed once to glide away.

"Oh it's beautiful, so graceful, and those pretty spots, a leopard ray ?"

"Risking my reputation of fearlessness and manly courage, I will attempt a song," and sang to her,

"I'd like to get to know you ."

"I know that, I love that old tune, Spanky and the Gang, right ?"

"Look Out ! Here comes another one . . . ."

I put an arm behind her, hoisted her out of the water and ran for the beach.

As she rides she asks, " I thought you said they were harmless ."

"Well, mostly harmless, they do have a nasty barb at the end of the tail ."

"Thank you sir. Now please release me ." I placed her gently on the sand.

"So, where are you staying ?"

"Here on the beach. And you ?"

"I always stay up on the cliff. The west end has marvelous hideaways."

"Really? Hwow so ?"

"The establishments on the cliff were all configured from the last volcanic age. The properties are all different. Some few have swimming and coral diving included, right out back."

"And yours ?"

"The place I always stay has swimming, great reef snorkeling, and cliff diving. It all comes with the room at the Coral Seas."

"Sounds nice, do they have a good restaurant ?"

"The best on the cliffs. May I have you for lunch ?"

"No, but if this goes well, you may have me for dinner ."

"I am blessed by a goddess, but please, may I protect you again ?"

"Maybe, how do you mean ?"

"I mean to protect your beautiful skin. The sun is deceptively hot. I happen to know the best protection on the island. Will you come with me ?"

"Come with you? Maybe later, or not, how do you mean ?"

I laughed out loud and so did she. " Not as you suspect; come on along ."

We walked the beach until we came to a straw hut with four poles at the corners and palm fronds up the sides and over the top. There were more poles in the sand leading outward covered with sarongs and beach towels.

"The first day I walked and swam Negril beach I started from the west end at the foot of the hill. By the time I got here I was pinking up some. Sharon saw me and rushed me with some glob in her hands and asked me to wait a minute. She slathered my shoulders with her hands and told me of her business. Her smile is a beautiful memory and her first words I shall never forget."

———vwoɑᘓᕼᕼᘓoɑvw———

The scene fades and we see my memory of meeting Sharon. She speaks,

"I am here to support my family by makin' sure you

go home tan and not burnt to a crsip." She got a little serious, "Dis here will make sure o' dat."

"It will ?"

"If you allow me treat your skin properly. You from Boston ?'

"No, New York ."

"The city or the outer islands? They usually get more sun than you got."

"The city, Manhattan ."

"And how long will you be here on de island?"

"A week, maybe more ."

"You need Me, more than I need You ."

"Probably true. So what's your name ?"

"Share-On. It's Sharon, but the accent is at the end."

"What do you recommend to protect and deeply tan my New Yawk Shitty skin ?"

"Me ." She smiled a wide white smile.

"Share On is a beautiful sentiment, passing positive actions forward ?"

"Just as I mean to do. Now, come in out of the sun, first thing you . . . . . ."

The back story fades into the beach hut as Shar-on emerges and speaks,

"Good to see you back so soon, and you've brought a guest ."

"Sharon this is the Lady Janet. She has just arrived to Negril and her skin will need your help ."

"And where do you come from Lady Janet ?"

"Well, today I came here from the airport in Mo' Bay. I arrived there from Montreal ."

"That explains your skin . . ."

I exclaim, " How do you explain that fabulous body ?"

"Never you mind, Mr. Ted. Or, if she's Lady Janet, might you be Sir Ted?"

"Right on both counts, can you do for her what you've done for me ?"

"No, for her I'll do better, 'cause she has better skin to start out ."

Janet says, " His skin looks pretty good to me ."

I say, " Hmmmm"

Sharon asks, " What's that mean ?"

"It means 'Hmmm' ."

"Sounds like it could be 'Yummm."

"Could be, How you gonna start her out ?"

"Let's do business first. Lady Jan, to get the best tan you must come here every day for the next 5 or 6, you gonna be on the island that long?"

Jan says, " Longer I think, but we are all over the place. I'm here working ."

"And what work do you do ?"

Janet looked at me and leaned to whisper in Sharon's ear. I leaned in to hear when Shar-on pushed me away.

"You men are always wanting something for nothing. If she wants you to know what you want to know, she will tell you herself. Go away and come back for her in an hour ."

Janet smiled at me and made a 'move along' gesture. Shar-on guided her,

"Come on honey, first we're gonna hydrate you all over with Aloe ."

As they disappeared into the inner hut, Janet looked over her shoulder and gave me a finger wave.

———∽∽∽◦◦∾◦◦∿◦◦∾∾◦◦∽∽———

I looked out to the ocean and saw a tree trunk canoe approaching the beach. Three beach runners arrived to help the older man who paddled ashore, so I helped out too. Mr Nigel was Sharon's father and a Conch diver. He was returning with today's catch. There were quite a few large shells in the canoe.

"Hey Mr Ted. You still paying my girl to help keep you all brown ?"

"Yes Sir, only today I brought her another body care for ."

Lionel directs, " You beach boys take these up Conch Hill for me, yes ?"

The canoe helpers gather as many as they can carry and after a few trips they had them all but one. Nigel and I dragged the canoe out of the surf and turned it over. When it was over, it looked like any other log on the beach.

Nigel took the last Conch and showed me a rare sight. He showed me a Queen Conch. She was beautiful. Instead of the crown and points that the males have, the female's tip and points are rounded and curved, and instead of the white outer shell the females have brown and tan striping the white. Also the sharp fluted opening of the male was a gentle curved lip along the orifice of the queen.

"Richie !" Nigel called. A young man ran back from the hill and Nigel gave him the Queen. " Take her to the farm ." Richie ran to a jet ski on the beach pushed off into the water, started the machine and took off.

"We be seeding some conch beds down by Bloody Bay where the tourists don't go. That one will provide 50 males and 1 female every year. So she gets kept and protected as a breeding Queen ."

The beach boys were separating the other Conch by size. They both had a machete close by. Nigel asked,

"How many ?" the reply came " 23 Papa ."

"Okay, not bad for an eighty year old man by himself." I smiled and lowered my head in respect.

The boys began to separate the conch meat from the shells by hacking a slit at the top edge of the crown and then using a thin flexible knife to work the meat loose. Each conch was taken by Nigel and placed in a salt water bath to rid it of sand and waste, and then into a fresh water bucket.

I noticed that Nigel and the boys would cut away a long slender shiny section from the meat. The first couple they ate and after that they left them in the salt water bath.

When I asked what the piece was Nigel told me it was " A man thing, good for men" and he indicated his genitals.

"But I guess no good for the visitors at th' hotels. The

cooks dere, dey just throw it away. So we keep that for ourselves, our families." He smiled and offered me one. I took it, smelled it, and ate it as they laughed at me. It was good, lightly salty and slippery like fresh oysters.

Lionel asked, " Dat one in dere, Man or Woman ?"

"Woman" I replied, he yelled, " SharOn ." She emerged and came to her father's side. He handed her a couple of parts and said to me, " For her skin ."

Sharon smiled and left without looking at me. Nigel said, " The man part for men to eat for their man parts. For the woman, it's good for their skin."

Dozens of empty shells were set in rows by the tree line. The new ones were set apart to dry and be further excavated by crabs and birds. The old ones were there to be taken by anyone who wanted a souvenir. A sign on the tree partially covered by Conch Hill read.

"$2.00 each Please pay Sharon."

The beach boys took the fresh water bucket of conch away, one by each handle, toward the nearest hotel. Nigel had kept a couple of large Conch and began to slice them into strips. He smiled at me and said,

"Dis our lunch here, you can't eat money."

Richie came back from the farm with three large fish on a stringer. He handed the line to Nigel. He went further up into the tree line to a cook pit. He took some twigs and wood from the scrub, tossed them into the pit. He used a palm frond and fanned the pit until a small cook fire and smoke began to build.

Nigel had pulled some fresh leaves from a nearby

banana tree. He eviscerated the fish and stuffed the conch strips inside. He rolled each stuffed fish into a big banana leaf and gave it to Richie who laid them close by the smoke, but not directly over.

"You hungry ?" Nigel asked with a smile. " Yeah." Sharon came from the hut and walked to the surf to wash her hands and then came back and sat in the braiding chair.

"How's Janet ?"

"Her skin is absorbing all the Aloe I could put on her. She was snoring so I left her here to meditate. Theo, that woman has an amazing body ."

"I noticed, and I think I got her to you in time to protect that fair skin ."

"You did, she was soaking up the Aloe as fast as I could put it on. So I had her turn over and did the other side. When she wakes up I'll send her to wash off and do it all again. Where did you meet her ?"

"Here on the beach just this morning. It was kind of a moment for us both I think. We started talking and I took her wading, then I brought her to you ."

The beach boys returned with the bucket empty of conch but full of money. Sharon rose and went into the hut and returned with a cash box. She opened it and counted the conch money.

"Nice catch today Papa, the boys got $75.00. How much do you need ?"

"Not much, give me $15 ." Sharon gave him some bills which he tucked in his swimming shorts. She gave the beach boys another $10 and closed the box on $50 to spare, all the time watching some tourists as they checked out her wares. She waits a beat, and then does her slow and easy pitch.

"If you see anything you like, just ask for the price."

Los touristas did not seem to notice any of us until the curtain parted and Janet came out buck naked. That they noticed. Sharon looked back at Janet and said, " Go wash off honey", indicating the water. Janet ran to the surf and splashed as she rinsed her body.

I sat beside Nigel and the beach boys watching to our mutual satisfaction. Two female tourists lingered enough for Sharon to ask, " You want a Hair braid? How about a beach towel, or maybe a beautiful sarong for the evening ? "

They both shook their heads and chatted in German as they watched Janet return and pass us entering the hut, calling, " Ready for round two SharOn ." The tourists asked the price of a wide brimmed hat, " That's $10." At which they shook their heads, so Sharon pointed to Conch Hill and entered the hut.

The German tourist women were delighted and examined the shells and chose two shells each. They returned and looked back and forth between us men. Nigel said " Okay that's $5 dollars please."

The Germans looked at each other and shook their heads pointing to the sign on the tree. Nigel simply said, " Sales Tax ." This they understood and paid him.

We heard Richie call, " Soon Come ." The beach boys

took banana leaves to the cook pit and received a portion of baked fish. Nigel did the same and returned handing one to me. Richie served two more leaves and passed them in to Sharon and Janet.

One of the beach boys opened a cooler disguised as a foot stool and withdrew two Red Stripes for Sharon and Janet. He withdrew three more and handed them to Richie, Nigel, and I. Then he took two more for him and his mate.

We all sat in the shade and ate in the silent respect a fine feast deserves. From inside the hut we heard a rather large belch and the laughter that followed. After a time, Sharon came out and requested Richie to come with her. He did and after some commotion she emerged again to announce,

"Sir Theodore the Perceptive, You may have noticed that I am here but Janet is not. Her daily treatment is done and I have sent her off to her digs for the coconut and aloe to set. And I sent Richie along to get her there safely."

"Did she like your massage?"

"I think she did, she snored for a while, and then ate like a hungry tiger after she woke up. She's had two Aloe rubs and a full coating of Coconut oil mixed with Conch, you know, stuff.'

My eyes widened at the mention of the Conch sperm. I stammered out the next words, " Where did she go ?" The four of them began to laugh and point at me, as they knew the joke I could not fathom.

Sharon said, "I'm not to tell you, Sir Perceptive, but she knows where you will be, at the Coral Seas Cliffs."

"Okay, all that ends well, . . . and all that other shit. Thanks, what do I owe you, for her ?"

Sharon answered, " Nothing, she paid for a week's treatment," and showed me a couple of hundred dollars which she put in the cash box. We met eyes and then smiled at one another, " Tanks." She smiled and rolled her eyes.

I ran and dove through the surf and swam down the beach for a mile or so to clear my head. I stopped to relax and drift for a moment before I made my way in past the breakers. I caught a good bodysurf ride and came back to the beach at the bar for the Coral Seas Beach. As I came up to the bar I saw the first friend I made in Negril; one Mr. Jinx Daley.

Jinx smiled at me and ordered me a Red Stripe, " Have a good swim ?"

As I had no towel, I shook all the water from me and scrubbed my hair with my fingers. I thanked Jinx, took the beer and drank it all in one swig which immediately went to my head. So I laid my head on the bar and rolled it back and forth until the throbbing stopped.

"Jinx, I met and lost the most beautiful Female I have ever met, and lost ."

"Boyo, after all these years, I say to you again, Welcome to Jamaica ."

The first time I came to Negril I was looking for a smaller tourist destination off the mainstream of Americans in need of a quick epidermal burn. Never had been to Jamaica, wanted beach time and sunsets, and as Negril had a seven mile beach, and is the western point of the island it qualified.

I had chosen the Christmas holidays to take some time in the sun. I didn't consider how many thousands of others had been doing so for decades. But I became aware of these facts by watching the passengers around me during the flight to Montego Bay. This was also pointed out to me as I found the bus to Negril when the driver asked where I was staying.

"I'm not sure, I thought I would get there and find a place, you know ?"

He looked at me as if he wanted to say, 'What are you, Stupid?'

Instead, he said, "All the Good Places are booked through the New Year."

"Where do you stop along the beach?"

"At all the Good Places Mon' ."

"Okay then, how about the Not so Good Places, the alternates,"

"There are several of course, but you have to get to them from the Good Places by taxi or by foot."

"Okay. Do you go up the cliff?"

"No Sir, I stop just forward of there at the Tea Water."

The entrance to the Tea Water Inn was about 100 yards from the bus drop off to the front desk. The rain was shed, but the light was framing a man sittin' and pretending to read a magazine. I disembarked and gathered my belongings, wheeled past him to the desk where I was asked,

"Good Evening Sir, do you have a reservation ?"

"Ah, no I forgot to make one. I would like to stay through New Years ."

"I am sorry, we are booked full ."

"I see, how about just a night or two, until I find a place ."

"Sorry we are fully booked ."

"I see, too bad, it looks like a nice place ." And I rolled back out front.

The magazine reader looked up and said, " No reservation ?"

"No, I didn't think to make one, didn't think I'd need one ."

"What were you tinkin' mon. Tinkin dat maybe Negril is a small deserted town at Christmas time ?" His amusement is as obvious as his big ass grin.

"I guess you could say I wasn't thinkin', not tinkin' right anyways ."

"Dere you go, Now you be lookin at tings better. Tell me mister, can you see a ting for what it is ?"

"Maybe, I'm not so sure just now, What would have me look at ?"

"Yo' predicament young man. You have come here with no rooms reserved during the holidays. You have put yourself in a predicament ."

"So I have, Mr —"

"Jinx, Jinx Daley, Mr-"

"Wallis, Ted Wallis, just in from New York."

"Well then, you may see Negril as smaller than your town, but it's a big town to all of us. First time here ?"

"First time on the Island. Only seen what could be seen from the Jitney ."

"My cousin Horace was driving tonight. Did he bring you through the hills or around the coast ?"

Reflecting I said, " A little of both, we climbed into the hills as we left Mo' Bay and then hit the coast about thirty minutes later ."

"Horace is a good driver, but he likes to travel through his home when he can. Did he stop at all ?"

"Just a couple of quick stops, he let off some men and picked up some women. One place he called, Cool Running Bridge. We stopped a while."

"Sounds right. The men, dey work at the airport, The women, dey work here on de beach. They all rode for free, well actually you paid der way by paying your own. How many more like you on the bus ?"

"Maybe ten, this was the last stop, they all got off before ."

"Good, he made a profit and did others a favor as well. Now back to you. Why do you tink I'm here ?"

"You work here ?"

"No guess again, cause dat's what you be doin, guessing dat is," he smiles.

I ask, " Does it have anything to do with my Predicament ?"

"Now you tinkin'."

"Then I would guess that you are here at the end of the bus line to round up the strays, and find them a place to stay ."

"Well said, 'Findin' De Strays a Place to Stay.'"

"I suppose you have some ideas about that, eh?"

"Supposin' I do, but not dat many, not durin' dese holidays, jus' de one ."

"I also guess is that you are a native to the region, uh, Parrish ?"

"You guess rightly. Born, bred, and raising my own children in de family compound just up Orange Hill. And in truth, I'm related to a good many folks around here ."

"And would it be fair to guess that one of your relatives has a place for me to stay until I find something better ?"

"Dere's some truth in what you say, But you won't want nothing better ."

"Excellent, I'm here for 10 days or so, You have a car for hire ?"

"Just this way ." We stepped around the side where I found a small van. Jinx buzzed the rear door open and said. " Put your rolly in de back and ride in de front with me so we can talk some more ." I did so and got in the front .

"So, before we roll, let's talk money ."

"Where do you intend on taking me ?"

"Up the west end road to my cousin's place, The Coral Seas Cliffs ."

"I saw another Coral Seas from the bus window ."

"Yeah dat's his too, He has three of dem, de Cliffs, de Beach, and de Garden. The only one with a room to let is on the Cliffs. But you stay dere, you have guest privileges at all three ."

"Sounds good enough to see. If it's like you say. How much for the ride there ?"

"Is this a one time ting, or 10 days worth of service ?"

"You can quote me both, if you are prepared to do so ."

He smiled as we left the car park, " Now you tinkin right. One way one time is $15.00. Daily service to and from the beach is $5.00 each way ."

"Let me think about that until we see the place you have in mind ."

Jinx smiled, " And Wham, jus' like dat, 'dere is no more predicament ."

We climbed away from the beach up the west end road. The garden side hotels were nice, but the water side places looked more interesting. The light rain had stopped and the moon was half up three quarters lit.

The Coral Seas Cliffs was on the water side. We stopped at the top of the hill by the check in and car park. Jinx got out and motioned for me to follow. The moonlit pathway ran down hill. I saw a central building with a swimming pool, a shaded restaurant beside the pool, and several doors for guest rooms.

There were three other buildings of guest rooms.

One faced the pool, the other two faced the Caribbean. The pathway between continued down to a cove with moonlight sparkling from the water. Is this guy a good salesman or what?

Jinx spoke, " The cove is about seven or eight meters deep in the center so don' jump close to the edge. This ledge up here is three meters off de water. The lower one dere is only one meter for the scare-dee-cats. There's coral around both sides so you dive the center, and use the ladder in and out to save your feet ."

"How's the food ?"

"Good as it gets. The Jackson family dat owns the Coral Seas also owns the Tea Water Inn and The Tree House Resort down the beach. Lots of de farm land you drove through from Mo' Bay is owned by the family as well. They supply all of their own meats, fruits, and our special local produce."

"Thanks, don't smoke. How much are the rooms?"

"You can negotiate 'dat at de front desk ."

As we walked up the hill I stopped to take a better look at the pool. The pool and it's water were clean and clear on top reflecting the moonlight.

"Okay Mr Daley, a couple of things. I would like to hire you as driver for the ten days I will be here." I took out a single $100 bill and gave it freely.

"As my wife's mother once said to me, you may be smarter than you look ."

"Ha, I already liked you Jinx, but that makes me like you more. That bill is just for the back and forth to the beach, ten bucks, ten days. I expect some day trips to local attractions to be extra. Next, I would like to ask you to negotiate the room for me as your poor long lost friend, but poor, okay ?"

He's nodding as he listens and smiles, " You get your bag, I'll get the room."

He completed the negotiations with a minimum of arm waving as I waited outside. He stepped out and handed me a key for the room and another key for the safe in the room.

"All yours, cheaper than usual, $500. I gave them the bill you gave me to secure the room. You can re-negotiate for food and beer inclusive if you wish."

"I'll leave it the way you set it up. Thanks Jinx ." I extended my hand to shake his. He smiled and asked,

"What time tomorrow ?"

————ᘛ◦◦ᘙ————

As the memory faded I looked across the bar at Jinx and asked him, " How many year we been doin' this now, Jinx ?"

"Dis would be year number Five ."

"And all that time have you ever known me to be love struck ?"

He pulled back and thought out loud,

"You mean other than the one three or four years ago? The one you flew down here to join you on Boxing Day ?" I waved and ordered another beer,

"Other than that one,"

"There is no 'Other than that one'. I used up a family

favor for you. I went to my elder, Jimmy Jackson, Ricky's dad to help you out of your predicament."

The scene fades to another memory

———⁓ꞈꙮꙮꙮ⁓———

I sit in front of a desk trying to explain myself,

"Sir, I have been very happy at Ricky's place up on the cliff, twice now,-"

A bleary eyed business man looks back, " . . but . ."

"But my friend, lady friend, would rather be staying at the beach."

"Is this the lady my cousin Jinx drove to pick up on Boxing Day?"

"Yes sir, that's her. Anyway, uh, if there is any way . . ."

"He's family, and we all missed him."

"I understand, but he wouldn't let me borrow his car."

Jimmy Jackson choked at the thought, and then laughed,

"Mr Wallis, I may have a small beach bungalow for you tomorrow, how many nights do you require ?"

"– uh – six nights ."

"We can do that by movin' Bungalow B's inhabitants, they're older and have complained about the, uh nightly noises. As a point of interest how did you leave your arrangements with the Cliffs? Are you planning on leaving soon ?"

"I am paid through the 1st. The rooms are yours to use ."

"Good. All good then. I'll put the aging couple up on

the cliffs for the same price and deduct the profit from yours down here, okay ?"

"Yes sir. Mr Jackson, I always like dealing with local owners rather than an off shore concern. My family has been around for a couple hundred years in America. How long has yours been here ?"

"A bit more than that, thank you sir ."

"I would prefer that the money I spend on this island, stay on the island and promote local growth ." He looked up at me and smiled as he said,

"And that is precisely why we are talking. We both have come upon an opportunity, I feel we should act in accord, 'Carpe Diem ' No ?"

———⁓⁓◦◦e⦿⦿⊙e⦿◦◦⁓⁓———

Pulling out of that memory I looked at Jinx as he said,

"Yeh mon', and then after you got her there, you found out she couldn't swim and was terrible afraid of water altogether."

"Yeah, but I wasn't in love. This time I think I am ."

"You really 'tink so ?"

"I'm pretty sure, it's been hours and I can't think of anyone else ."

"What about that German Olympic swimmer, couple a years ago ?"

A smile crossed my face as I thought of Frauline Ernst, 'DD'. What a beauty she was.

I met her when I was cliff diving from the three meter step before breakfast one morning. As I climbed from the water and up the ladder I felt someone watching me. I pretended not to notice and went up to the three meter position.

Cliff diving into a small cove takes some patience and intelligence of knowing the best time to dive. Namely, that you should wait until the water is at its highest before you go. As I watched and waited I heard a female voice say,

"Is this where the line forms?" I looked over my shoulder and saw a young woman in terrific condition looking at me with her hands on her hips.

"Are you going to dive? Others are waiting " I looked around to see no one but she and I.

"What others do you mean? I only see you, and while you are worth looking at, maybe I'll make you wait your turn so I can see more ."

She rolled her eyes," The best way to see more of me is to let me pass ."

So I stepped out of her way. She stepped onto the platform and paused as she watched the ebb and flow of the water.

"Is this your first time ?"

"Yes. How deep is it ?"

"Plenty deep at high water. Maybe 7 meters in the center."

She nodded as she watched, nodded again and executed a perfectly arched round dive into the center of the cove. I stepped up and waited for her to surface. She did so with a huge smile, submerged and came up in a smooth stroke toward the ladder. I waited until the water was high again and followed her dive exactly.

Swimming toward the ladder promise was fulfilled. She had taken long enough for me to follow her shapely bottom up and out of the water. It was a lovely side of her, from her butt and her hips, to her strong thighs, and down her muscular calves.

She stepped out of the way so I could top the ladder.

"That was a magnificent dive, Ms uh-" I stuck out my hand.

"Dee Dee, Dee Dee Ernst, and you are?"

"Theodore Wallach," I took her hand, " You dive very well."

"As do you, are you going again ?" I looked at my watch and said,

"Yes I have time for two or three more ." We climbed back into place.

"Are you on a schedule this morning ?"

"Only my own, after you ." She smiled and mounted the rock.

This time she dove flat out and then tucked into a ball rotating forward for a full turn and a half. She opened early from the flip and slid in between the water molecules like sunlight.

I waited for her to surface and then jumped straight out and tucked my knees up tight and yelled, 'Cannon Ball!' and landed beside her to swamp her with enough water to wash her ashore.

As I emerged she was laughing and once again climbed the ladder to my great visual delight. " That was a terrific one and a half and your entry was perfect. You dive very well ."

"Your blunderbust was fun but you might have drained the cove ."

I heard a bell ring once and looked up the hill to see a person waving at me.

"Will you join me for breakfast ?"

"Why, yes, but I would like one more dive ."

"Good, I'll go ahead ."

I walked up the hill and turned to see her waiting while watching the water. At the right moment she backed off a bit and then ran forward attempting a flying swan dive. Her head was up, her arms outstretched, and her chest was held high.

As she flew in that position she arched over slightly for her body to follow. She entered the water without so much as two ripples.

I couldn't help but applaud as she shot from the water. From up the hill, I heard another person clapping, Desmond the provider was standing and applauding from behind me.

I signaled him an OK sign. He signaled OK back. I held up two fingers palm forward. He pulled two fingers toward the pool. I pointed a finger at me and then at DD. He signaled OK and departed.

From the top of the pathway I held our towels. She reached for hers but I withheld it, " We must rinse off. I use the swimming pool," we walked there.

"That was an amazing Swan."

"Thanks, I worked on it for weeks."

"Are you a competitor?"

"Yes, Swimming and diving, Olympic class."

We were beside the pool and I put our towels over a chair, " Wow."

"And you ? What do you do ?"

"I uh, I am uh, a Judge, yeh, swimming and diving Olympic class ."

She laughed and pushed me into the pool. She dove after me and I floated face down. She swam down under me and turned over to look me in the face and dig me in the ribs. Which made me blow air and grab for her. She pushed back swimming toward the shallow end of the pool. I followed in joy.

As we stood and laughed at the shallow's steps I hear a bell ring again and saw Desmond laying out breakfast in the shade of a large umbrella. We both dove and swam the distance. We pushed out, took up the towels, as we appreciated the table Desmond had laid out.

It was perfect all the way to the flowers in the center bowl. There were large servings for two of fresh fruit slices, two goat cheese omelets, a platter of spare meats, tall glasses of guava juice, and a carafe of coffee with sweet cream.

This time it was her turn to say, " Wow! Were you expecting someone?"

"No, but I'm glad I found someone. I just pray to God you're here alone."

She raised her juice glass in a toast, " Here's to being alone, and then not."

————《wᴏᴏᴄᴇᴙᴏᴏᴄᴇᴏᴏᴡ》————

The images fade within the drink. We see Jinx's face smiling,

"Nobody saw either of you for three days, except at breakfast ."

"Yeh DD, she was great . . . ."

"And you weren't in love 'dat time either ?"

"Well, maybe a little, but not like-"

"Didn't you tell me, that you visited her in Germany ?"

"Yeah, but she invited me ."

"You took your Son ."

"He wanted to go skiing, you know, in the Alps ."

"You were in love ."

"okay, yeah, maybe so."

"'Sew Buttons', So nothing, I was happy for you then, I'm happy for you now. You have the luck to easily fall in love. . . . And I might add the luck to easily fall out of love too. So, the diver, why did it end ?"

"Well, it wasn't to be, you know, She didn't want to leave Germany. I didn't want to leave New York City, so, it just has kind of, you know . . ."

Jinx watched me over the top of his sunglasses " Did it end ?"

"Not completely." I threw some cash on the bar, He shook his head and walked away. We got to his van and started to drive. " Take me up the Cliffs ?"

"uh huh, and when was 'de last time you saw her ?"

"A couple of months ago ."

"Oh god, you got de worst case of horny pants I ever seen. But now you also got a predicament, don' cha ?"

"How So ?"

"You're in love again, aren' cha ?"

———∿∿∾◦◦♥◦◦∿∿———

The next day I went diving early and called Jinx to pick me up. I asked him to have breakfast with me and discuss things I had not done, or places not visited.

"You never been to Hogg Heaven. Some of best coral diving left."

"Where is it, far from here ?"

"Naw, further out west from here, way out the end ."

"I got to go see Shar-on early I guess ."

We finished and he drove me to the beach hut. I walked round.

"Ah there you are, early just as I hoped. Go in and strip I'll get ready ."

I did as requested and soon felt the strong warm hands rubbing my back with a very slippery substance. She worked my back and shoulders and arms. She worked my butt and legs and feet. Then she slapped my ass and I turned over.

Sharon stifled a laugh and threw a towel at my erection. I covered it as she went to work on my front. She hardly ever talked as she worked, but today,

"Today, Sir Ted, you get a combo rub of Aloe and

Coconut oil, so Yo' skin absorbs the oils and the sun bakes it brown. Speaking of which, your Princess is looking pretty good for her second day here. She baked yesterday and then came back late for another rub. I hate to tell ya, but She brought a friend with her."

"Oh " I said without trying to show interest but willing the towel down.

"Yeah, the friend said She wanted to be as tan as Janet ."

"Oh ?" Sharon laughed as she smacked me on the stomach.

"Yeah, dey comin' back dis morning so dat's why I'm glad you're early ."

"I could have waited if they were here, uh what time did She, they say ?"

"ummm," looking up as if hearing, " Jus' 'bout now."

Outside the Hut I heard the sound of two women talking and laughing and Jinx asking, " Ladies my name is Jinx, SharOn is busy, may I be of service ?"

"Oh is she? We have, uh, appointments?" SharOn threw me my suit.

"Put on your pants you." SharOn hissed, "I'll be back, soon come ."

After lacing up my baggy surf shorts, I swept the sarong aside,

"Well, Lady Janet, how pleasant to see you, and you Miss-"

"Sir Theodore, this is my friend and working associate, Nickie, Nickie-"

"Sir Theodore, the Perceptive I assume, she has spoken of you."

"The pleasure of our acquaintance has been mutual. Ladies this is a personal friend, confident, and local specialist, of many years, Jinx Daley."

Jinx removed his Kangol and swept it before him, he bowed, and held out a hand low, in order to receive and to kiss the back of their hands. They giggled and allowed him to do so.

SharOn came from the hut and said, " Who's up First ?"

Nicky stepped forward, " Jan told me to go first and last while she would do in between, okay ?"

"Okay, in and strip down for an Aloe rub. Lady Janet, I will be with you momentarily." She turned to me, " You are done my dear. You may leave; as if ."

She turned her back, entered and began to work while she began to hum.

We looked upon each other with attraction so obvious that Jinx said something about being in the van. I could only look at Janet and manage to say,

"You look great, I mean your skin looks very healthy, uh robust, you might say, or you might not, depending on how far gone your mind has, uh gone."

"You look pretty good yourself, and your skin is almost glowing," As she touches my shoulder, my knees went week, " Did you just shudder ?"

Smiling like an idiot I bit my lower lip and nodded

Yes as I blinked. She laughed and took my hand. We walked to the surf.

"I'm going coral diving way out west end today, would you care to join us, you and Nickie, of course ?"

"Love to, can't, working a long day today. When we go back to the hotel we'll be on our feet 'til after sunset."

"Which Hotel ?"

"Hedonism ."

"What are you working on with Nickie ?"

We hear the squeal of Nickie as she dashes from the hut into the surf. My eyes went wide as I saw a body as fantastic as Janet's fly between us. Janet said,

"My turn." And kissed me on the cheek, turned and entered the hut. Sharon handed me a towel and gestured to the surf where Nickie was splashing and rubbing her body partially under water. I turned again and Sharon was gone.

I looked back toward the surf and Nickie was strutting out trying to cover her breasts with her small hands. When she got to me, she turned for me to put a towel on her shoulders. She took it hooked it under her arms and tied it in front.

"I think Mr Jinx should get out of here, before he and I do something we will regret later ."

I say, " I can't think of anything he would regret later ."

"That's because you're a guy. You weren't born with any common sense to begin with, so you can't gain any from experience. Go now, get on with you ."

"Of course, will you give Janet a message for me ?"
"Maybe, what is it ?"
"Tell her, please, " and I sang to Nickie.

**'Well, I'd like to get to know you,
if I could.'**

Nickie laughed and clapped. I stopped, but from the
hut I heard Janet,

**'Yes, i'd like to get to know you, know
you, knoooww youuuu'**

Sharon stepped out and took two Red Stripe from the
cooler. Then she picked up the cooler and tossed the rest
of the ice water at me.

———∿∿∽o∾c⊕⊙⊕ↄ∾o∽∿∿———

Hogg's Heaven was difficult to drive to. The broken
terrain was so uneven that dis-connected paths had been
made from the road. I had to walk a bit to get to the water.
Old man Hogg owned miles of beach front as it edged
along the point. In some places there were a few feet of
land before the short beach. In others it was acres of coral
waiting for high tide.

Of the few houses which sat on Hogg land, about half
were for sale. According to Jinx, if I wished to have a home
here, Mr Hogg would lease you the land, then build or re-
build any structure you could afford. And he would help

finance the project in order to take receivership when, and if, you wanted out. I had an uncle who did that with hunting and fishing cabins.

Fifty feet off shore were the most impressive coral beds I have ever seen. The water was ten -fifteen feet deep with crystal clear sunlight illuminating the beds of living coral which grew below. There were huge bulbous brain corals rolling along in humps and curves. There were acres of fire coral rimming underwater rock shelves. There were racks upon racks of antler coral and longhorn coral. There were huge bedrock sea fans flowing with the current. Swimming one reef I saw a perfectly camouflaged fish the size of a Volkswagen.

I stayed and played for a while. When finished I was withered.

———❧———

Later that day, I had Jinx drop me at Sharon's only to find the hut empty. The tree trunk canoe was there, as were a fresh set of shells beside Conch Hill. No festive beach towels hung out along the rails. There were no sultry sunset sarongs hanging about upon the driftwood poles. There were no beach boys running errands, playing dominoes, or hooking tourists.

Mr Nigel was sitting on his stoop carving a flute. He stopped carving when he saw me and blew a note. I waved and asked, " Where is everybody ?"

"Dey all off wit 'choo ladies, doin' de browning ting."

"Uh Sharon left with Janet ?"

"Irie mon' her and the other one, and the others too."

"Others? Off with Nickie and the others, other girls ?"

"Girls and Boys too, all of 'em very pretty people ."

"Do you know where they went ? When they would be back ?"

"No, none a 'dat. She asked me to feed 'de kids and not to wait up."

I called Jinx on the link to ask for a ride back to the cliffs. His link answered for him and offered to take a message. So I went for a swim as far the Coral Seas Beach. Sitting at the bar bullshitting with Beaufort I felt my link vibrating in my pouch. It stopped as I fished it out, but I saw Jinx's number crawl from the screen.

I harrumphed at the sight, I admit to being in a pissy mood. I was denied an afternoon massage / skin treatment because Sharon had been hijacked by the person I introduced her to. I was grouching because Sharon got to go with Janet. Beaufort was saying something that I was not listening to when I looked up and saw the Coral Sea shuttle bus pulling in the car park.

I took my beach pack and walked to the bus. We pulled out onto Manley blvd at sunset and trundled toward the Coral Seas Gardens. A short stop later as we left the Gardens we sat waiting at a traffic stop, I saw Jinx's van go by full of people and a fleeting glimpse of Janet in a rear passenger seat.

I started sucking air like a gasping fish. I didn't want to see what I had just seen so quickly pass by. Jinx and Janet and many others were in his van. Then suspicion hit me again, somewhere in that van was most probably Sharon. As the shuttle began the climb up the west end road I was being eaten alive with jealousy, Sharon, and Jinx, both where I wanted to be, with Janet. It was a low dark evil thing which started me scowling.

When we got to the Cliffs I went straight to the shower and stayed until the grime of those low thoughts had washed away. Jinx and Sharon had every right to join the show biz party if they wished to, or whatever they wanted to do.

Fortunately my shower ran out of hot water just as I heard my link chirp. And as before, stopped chirping as I got there dripping wet.

I punched redial and was sent to Jinx's voice mail, and was stunned again by the message that played. It wasn't Jinx's voice, it was Nickie's.

"Jinx can't answer you right now. He is driving and being distracted by seven beautiful actors and a superb massage therapist. You can leave a message or eat your heart out in silence. 'Jinx is da Man, da Man wit da Beauty Van'. BEEP ."

I was in a mental state beyond reason, so I didn't leave a message. I dried myself, dressed, and walked to the pool side bar. Dianne was there with a Red Stripe before I found a seat. I took the bottle and rolled the cold glass back and forth along my forehead. I took a short drink and walked out onto the terrace. I looked about and found a large woven wicker cane chair with arm rests.

From there I could see the wispy cloud line being

lit from below the horizon by the falling sun. The rivers of color continued their slow cross fades as I rested my head against the cane weave of the chair. At some point I must have dozed off for I began to dream a dream of still photographs; all of Janet.

The dream ended with just her face saying,

"Ted ? Theo ? Theodore ? Ted ? . . . " and I could see her face very clearly.

"Ted ?" It was she, I mean really her, sitting on a lounge beside me.

"Janet ?" My hand reached out to touch her face, " Are you really here ?"

She took my hand and brushed her cheek

"I am. I have come to you to ask a favor ." My mind reeled from the past.

"Lady Janet, you've already taken my driver and my masseuse, what else do you want, my rooms?"

"Why, Yes, Sir Perceptive. I Thank you, Would you do that for me ?"

I shake my head sideways while maintaining eye contact and said,

"Yes, I would. I'm not sure why, but I probably would . . . say Yes ."

She looked into my eyes and smiled as she glanced down at my lips. Our eyes met again and we both moved in to kiss. This kiss seemed to induce a trance, a wonderful taste of bliss, and great promise.

Sometime during that eternity I needed more air, so I broke the spell,

"I need you to come with me. Please ?"

She allowed me to lead her from the terrace and across the lawn.

"Are we going to your rooms ?"

"Yes, if I am giving them to you, you should know where they are ."

She says, " Good, We've waited long enough. God I'm hungry." I smile.

When we rounded the side of the pool I saw, three pair of feet sticking over the railing of my little porch and clouded by smoke. I had to smile as I said,

"Jinx ?" and saw the center pair of feet drop .

"Right here Sir Teddy ." His face replaced his feet at the rail.

"I see you are having an appetizer. I'm taking Janet to dinner, would you and your guests care to join us ?" SharOn and Nickie's heads appear beside Jinx's.

Janet said, " You sure know how to treat a girl, or three," and we doubled back to the terrace and crossed to the bar where I ordered.

"Darling Dianne, this is Janet, we are dining with three others. We will share 3 large seafood combos. And 3 orders of jerk chicken and a bucket of cold Red Stripes, Oh, and if you wish to, You may join us."

Janet looked on and said nothing as I led her to a bar stool.

"So, First you kidnapped Sharon-"

"Convinced would be a better term. She wasn't taken against her will."

"Did she have a good day?"

"She had a very good day. She said it was her best day ever."

"She does okay at the beach."

"I thought she might be an asset to have around ."

"I've always thought so, until she wasn't. I got a little jealous, actually a little mad that she got to be with you while I had to wait."

"That is so sweet, I love that you got jealous, But, she was working those arms and hands swollen until I had her take a break. She must have done twenty people today."

"May I ask, and be answered this time. What are you working on?"

"Just a photo shoot. We're swimsuit models."

"You've just made me a very happy man."

"Why is that?"

"Because I guessed correctly, and I won fifty bucks."

The bucket of Beer arrived along with Jinx, Sharon, and Nickie who said,

"Sir Teddy Boy, you saved our lives today, I owe you a kiss ."

And she did so. And so did I, with whistling approval from Sharon.

"Thanks, I do what little I can, with what little I have. What did I do ?"

"First, we took Sharon, the goddess of tan, without asking permission-"

"She's a free woman, she doesn't need my permission ." SharOn added,

"That I am, and that I'll stay. Got married once and found I was too much for any one man. So I've been me own boss and same to others for years now."

Nickie says, "And when we needed a fast get away, we took Jinx's number."

Janet adds, " And of course, he said he thought you would understand-"

I have to ask, " Get away fast from what ?"

Jan confesses, " I'm being stalked ."

"Wait there a moment. Sharon, did this pack oh hyenas treat you well ?"

Sharon adds with a toast of Red Stripe, " That they did, best day ever ."

"How much ?"

"A little over 2k ."

"And did they tip you as well ?"

Nickie says, " I did so personally ."

"How much ?"

"I gave her another 200 for excellence, and being a good spirit ."

"Okay. Then you hijacked, 'commandeered', Jinx. Where were you ?"

Janet says, " We were shooting out at Ricks ."

"How much did you pay Jinx ?"

Nickie objects, " Pardon me Sir Teddy Boy, is this your business ?"

"Yes, these two local people are under retainer from me, therefore I am responsible for making sure that anyone I introduce them to treats them well ."

Nickie says, " One rarely sees nobility from an American ."

Janet admits, " Noblesse Oblige at its finest ."

Nickie offers, " I paid him 200 and was intending to tip him another 50 ."

"$ 250? I thought you said this was a rescue from a stalker. Cheapskate ."

Janet says, " Okay, you're right, Jinx, How much ?"

"Talk to me manager dere." Nickie takes the beer I offer as I ask,

"How many people in the van that passed me?"

Nickie asks, " We passed you?"

"Ten passengers, and myself very much distracted at the wheel."

"You should pay him $40 dollars a head and a twenty five percent tip."

Jinx brightens, " $ 500.00? I'll take it."

"Good even up. Here comes our dinner to the big table. Let's eat."

———∿∿⊙⊙⊙∿∿———

We ate until we needed to get up from the table and digest.

"So Sharon, how did you like your first day in show busines?"

"Well, the talent here is pretty nice, it's their handlers that were bossy. The top people are okay, not too full of themselves, but it seems that the assistants are too pushy, and even a bit snarky, if it means getting something the boss wants."

Nickie says, " That is, the best, dead on description I have ever heard. I mean, My suit designers, Sweethearts; their assistants; bitches, except the one who isn't a girl, but he's a little bitch too."

I ask, " How about you Jinx?"

"What do I know, I made one run to Ricks and back, the way I see it, everybody is somebody's bitch ."

Jan asks, " Oh yeah Mr Jinx, whose Bitch are you?"

"It's a toss up, either my mother in law, or her daughter ."

Everybody gets a good laugh. Sharon excuses herself and stumbles toward the pool to drop over the side into the water. I head toward the pool as she pops up and extends a hand. I take it and pull her out. Janet looks at Nickie and says,

"To nobility." Nickie nods and raises a Red Stripe for a toast.

"To nobility, wherever it appears, a trait rich enough to be savored ."

Their bottles are raised, " To Nobility !" The bottles clink and they drank.

As I returned to the table with Sharon on my arm she asks,

"Where's the Loo ? My back teeth are floating ."

I took out my room key and tossed it to her.

"Don't forget to leave the seat up ." She tip toes away.

"Now down to cases, Who is stalking whom?"

"The assistant director has been stalking me."

"The assistant? Well now, the bitchy theory holds water. Male or female?"

"Female, although there are rumors that she morphs after darkness falls."

"Same sex stalking. Ah, that's got to be different then."

"But not as obvious, it started as 'We're all sisters here on set', you know with a friendly touch or hug, usually followed by a personal compliment."

Nickie is laughing brandishing a jerk chicken part,

"You know the difference between a rogue elephant and a bull dyke ?"

Everyone just looks at her inquisitively.

"Fifty pounds and a flannel work shirt."

"Okay funny but not to her. Okay, What happened today ?"

Janet says," Well, near the end of the shoot at Ricks, She has the costume department pack early and then sends them off, without the final shot costumes ."

Nickie says, " Knowing we'll be a van short for the return, which of course she can cover by offering Nickie and I a ride back to the hotel in her private van."

Jan adds," Making the other talent wait for a second run from the beach."

Nickie admits, " So, I got on the link and asked Jinx for a ride. He said he was waiting for you at Sharon'. Knowing she was with us, he said yes and that even if he was a little late to pick you up, that you would probably understand."

"Irie. I'll vouch safe as to all of that, knowing you would; probably. I mean knowing you as I do, for as many years as we have . . . I said okay ."

I raise my bottle and said, " Salute! " And we all drink.

Sharon comes back to the table, " Thanks," and holding up the key; asked,

"Anybody else? "

Nickie stood shakily " I'm next ." Sharon tossed her the key,

"Beware Luv, the seat's up ."

"Okay, thanks for that, I'll never forget this one time, I uh, . never mind ."

As Nickie departs, I considered the coming night and all the unknowns.

"They need to go back. I don't want to . . . . . that woman,"

"And, will you stay with me ?"

"I thought it was wrong of me to presume, so I got a room."

"Good choice. Jinx?"

"I heard and ready to go."

"Two for the beach, individual drop offs; Sharon at her cambio, and then to her home. And then drop Nickie at hedonism."

Jinx asks, " Which reminds me, the show tomorrow. Can we get tickets ?"

Sharon comes back to the table holding the dinner bill.

"Ms Thing, are you expecting me tomorrow ?"

I said, " That's my check ."

Jan says, " Based on today I would guess 'Yes', but I don't really know ."

"Good, cause I got other clients at the beach that have requested time ."

I ask again, " Will you let me have the check ?"

SharOn says, " No, I've already paid it, plus de tip."

Jinx says, " Even though you saw she was a little one, there's nothing small about me cousin SharOn."

Janet speaks, " Here's a couple of thoughts, Jinx can you take me down tomorrow at 8am? I won't assume Sharon can work the shoot and didn't ask her. If they want her, they'll make a fuss and have me call. Sharon, did anyone take your link number?"

"No."

"Perfect, they have to get it from me. I will tell them that I was lucky to get you today. And that if they're lucky they might get a half day sometime soon."

"I get'cher tinkin' Jan honey, what is your link ?"

Nickie comes stumbling back to the table, " Here ya go, the seats up. Are we square? Do I owe anything? Are we going soon ?"

"Sharon got dinner,"

Jinx calls, " All aboard to da beach, " as he starts for the car park.

"Jinx will drop me off before de bottom, round my way. You be good ."

Jan says, " Nickie, baby, I'm staying here tonight. I want you to stop at the desk, tell them you're me and tell them you dropped your room key at the desk this morning. That way anyone who checks on whether I returned, will be told yes."

"Well, the plot thickens. You gonna' sing to her Sir Ted ?"

"Until she asks me to stop. But that won't take long. See ya Nickie ."

As Nickie dashes the path after Jinx and Sharon, we hear Janet ask,

"Where's 2G?"

"Over there."

"And where are you?"

"Over here."

"Why don't we start over there and end up over here?"

"Something to look forward to."

"Hey mister, wanna walk me home ?"

"Thought you'd never ask." He takes her hand and strolls, and sings,

"This could be something wonderful ."

She opens the door with her key, stands aside as he enters, and shuts the door behind him. We hear a muted reprise.

———⁓⁓◦◦⌒◦◦⌒◦⌒◦◦⁓⁓———

Janet left early and I slept late. Then I went cliff diving and met Jinx on the pool deck for breakfast.

"Are you still in love?"

"More than ever."

"Is it bad?"

"Worse than ever."

"It that good?"

"Better than ever."

"Better than the veterinarian from the ostrich farm?"

"Way better, but way different, no comparison."

"Different how?"

"Janet doesn't do animal imitations. Did, uh, did she say anything about, you know, about last night?"

"Nope didn't say a thing but good morning and thanks, see ya later."

"That sounds encouraging to me,"

"No doubt, so what's the plan today? Wanna see de car wash?"

"Maybe, does the van need to be washed?"

"It's a taxi mon, needs to be washed every day."

"How far is it?"

"Out about half way to Black River. Off in 'de hills."

"Let's do it after I see a woman about some browning."

———∿∾⊙⌇⊙⊙⌇⊙∾∿———

When we got to SharOn's the renovation was just finishing. The beach boys had expanded the hut sideways and added enough room for a second massage table and a second cooler for Sharon's custom blended items.

The outside spans of poles and rails were spread wider apart but hung much the same. There was a younger woman working beads into the hair of a client who sat in a semi coma watching the surf roll.

Sharon was on the link saying,

"No, 'fraid not, I have a One o'clock. Could you be here by Two ?"

I smiled at her and went to wash in the surf. When I returned, she was off the link and watching the thatch roof being woven.

"Busy day ?'

"So, far, yeah. You here for your usual, or, you here for the unusual ."

"The usual, unless you know something that I don't know ."

"Like, Something Wonderful, perhaps ?"

"Did you see her today? Did she say that? Was she okay, I mean did she seem alright ?"

"She seemed right as rain to me, didn't talk much, but she smiled a lot, especially with her eyes closed ."

"Was Nickie with her ?"

"No, a big blonde was with her. She told me to hurry, and that, 'Time was of the Essence' whatever that means ."

"It's Sho Biz BS meaning her schedule was more important than yours ."

"Yeah, I guessed that. I told her to wait, or go swimming to cool off ."

"How did she take that ?'

"Not well, not sure. But she offered me a 20 to watch,"

"And you said ?"

"I told her to get her fat ass outa here before I set my dogs on her ."

"What dogs, there aren't any dogs here ."

"She don' know dat, so she got mad and got away from here ."

High fives and down low too.

"I like the expansion, You still got time for a faithful customer ?"

"Lord Wallach, You are the inaugural customer, step right this way ."

I stepped in, dropped my beach baggies, and laid face down on Sharon's table. I felt her fabulous hands pushing aloe and coconut oils into the pores of my back She was working on my shoulders, and onto my arms, wrists, and hands.

I must admit, I was snoring when I was awakened by a slap on the ass.

"Turn Over, I'll be right back ." She left as I regained reality; somewhat.

The palm fronds were covering the top of the hut admitting small rays of light. The beach boys were climbing and adding more fronds as they watched. I smiled and waved, they did the same, and I drifted into the feel of Sharon's hands rubbing my toes and feet, distant neural synapses fired as she worked her way up my calves.

The front of my thighs were evidently fore play, for I heard her exclaim,

"Down please, Now is not the time for that kind of fun." She toweled me.

Sharon continued along my torso and finished with my shoulders, arms, wrists, and fingers. Sometime during the end I dozed off again. She evidently left me there a while because I woke up with the sun shining directly down.

There was a person, a female person, snoring on the table beside mine. I shook my head, swung my legs off the table, and felt the towel which had been placed over me drop to the floor. As I bent to pick it up I realized I was naked. I took my surfing baggies hanging from a hook and put them on.

Outside I found the aroma of some cooking fish wafting toward the beach. Richie was at the cook pit. Mr Nigel was washing out his canoe. The beach boys were gone. And Sharon was on the link down the beach some. I took out my own link to find the time to be 12: 45. Sharon was walking back toward me.

"If you gonna sleep like that, I gotta raise my rates."

"It might be worth it, how long was I out ?"

"A couple of hours, good thing I put out the money for that extra table ."

"Yeah, you could have saved it all and just leave it in the bank ."

"Maybe, dis one time Papa and I were out walking and a car stopped to ask directions for somewhere. Me 'fodder gave them instructions and as they drove away I saw a sign on the bumper that read 'Jesus Saves'. Me 'fodder add, 'Jesus Saves, but Moses Invests'. That's all I'm doing here, building by gradual degree. Not too much, just enough for dis week, maybe dis season ."

"Where's Jinx ?"

"Not here now, but he'll be back, You never know with cousin Jinx ."

"True dat. Did Janet call for you ?"

"Oh yeah, well one of her Snarkies called, and I told him that I only had time for Jan and told him to have her call when she could do so herself ."

"How did he take that ?"

"I don' know, I hung up after I spoke ."

"Did she call ?"

"Yeah, she wanted me to come to the shoot for the rest of the day ."

"You gonna do it ?"

"Sure, I could use another four figure day."

"Where are they shooting today ?"

"Up the west end again, The Rock House and the Pickled Parrot ."

Just then Jinx walked onto the beach wearing a new Kangol

"There he is, sleeping beauty, You a little browner, but no prettier ."

"Same to you little brother. Are we doin' the car wash ?"

"Do we have time for lunch? I smell something good with Richie ."

"Sea Bass stuffed with Crab and conch fritters. Me 'fodder's a damn fine provider ."

Sharon's link chirps and she answers,

"Who dat calling me? Who, Oh we did, Yes she did, No, 'cause I haven't had lunch yet. Who gave you dis number? Well, let me give you some advice, Loose this number and never ever call me again," and she disconnected.

"lemme guess, your morning acquaintance?"

"Well, Lookee 'der, 'dat woman was calling me from Janet's link."

"Is that her link number?"

"You don't have it? "

Jinx smirked, " I do, Janet called me and asked me to give Sharon a ride to the Rock House."

Something did not make sense, so I asked, " Do you think Janet knows that the stalker is using her link?"

"Anybody have Nickie's number?"

"Sure do."

"Sharon, would you call Nickie and tell her that the stalker has Janet's phone. Probably cloning Janet's phone, and probably her contacts. Probably as we speak ."

"Will do, " She turns away as I say to Jinx, " Let's drop Sharon off."

"Nickie was pissed and hung up on me."

Jinx asks," Mister Nigel, can we get some fish to take away with us?"

—⁓⊙⊛⊙⊛⊙⊛⊙⊙⁓—

We dropped Sharon and her bag of tricks off at the Rock House. It's a nice place with cabins strewn along the cliff face. There is a central bar and restaurant over looking several tanning and diving areas. It's pretty much perfect for a swimsuit shoot. We did not stop long as we were on our way to the 'Car Wash'.

There is a church on a hill close to the Black River. The Church of Holy Waters is blessed with exactly what she praises. The water coming from underground runs strong, cold, and clean after traveling the length of a mountain. The church owns the land on both sides of the stream from up the hill all the way down to the Black River.

There is a particular spot where the underground stream shoots out the side of a hill becoming an above ground stream. The water shoots 8 to10 feet this time of year. The church's patrons have built a large wide driveway across the stream. There is room for two vehicles in the shooting stream of water.

So here's what you do. You drive through twice to get wet all over. Then you wash one side and drive through. Then you wash the other side and drive through. Then you drive back and forth another time for luck and park to wipe down. In the course of this effort, you and your assistants may get as wet as you wish.

In the meantime, you pay whatever you like. There are donation boxes with a bell to ring on both sides of the stream. The suggested donation is $1.00 per trip. Jinx gave up $ 5.00 and rang the bell 5 times. Several people looked our way and waved their, 'thank you' waves.

He had all of the stuff to wash the van in the back. There were a couple of wide buckets and long handled brushes. There were short handled brushes and a single bar of Castile soap. There were dry towels and a chamois cloth.

We got soaked three times. Twice were from the actual washing and rinsing of the Van. The final time was from the water fight that broke out because one of us had splashed some water on the other one. I'm not quite sure who started that one, or who won that one, but, it seemed like fun at the time.

As we drove away, I asked Jinx if he knew of a local jelly nut stop. We cut across the ridge lines of several hills through a series of unmarked country and farm roads. When we emerged, we overlooked Negril from a mountain road precisely beside Jinx's favorite jelly hut. Maybe it was favored because of Sally, the large eyed beauty that ran the place. And maybe it was because she was another of Jinx's cousins.

The Coconut is a wonderful thing. Something like 95% of the tree, fronds, and nut itself is used or consumed by the people of these hills and many other hills like these throughout the world.

The young nuts are best served cold. So the beautiful Sally had several in a big ice cooler. She pulls one out and sets it on the counter. She takes a machete and cuts a small scooping spoon from the outside of the hull. She cuts off the top end to expose a hole small enough for a long straw to draw out the cold milk.

Then comes the fun part. After you have held the nut upside down over you mouth to get the last drops, you give the big green nut back to Sally who splits it down the middle. This allows you to scoop up the creamy cold thick liquid pulp with your spoon. Both sides scoop five or six laden pulp swallows of gastro intestinal pleasure.

The cool liquid milk that has already entered your system is now followed by the cool pulpy meal which fills your stomach. Heaven, did I say 'Heaven'? Well, I meant to quote Jinx, 'Fuckin' Hevan' Mon'.

I was sitting in the shade by the van day dreaming when da Jinx link began to chirp. He answered,

"Yer time, the meter's running. Oh Hello there Princess. Yeah he's with me, I don't know, Boyo, Do you have your cell ?"

"Yeah, well sort of, it's in my beach bag, in the van."

"Not on him Jan, what's up? Uh huh ? Oh Ho, ... maybe an hour or so. right, layers then ."

"Do tell the latest ."

"Janet says to tell you thanks for letting Nickie know about the phone. They decided to declare the phone stolen. A security person found it on the assistant director. Jan wanted to know when you would be back in town, and if it was okay for you to pick her up at Sharon's. I told her yes."

"Good enough, they found her link on the stalker. Let's shove off ."

———∿∿◦◠◯◔◯◯◠◦∿∿———

When they got to the hut, they found Sharon working on Nickie's well tanned skin and Janet out front lounging topless in the braiding chair.

"Well, well, what have we here? Jinx avert yer eyes."

"No can do boss man. They seem to be stuck where yours are."

"Oh, well, yeah, hello there beautiful."

"Hello yourself handsome, Hey Jinx, thanks for meeting us here ."

"The pleasure is still mine. You're looking pretty good."

"Thanks, Sharon said that 'The Girls' here were undernourished, so I thought I would give them some fresh air and sunshine ."

I say, " Yeah, well I suppose only one word would suffice."

"And that word would be ?"

"Impressive. Like howl at the moon, impressive."

She laughs, takes off her shades, and shoulder rolls into a bikini top that covered a fraction of the acreage.

"The three of us, my tits and I, thank you both for the compliments."

I admit, " Well, uh, okay then, sorry to stare."

"Don't be, most women can take it one of two ways. I choose to take it as compliment when a man is stricken speechless by a pretty pair of breasts ."

"What's the other way?"

"Insulted, rude, and generally un-accepting of such simple behavior."

With palms up I confess, " What can I say, we really are quite simple."

"Ain't that the truth-" says Nickie as she runs naked into the surf.

Sharon comes out of the hut wiping her hands on a towel

"Is 'simple' another English word for stupid?"

. "Sometimes," I admitted, " But not universally the same, it's a matter of context, you see-" Jinx interrupted,

"According to me wife, they're the same when it comes to men ."

"Jinx's wife and I are cousins. Most Jamaican women think alike. You guys can get terrible stupid over a nice pair."

Nickie emerges from the water and walks back to the four. Two guys are watching every step as she passes wide eyed and mouths open. Laughing, Janet enters the hut and Sharon follows her inside.

"May I treat us all to dinner ?"

"Here? I mean at Hedonism ?"

"No, not here, or there. I was thinking more like out on the Cliffs. You mentioned there some marvelous hideaways."

"Sharon, when you and Nickie are done, let's all go to dinner, okay?"

Sharon emerges from the hut opening wiping her hands and wrists again.

"Okay by me." She surveys and picks out a sarong, She skies it through the opening. " Nickie's gonna change and I'll find one for you – ah, here's the one."

She takes a sarong in deep Greens and Blues and hands it to Janet. who nods in approval and steps inside.

A worried breathless production girl arrives running, and carrying clothes on her arms. She stops, looks, and stammers,

"Pardon me, are Janet and Nickie here?"

"It depends, who you are you?"

"I'm Shirley, wardrobe? I need to get the suits back to the designers. They sent these summer dresses in exchange, if I found them; did I?"

"You did, Yo, Ladies in the Hut. Your costumes are required to be returned to Wardrobe. The mistress, Shirley, just arrived. She brought adequate coverage for you both. Please hand out the suits."

I handed the summer dresses in, and got a miniature tangled ball of a swimsuits in return. I handed them over to Shirley. She almost wept and tried to flee, but for Janet yelling,

"Shirley, Stop. " Shirley did so and stood quivering awaiting the voice.

Jan stepped out in the sarong. " I just wanted to thank you for looking out for us. May I ask you for another favor?"

"Well, uh thanks, ok, sure,"

"Tell us what happened after we left."

"Well, the day was done at that point. I mean, the AD was in possession of stolen goods. You and Nickie left the scene. With the possibility of prosecution, security also confiscated Charlotte's link for, you know, further investigation."

"And ?"

"The BFD skipped, actually she ran and dove right off the cliff. Well, that left us in quite a mess. We couldn't finish. We had to shut down for today."

"Excuse me, what does BFD mean here ?"

"Well, Big Fat Dyke, although to be honest she's big but not that fat. The other was the staff's name for her due to her, uh, preferences? May I go now?"

"You may go with my thanks for your service. See you soon."

———∽∾∾∾∾∾——

Jinx' idea of a private dinner was a place further up the west end road called 'Roy and Tony's Serious Chicken'. It was maybe 60 feet wide by 120 feet deep with a picket fence framing the entrance. Every corner post, both ends of the bar, and entry posts were adorned with carved wooden birds. Both Chickens and Roosters stood or flared in various positions.

We chose a secluded corner. Sharon is on the link. The ladies are both texting, the server is approaching and Jinx orders,

"Three full jerks with Red Stripes here. Two half jerks with iced tea there. Extra potato salad all around and one order of sweet potato fries."

"Well, here's some news from my agent, Murrry. A warrant has been issued for the AD, full name of Charlotte

Masters. It seems that a couple of other crew people have now filed official complaints of sexual harassment. It also seems that her phone had several photos of naked talent in the dressing rooms, fitting rooms, and changing areas ."

"Oh, she's is such a goner."

"Sounds too good to be true."

SharOn asks, " What's a goner?"

"One who has left for good."

"I don't know. How will she get off the Island?"

"Maybe the same way she got off the cliffs, by swimming."

"Here's food. I ordered half portions for the models and full meals for the rest of us. Knowing they will mooch as much as they can after they finish theirs."

At one point the owners came out back to check on us five and to get a photo taken with all of the girls, Sharon was asked to stand dead center flanked by Tony and Roy with Janet and Nickie outside.

———〜〜∘◦⦿◦∘〜〜———

Afterward, as we walked back to the hotel, Jinx and Janet made the same deal for morning transportation, Nickie and Sharon talked babies, I just marveled at my good fortune. When we got to the car park the night guard asked if our friend had found us. He had his guard dog on the short leash.

"What friend? " asked Janet as she reached out to pet the dog

"De one dat came askin'for you. I told her you were

taking dinner at Serious Chicken." The dog is loving the attention from Janet. " Bruno, sit!"

"I wasn't expecting anyone. What did my friend look like?"

"She was a mess, looked like she just got out of the pool. Said 'dat she locked herself out of the room and asked me to let her in." We all looked at one another wide eyed.

"What did you do?"

"Well, I know you and him be staying here. Jinx here, he's my in law. But him and these other ladies got no privileges here. So I told her 'No' and 'dat she had to get the key from you."

Jinx said, " Well done Trevlan, you do me proud, can you describe her?"

"Sure enough, although it wasn't a pretty sight. Big woman, almost two meters, dirty blonde hair, brown eyes, had a limp, de foot was bleedin' some."

"I think we know that woman from somewhere."

"Bruno, he don' like her he bared his teeth and snarl. She backed off, I thought she went to find you. Dat's why I ask if you seen her, an' to let you know she came lookin'."

Jinx says, " You did just right Trev, dat woman is no friend, in fact she is wanted for some crimes. We need to do some'ting here. Let's go in the office."

Nickie asks, " You think she's still here?"

I say, " One way to find out, Sharon can you go round the kitchen where you can see Janet's room from the water side? " She smiles and leaves the group as they go in the office.

"Trevlan, you got Ricky Jackson's link number? Can you call him and let me speak with him, I got a favor to ask." Trev takes out his link and punches

"Nickie, if this goes right, we will need the photo shoot security to collect the criminal from Coral Seas security, do you know who to call?"

She nods and takes out her link, as Trevlan hands his link to Jix,

"Hey there Ricky Boyo, have I got some fun for you . . . ."

During his conversation Sharon comes back to report,

"I don' know who, but dere is someone aside the steps to your porch."

Jinx says, " The owner is comin' with a couple of guards from the beach."

"Shoot security force says they would like to be involved. They said to give them about 20 minutes."

"Good, Here's what I think we should do . . . ."

———

Janet and I went to the bar to have one more and give the others time to get set. We were intentionally louder than usual seeming a bit drunk. We had a couple of shots of Anejo tequila and chased them with limes and a Red Stripe.

We stalled until Ricky Jackson arrived and joined us at the bar.

"Ricky, welcome, Jan this is a recent friend Mr Richard Jackson, the owner of this fine establishment. Ricky I would like you to meet my new friend, Janet."

"Pleasure to finally catch up with you Teddy Boy. Ms Janet, welcome to the Coral Seas Cliffs, my favorite hotel. Are you perhaps a model for the photo shoot around here this week ?"

In the shadows we see a head turn toward the bar.

"That I am Mr Jackson. You have a lovely place here, I like it much more than the slime hole they have us booked in, you know the place."

"I do believe I have heard of Hedonism, but I have never been there."

"Talk about leaving a bad taste, filled with over age, panty waist men, and their closet lesbian girlfriends." Jan goes snarky.

We see the head in the shadows jerk as if slapped. We see the dim grim face of Charlotte twitch and snarl.

"We don't allow that sort of trash. The place is little more than a bordello."

"On the money, Cheers." Jan hoists her beer and we toast.

"Well, that's it for me. Ricky, nice seeing you. Jan are you ready?"

"Honey, ah'm always ready! Mr. Jackson, a pleasure, Ciao!"

We waved goodbye and I led Janet to the front door of her place. As I opened the door she placed a hand around my neck and leaned in for a kiss. And what a kiss it was, all warm and wet with an adventurous tongue. I struggled to stay focused on the scenario we had devised.

The shadow crept closer to the porch watching through a window.

Janet pulled back from the kiss and said,

"I want more, and I want to be clean. Want to start with a shower? I'll wash you if you wash me . . . . I'll start the shower ."

We see the face contort and then bite her lower lip.

"If we're gonna fill this place with steam, I'll open the porch door."

I went to the sliding door, unlocked it, and slid it open 'bout halfway.

Falling off the porch we see the shadow hit the ground. She rolls over and picks up a Conch shell.

———ᘟᘘᕳ᙭᙭ᘛᘚ———

Outside the front door we see Nickie and Sharon sneaking toward the building, each trailing a rope behind them. They stop about ten feet shy of the open door, and throw the ropes up to the second level railing. Rickie draws them tight raising a net across the door.

———ᘟᘘᕳ᙭᙭ᘛᘚ———

Creeping back onto the porch Charlotte takes one last look around, and the pushes the curtain and door open a little more.

We see steam coming from the open bathroom door.

We hear squeals and moans of passion coming from within.

As Charlotte warily passes through the living space she sees the back of Janet's naked body in the steam. It's almost too much for Charlotte as she blinks and stops.

I say, " Hey come back here, You missed a spot ." Janet is pulled back into the bathroom and the door slams shut. As we hear more sounds of delight, Charlotte's composure snaps. She moves to the door and shouts,

"You let her out of there!" All sounds inside stop.

"Who is that? Who's out there?"

Charlotte fakes, " Hotel security Mam, we have an intruder. Open up!"

"Not on your life, Charlotte, baybay!"

At the sound of these words, Charlotte slams the Conch shell against the bathroom door. It comes half through and sticks. When it wiggled, I crashed the door open striking something on the other side.

We only hear, " Ah, mother- jeez! What the fuck, that hurt,"

I slammed the door again.

"You bastard! I'll do you for that."

As the shell began to move I shoved the door open again. I spiked her with one of points off the crown of the conch and it came loose from the door.

She stumbled back screaming and holding the red conch, The blood from her forehead was covering her left eye and cheek.

Janet looked out at her and then slammed the door again shouted,

"Fuck off bitch!"

A scream of rage was followed by the words,

"I'll kill you both before he can have you!" She slams the conch again.

Her scream and the blow on the door were accompanied by the barking and snarling of a guard dog.

Bruno and Trevlan had come up the porch step with Ricky following, both waiting for the right moment. When he heard the words, 'I'll kill You', Ricky told Trevlan to enter the suite.

As Bruno advanced, snarling and barking, Charlotte shrieked and threw the shell at the dog. It bounced off the Rottweiler's cinder block head. He snapped his jaws and kept coming for her.

She shrieked again and fled through the front door and into the fishing net thrown up to prevent her escape. She was caught in the net and twisted back and forth to get free. This only made her more firmly entrapped as she fell to the ground. Bruno was delighted with the reaction

Trevlan and Jinx walked to the security officers of the photo shoot.

"Is this the woman we were told about?"

The captain of shoot security looked and said, " Looks like her . . . ."

Mr Jackson says, " If you want a better look, throw her in the pool."

"And who are you?"

Trevelyn is in his face saying, " He is the owner of the hotel, he my boss."

"Trevlan, give me Bruno, you and the others throw her into the pool."

Photo security says, " You can't take my prisoner."

"Yes I can, actually she is my prisoner until released to you. Under Jamaican law . . . I have the right to question her. Do you, by any chance have the warrant issued for her arrest?"

"Yes."

"Good, let's go to the pool ."

Trev and a shoot guard swing the net over the water and let go. Jinx and Sharon dove in after and detach and unwind the net. Being freed, Charlotte thrashes to the surface to see Janet being questioned by the guard.

"Ms Janet- You can identify this woman to be accused of the charges?"

"Yes I do identify her as the guilty person."

"Take her away,"

Charlotte screamed, " You ungrateful Bitch, I helped you get here."

Nickie chimes in, " They all say that."

Two sets of guards leave with Charlotte in handcuffs.

Jinx says, " Well, tha's 'bout enough fun fo' one night. One fo' de road ?"

We re-entered her room to find the water still running. But instead of steam, we found the hot water had run out and the water running cold.

"This is not the time for a cold shower."

"Can we use your place?"

"Is there water at the bottom of the ocean?"

Janet walked through the room and picked out some clothes. I picked up the bloody Conch shell and we walked out through the porch door. As we walked the path by the cove I pitched the shell into water.

When we reached my door, I unlocked it and bowed aside as Janet entered. She threw her clothes onto the bed and turned into my arms.

"There is one thing I would like to get straight here ."

"What is that ?"

"You."

————ᴡᴠᴏᴏᴇᴛᴏᴏᴛᴇᴏᴏᴡᴠ————

We should always find a way to express our appreciation of something wonderful.

end of story

Water Songs 3

Feathers

The Piers of Pearl Isle

Feathers

by

T K Wallace

1

A delivery person walks down the gangway onto a floating wooden dock. She carries two bags of groceries to the stern of a boat named Feathers. As she looks forward, she appreciates a ketch in good condition. Due to her connection with the owners, she has permission to board.

There are two coolers on the starboard, or the right, side. She opens one, loads a bag, and closes. She unlatches the other to see a cold mist emerge. She stows the other bag and re-latches. In between the two coolers hangs a small cloth bag from which she pulls a tip. The money is tucked away in a pocket. As she disembarks, she stops to ring a small brass bell twice, and continues on her way.

Down below and inside the engine room a large man is cramped into a small space. His hand extends behind him holding a used pump. A smaller hand takes the old pump and places a new and bigger pump in his hand. It disappears into the compartment as we hear vague swearing and the clatter of tools.

An attractive middle aged woman goes to the control panel. She stands reading a manual in one hand and places the other hand beside a switch labeled 'Bilge'. After some more swearing we hear, "Okay, try it." She trips the switch and we see water begin to flow out a side port. Angelina goes top side and makes sure the flow of dirty water changes to clean water. "All good", she yells and goes to the coolers on the starboard side to extract the delivery.

The large man extracts himself from the small engine room door by hitting his head as he backs out. Angel returns with the groceries and begins to stow the goods with the exception of a couple items; "Lunch in thirty." Wiping his dirty hands with a cloth, Joe stops to kiss one of Angel's cheeks and wipe a dirty hand on the other. As he continues on, she wipes off her cheek and backhand snaps his ass with the towel.

Joe jumps from the snap and goes topside to check the water flow. He hears, "Lookin' good", and looks up to see a sailor carrying a wrapped box.

"Permission to come aboard sir."

"Granted," says Joe. "Whachoo got there"?

Teddy fakes, "I'd tell ya, if I weren't so thirsty, ... the sun is so bright . . ."

"There's a long neck waiting right here. . . ."

"Well then, I can't say no after begging can I. Good stuff, ahhh, good as it gets", he drinks, "Much better. Now then, I have a thing for you two, something that will help your communication process."

"Hey Angel, Teddy's here for lunch."

"She knows, I called. You remember a few weeks back to boxing day?"

Joe admits, "Hard to forget that sail. She didn't talk to me for a day."

"That's because you two started yelling at each other."

"She started it."

Angel comes up from below and says, "For the record, you started it."

"Let me referee this one." They both stare at him in silence. "Okay, good."

"Remember it was boxing day, and by tradition officers and crew trade places. You and Angel traded Captain for the day, and I promoted Roxy to 1st mate. The day trip out went well enough, although you made a few maneuvers without permission. Then coming back to the mooring, Captain Angel took the helm and sent you to the bow for the mooring pick up. Only you didn't use hand signals, instead you were yelling directions while facing away from us, and we couldn't hear You."

Joe says, " We've been through all that and I apologized, didn't I?"

"Yes you did, after a couple hours of arguing, some separate venting, and Roxy's cocktails. And, uh, by the way, Roxy says she doesn't want to go sailing with us, if you two are going to behave like that, you know, uh, to each other"

Angel speaks, "Oh dear. Teddy, I'm sorry. Did we behave that badly?"

"Didn't you?" We have an awkward silence. "Yes, you did, So . . ."

He hands the bag to Angel. "This is our boat present for the two of you."

Angel opens the bag and pulls out a box.

"These are a pair of wireless headsets, one for the person on the bow and one for the person steering. These should help eliminate misunderstanding,"

The two of them look at him, and then at each other. Joe speaks first.

"Angel, I know I apologized before but I wish to again. I'm sorry."

"Joseph, you will be the death of me. You know I can't stay mad at you."

Teddy says, "All good then? What's for lunch?"

"Thanks Teddy boy." Joe takes the box to look it over.

"Grilled ham and cheese with hot and sour soup. And a kiss for you."

Angel kisses him and then asks, "Will Roxy give us another chance?"

"Probably. She wants to see if our idea works things out."

"I have to plug these things in to charge them." And Joe goes below.

Angel follows him and Teddy speaks to his smart phone, "Roxy."

As the link dials Teddy hits the transmit button. The wireless speakers below pick up the signal and transmit the call for all to hear.

"Hello?"

"Who's smartest guy you know?"

"Dunno, Who is this? Just kidding. Did it work?"

"Funny, Yeah I think so."

"I hope so, you know I really hate yelling."

"I know baby. It's bad enough in private, but in public it's embarrassing."

"So, they like the gift?"

"I think it will change things. Wanna go sailing tomorrow?"

"Let's give it another try."

"Okay then. Oh, and Roxy?'

"Yeah?"

"I'm transmitting this conversation to the wireless speakers down below."

"You sneak, can they hear us?"

From below they hear two voices yell. "YES !"

"Was that yelling?"

"NO !" and then laughter from below.

"See ya later sailor boy?"

"Yes you will."

2

Feathers is under sail with Roxy at the helm as Captain Joe instructs.

"Okay that's good, she responds best to small moves. You adjust, observe, think, and evaluate. If you're confused, ask questions, We're right here."

Roxy is nervous, "Okay."

"Good. Now look at the top of the mast, read the windex, and show me which way the wind is coming from."

She scans the wind and points. "Okay the wind is coming from . . .there."

"Correct. We're going to learn about trimming the sails to help the boat go a little faster, okay with you?"

"We're not going fast enough for you?"

Angel asks "Would sailing faster make you uncomfortable?"

"Well, no, not as long as I feel like, I'm able to control, uh,. . . . you know."

"Joe and I like this boat a lot. We won't let you do anything to harm it."

"Well, okay uh . . . . what should I do? Uh, Captain ?"

"The wind is coming from the port side, your left side. Your main sail is flowing away from the mast to the right side, or your starboard side, okay?"

"Got it."

"To increase boat speed we will pull in the main sail here, and then pull in the front sail, the jib, and steer a little more into the wind. Ready?"

"Ready."

"Main sail trims first, sailors, draw the sail in a bit and hold fast." Angel and Teddy draw the main in and they feel the boat speed increase. The Cap'n instructs,

"Secure that line."

Roxy begins to smile and Joe coaches further.

"Now, very slowly turn the wheel to the left, or to port, in a small move. Say about 10 degrees."

"How do I know how much is 10 degrees?"

"There's a compass right down in front of you. Tell me what it reads."

She looked down and said, "Looks like 30 degrees, right?"

"Very good, now steer slightly to port, to the left until it read 20 degrees and see if our speed increases."

As she steers to port, the boat speed increases, and her smile gets bigger.

"Now crew, trim the jib sail and watch the speed again."

They do and all exclaim approval.

"Very good. Now hold this course while I get coffee." And he went below.

"Joe, JOE, Where are you going?" She almost yelped.

Angel goes to her and asks, "Were you yelling? By the advice of a good friend we've been trying not to yell. It scares some people."

"No. No, no, no, I was, uh, uh asking a question loudly."

"Good, that's permitted."

"Okay."

Angel offers, "Okay, want coffee?"

"You're not leaving too?"

"Sure, you're doing great sailor." and she goes below.

"TEDDY!" He looks out and climbs up from below.

"I'm here babe. Was that yelling?"

"No !" she yells.

"Good, want some coffee?"

"PLEASE, . uh, No coffee, just please don't leave, uh, don't go."

"Where can I go? We're all on the same boat."

Angel and Joe return with 4 steaming mugs. They all settle in for another hour or so with Roxy getting more comfortable. Eventually Joe asks if Angel would relieve Roxy at the helm. After she was relieved, Roxy relaxed with a smile of accomplishment, and sometimes a grin on her face.

3

The Good Ship Feathers sails comfortably up the eastern side of Long Island sound with Captain Angel steering. She is in command and directs her crew,

"I'm powering up the engine to maintain steerage. Teddy, you drop the Jib. Joe, you and Roxy drop the main sail." Joe had chosen a secluded cove in Huntington Bay to anchor. Teddy brought up the headsets. He gave one to Angel and gave the other one to Joe.

"Let's give this system a test. First you turn them on." They did so.

"There's a switch on the belt pack, it turns on your mic to talk."

"Hello?"

"Yes, hello."

"Yes good, okay, please go forward and look for a good place to drop."

Teddy and Roxy smile at one another. Joe goes forward and preps the anchor to be released. He then looks into the water for a clear spot,

"Anywhere around here looks good," She takes the boat out of gear, "Killing forward momentum,"

"Aye Aye, Captain, dropping anchor." He steps on a foot switch and the anchor plummets into the water.

Joe watches the anchor until it hits bottom. "Anchor hit bottom in ten seconds. Letting out another forty feet of anchor rode for good measure." Feathers coasts to a slow stop as the anchor takes hold and swings her bow into the wind.

Captain Joe returns and says, "I'd say that was a successful test."

Angel and he trade a kiss and take off their headsets. "Thanks Teddy."

"I'll take the credit, but to be honest, they were Roxy's idea."

Angel says, " And a damn good one Roxy, Who's hungry?"

They all go below and share in prep. As they do, Roxy says,

"My parents were both yelling fools. They used to scare us kids. It wasn't until I was out of the house, that I realized ayone who thought they won a family argument, had actually lost."

Angel says, "I only yell when I am yelled at, then I yell back."

"Hostility is like a psychotic boomerang." says Teddy. They all look at him.

Roxy asks, "And on that note, are we eating on deck?"

"Where else? I'll set the table." Angel goes top side.

Cap'n Joe says, "Enough yack, yack, everybody fill plates."

The choreography of three people moving about a ship's galley is always an interesting thing to watch. There is no way to move about without touching one another, so it may as well be done in a friendly way.

As plates were filled and passed top side boat drinks followed. The foursome sat and appreciating the peace of the afternoon bay around them.

At one point Joe commented, "We just had wind shift."

Roxy looked up at the windex, "So little, how did you know?"

Angel says, "He says, he uses the short hairs on the sides of his neck."

"I use whatever works."

"How does the windex work?"

Teddy says, "It points into the wind so the air streams equally down both sides. Like birds standing on the beach. Their bones are hollow and they weigh very little, They always stand with their beaks straight into the wind. Otherwise they could be blown over."

"Okay." Roxy is thoughtful, "So why is the boat named Feathers?"

"She's a ship, not a boat."

"How so?"

"Because a ship can carry a boat, but a boat can't carry a ship."

"Thanks for that, good to know. Back to Feathers, why?"

"Who wants pie? I've heard this part." Angel gathers plates and descends.

"Actually the entire name is The Good Ship Feathers, but that was too long for the stern. I'm going to help Angel." Teddy descends.

Joe says, "I think feathers have the same properties as a good sailing ship. Their shafts are hollow so they are very light and float easily. The outer feathers are water proof and we certainly want our ship to be water tight. And they create lift and maintain flight just like our sails as they move us across the water."

"Logical."

"Some cultures think feathers are magical, like sailing in the moonlight."

"I think you're a poet."

They look at each other for a long moment and Joe breaks,

"The wind just shifted again."

Roxy looks up, "Right again." And then looks at Joe again, "Amazing."

Angel emerges, and looks at the two of them. "Who wants cherry pie?"

4

Teddy is at the helm and the sails are full. Feathers is heeled over about 10 degrees and flying. Angel and Roxy are looking at a portable screen.

"One of the things that attracts me to sailing is the

combination of old and new. Sailing ships have been around for thousand years. Current technology continues to enhance the experience."

"What's the longest trip you've taken in Feathers?"

"To the end of Long Island and back. We've only had her couple years."

Teddy asks, "Anybody want the helm? I've gotta go."

Angel looks at Roxy, "Go on, you know you want to."

"You sure?" Roxy replaces Teddy at the wheel. Teddy goes below.

"Yep, besides we're going to head back soon. You'll get to tack the ship."

"Angel, you are so cool, Joe too, I mean, I love learning new stuff."

"Joe told me he'd like to teach you a thing or two." They look at each other

"He said that? I mean like that? Not just about sailing, but, um, like that?"

"Yep, just like that, and he had a big grin on his face."

"And you're okay, you know, with that?"

"Sure am, well as long as its' an even trade, you know, Joe for Teddy."

"My oh my. Now that's something to think about." Roxy grins widely.

Captain Joe and Teddy come up from below to see the conspirators laughing with one another. They are each carrying two bottles of beer. Joe moves to Angel and hands her one. Teddy puts Roxy's in the cup holder by the helm.

Roxy asks, "You want the helm again?"

"Not with the grin you have on your face. You're having much too good a time. Keep it, but drink up, that beer won't stay cold."

Joe asks, "We need to return soon. You want to learn how to tack the boat?"

"I thought it was a ship."

"She is, but I like the word 'boat' better. Ship always seems too formal."

"Hear hear. Let's be interchangeable." The ladies look at each other.

Teddy sits by Angel and says, "Different strokes for different folks."

Joe pulls a feather from his shirt and runs it along Roxy's face and neck. She preens at the helm as Joe moves in behind her and puts a feather in her hair.

Joe says. "You two, stand by to come about, Roxy, we're going to steer the bow of the ship across the point of the wind. Now, this is the key to a clean tack. Sail trim must wait until the instant the bow is across. Otherwise you lose momentum and stall as you come about."

Teddy says, "We wouldn't want that to happen."

"Okay begin your turn, nice and fluid, Teddy, Angel, wait, wait, NOW! You're across, slow your turn, and stop here. You two, trim sails and hold fast."

The crew buddies turned to one another for unspoken help in every way. Feathers returned to her mooring for the evening with plans for an early start the next day.

The foursome smiled and laughed their way through dinner, and then through the rest of the evening.

5

We see the Feathers from broadside anchored in the moonlight. There are lights down below only in the bow and stern cabins.

The bow lights begin to flicker as the song 'I Only Have Eyes For You' begins to play.

The stern lights begin to flicker when the song 'Smoke Gets In Your Eyes' begins to play.

The interior ports of the ship light up as if doors at both ends have opened. We see shadows run the length of the ship both fore and aft. The interior port lights are extinguished as we see and hear the cabin doors slam.

Both cabin lights flicker wildly when we hear 'Hot Fun in the Summertime', play. At the end of the third song both the bow and stern lights are extinguished.

6

The song 'Why Do Fools Fall In Love' begins to play as the day begins. Food is prepared, coffee and juices are poured, a kiss on a cheek, a pat on the fanny, arms are rubbed, and all hands touch one another.

As the meal is served and eaten on deck we see the

four obviously pleased with themselves. 'Green Onions' is playing softly in the background.

Roxy says, "I think we should take a trip together."

"Let's do that. Where do you have in mind, babe?"

She says, "I was thinking of a small town inside the north fork of Long Island; New Suffolk. It's about half way out to Nassau point. Teddy and I both know the place. There are some great orchards and vineyards out that way."

Angel says, "Oh right, there's a small island off there, Robbins Island. And further down is Riverhead where the north and south forks split."

Teddy says, "I know the place, spent a good bit of time out there."

"Hand me the Pad." Joe said, "Let's start this journey now."

"How far is it from City Island out to the end of the North Fork?'

"Says here, Long Island Sound is about 100 miles. It's another 15 miles back along the inside of Peconic bay to New Suffolk."

"So that's what in sailing time; two days each way?"

"Let's take a week and anchor out there for three days or so."

"I think you'll like it, small towns with public and private anchorages."

"How come you know the place Teddy?"

"It was there, I was asked to kill a person."

7

A month later Feathers left City Island for the longest trip her owners had undertaken. The destination was New Suffolk, Long Island.

The Captain had estimated the time on the water to be twelve to fifteen hours. Speed, distance, and time, are easier to calculate when you get to the day of departure, when you actually deal with the weather conditions you're given.

Joe and Angel were scrupulous about collecting weather predictions. And as an extra precaution, Angel convinced Friar Knapp from 'St Mary of The Sea' to take a dinghy ride to Feathers for a special blessing before departure. As he departed the Friar gave Angel a vial of Holy Water from the parish basin.

Provisioning was easy for an overstocked boat. Boat drinks were a must. Extra coffee and tea ran a close second. The evening before they sailed held a dusky red sky. They all slept on board Sunday night for an early departure. Joe and Angel slept in the Captain's berth aft. Roxy and Teddy slept in the 1st mates berth in the bow.

'Red sky at night' is supposed to be a good omen, and so it was, for the dawn on Monday brought a blue sky with a warm fifteen knot breeze from the south. No one slept past dawn. They were all too excited to get underway. The coffee maker was filled and set ten minutes before dawn, so there was fresh brew waiting for the crew when they rose.

No one had time for more than a mug of coffee as they prepped Feathers to sail. Captain Joe was at the helm wearing his headset and 1st mate Roxy was at the bow wearing hers. Teddy and Angel were standing ready to assist.

"Stand by to release the mooring lines."

"Standing by" was the response. Feathers engine had been running in neutral for a while to warm up.

Joe speaks, "Moving slowly forward. You may release."

"Lines released and remain hanging on the mooring. We're clear."

Captain says, "And we are away. As my friends would say, 'Andiamo'."

Roxy asks, "Any chance of rain?"

Angel assures, "20% toward the early evening."

"Standby by to hoist sails. Teddy show Roxy how to winch the main."

"Aye Captain. Come along love." They move to the main halyard line, untie it, free the coil, and wrap the line three times around a deck winch.

"Angel baby, can you hoist the jib?"

"Aye Cap'n, but I would love to have help tailing the line."

"Roxy, after the main is up, you move to tail the jib."

"Aye Cap'n."

"I'm bringing her around head to the wind to ease tension on the sails. Once they're up, we'll fall off the wind to the port side, take positions."

Three voices at once cry, "Ready!"

"Swinging to the wind, here we come, and haul away."

Teddy and Roxy haul the line as it rotates the winch. The huge white sail rises and luffs in the wind.

"Keep tension here so the winch can grab the line," Teddy begins to crank.

Angel wraps her halyard line around the smaller winch and begins to haul.

"Main's up Capt. Roxy, move over and tail the halyard for Angel ."

"Moving," says Roxy with a big smile on her face as she tails for Angel.

Angel reports, "Jib's up Capt."

"Most excellent, falling off to port, ease your sails out to a broad reach. Our general heading will be northeast a good bit off the coast."

Teddy and Angel ease the sheet lines allowing the sails to fill with the warm southern breeze. The Good Ship Feathers flies along the sound.

8

The routine established by the Captain was two hours at the helm and then rotate. The order was Joe, Roxy, Teddy, and Angel. They would sail for as long and as far as they wished each day.

Up on deck Roxy asked, "So why is the gibe harder than the tack?"

"It's not to everyone. You should become comfortable with both."

"You taught me to tack first. I have yet to gibe."

Teddy says, "Technically, a tack is moving the boat and the sails across the point of wind ahead of you. A gibe is moving the boat and sails across the wind while the wind is behind you, pushing you."

Angel adds, "Romantically, a good gibe, a safety gibe is fluid, like dancing with someone you enjoy, like a sweet and lovely kiss."

Teddy asks, "Like the ones we trade?"

"Exactly, you got one on tap?" She moves to him and delivers. They smile.

Roxy approves, "I like that music, what is it?"

"Appalachian Spring by Aaron Copeland." replies Angel.

"It's lovely."

As Teddy goes below Angel brought out two more plates. Teddy returned with cut fruit and juice for everyone. The ships clock ding dings.

"Shift change?" asked Roxy.

"Eat first, we'll change after." said Joe. "Flexibility is the key to happiness."

They rested after a short time and switched to Roxy at the helm with Teddy at hand. Angel and Joe take care of the dishes.

"Thank you for breakfast. I didn't know you could cook that well."

"That's because we haven't got past cereal yet. What's our heading?"

"Captain adjusted course when we got further out in the sound. We are now headed due east at 90 degrees."

"You are learning fast. How does it feel?"

"Great. I gotta pee. Will you spell me?"

"Sure," They switch and Roxy goes below. She isn't gone very long and when she returns with a smile on her face. "What's that grin for?"

"Our Captains seem to be in their quarters with the door shut."

"Ah so, take the helm. That would be under oriental bath house rules. 'Such things are often seen, but never noticed'."

Roxy smirks, "It makes me horny just thinking about it."

"I'm happy to hear that."

"Kiss me you fool." and he does from beside, "Thanks I needed that."

9

As they consumed lunch the progress report was discussed over a folded chart. Joe had marked waypoints to display the course at two hour intervals.

"According to our waypoints tracked through the GPS, as of 1 o'clock, we will have covered most of the north coast."

"Damn good time. What's the calculation?"

"We have been doing an average, ... never mind, long story short, We've come about 60 miles"

"Time flies when you're having fun. Who said that?"

"Too many people to count. A cliché becomes a cliché because of the basic truth. Let it be forever so."

The ships bell is heard and Teddy says, " Shift Change."

Angel says, "My watch. Move over cabana boy." Teddy yields the helm.

"So in another two hours we should clear the North Fork, and be ready to move inside the arms of the island; right Captain?"

"What's your course mate?"

"90 degrees magnetic, due east, and steady as she goes."

"Well then, we've time for a good yarn. How about it Teddy?"

"I might as well warn you, this one could take a while."

"Last I checked, we've got time to spare. Let 'er rip."

Angel added, "Tell the tale Teddy Boy."

10

"It all started at the graduation party of three PHD students that no one thought would ever graduate. There was a painter, a sculptor, and a photographer, all of whom were almost 30 years old. They said they were all in pursuit of teaching credentials, but the fact was, they just wanted to stay in school.

My room mates were all trust fund babies and even

though I was the only one who had a job we got along
pretty well. We co-rented a brownstone in the Fort Green
section of Brooklyn on Claremont between DeKalb and
Willoughby. My quarters were the ground floor with a
walk through to the back garden.

These three knew how to throw a party. They
specialized in a format they called the CAYABF&D.
The 'Come As You Are, Bearing Food and Drink' club
was years in developing party goers from the NYC arts
community. The only standing rule was that everyone
who wanted to get laid, got laid, which was FBM.

It was there, at that party I met Beth. I remember
it like it was yesterday. The tunes of Talking Heads and
Roxy Music, an electric blue punchbowl, and the prettiest
girl at the party asking me to dance, teasing me with
finger foods, asking me if I lived there, and then asking
me to show her the garden behind my flat. Life was damn
good on that particular night.

We saw each other most the evening and then through
the weekend. She had the most amazing eyes, mouth, and
body. By Monday, I was in love."

"Good God this is thirsty work. How about boat
drinks Captain?"

"Not for me, I have next watch. Go ahead if you want.
Roxy's not on til 5, she could have one if she wants."

"I'd be having a nap if it weren't for this story. Here,
take this beer."

"Ah, the pride of St Louis." He drinks and thinks
aloud, "Where was I ?"

"You were sure you were in Love."

"Ah yes, sweet Elisabeth. She thought she was in love too. Wanted me to meet her parents, see her home. Her folks had a place in Bedford Falls. Her father was city comptroller, Ivan was his name. Her mother, Willameena was a Gibner, old money. Her father had acquired the frozen food process for General Foods.

Elisabeth had an older sister, Gloria, an introverted alcoholic who was addicted to romance novels. She had this noisy little hairless dog, Mugsy, who wasn't house broken. They used to pour rum in its bowl. They were all alchys except Beth, she escaped by going into medicine and actually worked for a living.

Her Dad, Mom, and Gloria were sedentary boozers. They were barely out of bed by noon and back in the bottle by sundown, even the dog. But they were rich alchys so they could afford their existence.

The first winter we visited her parents in Bedford Falls I noticed their home was in terrible disrepair from neglect. Ivan and Willy could afford the repairs that were needed, but they were confused and paranoid wet brain drunks. They did not like strangers in the house. And Mugsy, the dog was always in the way, and yapping.

I offered to co-ordinate the repairs which needed to be done. The contractors I convinced to work were only allowed in certain parts of the house. So we had those parts sealed off from her family and worked out a schedule for repairs room by room. We made good progress into the spring of that year. I was told that we would have the entire place when the family moved to the beach for the summer.

Ivan's health was beginning to fail due to liver cancer, but he would not stop drinking. The mom, Willy, was emotionally unable to care for him. And what was worse, the older sister wanted some attention. She made retarded awkward moves like showing me her tits or rubbing her crotch when Beth wasn't around.

I decided this had to stop and told Beth about it. She told her mother and confronted her sister. The sister lied and professed it was I that had been the aggressor. The feud upset Ivan so much he had a heart attack. Due to complications of liver cancer he died within weeks. Willy decided to sell the house in Bedford Falls and move to the Long Island home. I suspended repairs.

At the loss of her father Beth started drinking. She blamed her sister for her father's death. I felt that the mother was not far behind. The entire family was falling apart . . .and one weeping drunken evening Beth asked me to kill her sister."

Captain Joe interrupted, "Wo! Is this a true story?"

"Unfortunately, yes, one I had to live through."

"Look over there. We are running out of island. It's about an hour until we clear the island and turn south into the Peconic. What time is it?"

Angel speaks first, "Says here it's 3:30. I'll extend my watch,"

Joe says, "We should be in good shape by 5. I think

we'll probably lose the wind once we're inside, we should plan on motoring after that."

"Where do you want anchor for the evening Captain?"

"Dunno, Angel baby, do you have dinner planed?"

"We always have plans Joe. And plans are made to be broken. I do have an idea for options."

"You get some good ones."

"Well, we're going to have a few hours of daylight left after we get inside the fork. Right? It how far to Greenport?"

"Not far, The wind has calmed. We'll motor the rest of the way."

Angel says, "So once our sails are down, let's break out the fishing gear and we can troll for dinner."

Joe asks, "All those for a fresh caught dinner raise yer hands."

Four hands go aloft.

11

Teddy and Roxy are on a beach looking across the water at Feathers. Their backs are bare. The sun is beginning a slow descent. He looks at her and she feels his gaze. She turns her head and looks down at his lips. They join in a slow passionate kiss with Roxy gasping and muttering,

"I'll . . . . give you . . . . . just 30 minutes . . . to . . . . . . stop doing that."

Teddy pulls back ."Stop doing what?"

"No, don't stop, why did you stop?"

"Didn't I hear you say, 'stop doing that'?"

"You are such a tease" She kisses him, "You know I didn't say that."

He kisses her, "Oooh, yeah, you are so hot. Ooh yeah," His eyes close.

"Yeah? You like that?"

"Ohh Yeah, don't stop . . . . don't . . . . . stop." he pants.

"Okay," and she stops. His eyes pop open.

"Now who's the tease?" They both laugh and kiss again.

12

Captain Joe comes from below with a pan and a bowl and hands both to Angel. He turns, picks up a Conch shell, and gives it a blow. He watches the two on the beach stand and walk into the water. Angel puts two large filets in the marinade. Joe places two more filets on the barby and arranges the prawns around them.

"How you doing down there?" He asks,

"Good, the potato salad is chilling in the freezer. Just waiting on these fine filets. Good catch by the way."

She returns and looks. "Good filet work, I'd never seen you do that."

"Worked on a fishing boat in college. The charter Captain had an arrangement with a local B & B.

Angel admires, "That was nice of him."

"He and his sister had a bed and breakfast. She would

book fishing charters for her guests. We would filet the fish and then cook the catch, adding before dinner cocktails, wine for the meal, and after dinner drinks"

"Good business. Let me turn these," She queries, "Joe, do you believe Teddy's story?"

"Sure why do you ask?"

"Well, for one, we know he's a writer, and you did ask him to spin a yarn."

Joe says, "Don't see that it matters much one way or the other. It's a story."

"I guess not. Oh, here come the kids. She went topless. I'm so proud."

Teddy climbs the swim ladder first and offers a hand to Roxy. She takes it and climbs up behind him. Angel turns and says,

"Hey there pretty tits, you're just in time to serve boat drinks. There's a pitcher of Cuba Libre chilling in the ice box. Joseph these are broiler bound."

"I'm all over that." She grabs a shirt and follows Joe.

Teddy steps behind Angel and gives her a neck nuzzle she turns into a kiss.

When they break she says, "I'm so glad Roxy is comfortable in her bare skin. It's a rare thing for a young woman these days."

Teddy says, "You're a good example. She said her parents were nudists."

"That would contribute to comfort" Roxy emerges with two tall glasses.

"Thanks Rox. Where was your parent's nudy camp?"

"The Sun and Fun, Swim and Sports club. Right on the gulf, Brownsville."

"Huh, Texas nudists, who knew."

"I grew up amazed at people with tan lines. Teddy noticed I had none."

"Teddy, be a love and take the prawns off the barby. Roxy, will you please go below and hand up the cole slaw and potato salad? Joseph how are you doing dear?" she calls

"Almost done, in a couple mo-'"

Roxy is half way up. "Here Angel baby, take these." Angel takes the bowls and puts them on the table. Roxy squeaks and slaps behind her.

"Something pinched me."

Captain Joe says, "Sorry, I was having the prettiest vision. I just had to see if it was real." He hands off the pan of filets to Teddy who says,

"These look great. Good idea Angel cakes."

They all fill plates and sit back to settle and enjoy boat cooking at its best.

Angel raises her glass, "A toast, To comfortable friends." They all repeat and clink glasses.

Roxy asks, "Okay, why are women's breasts like martinis?", they all look at her, "Because one's not enough, and three's too many."

Teddy's turn, "What's the favorite saying of Fishermen and Mega Yacht owners?"

Angel says, "I know this one,' Mine's Bigger' ". Boos and jeers . . . .

Roxy says, "Will you look at that sunset. See the shifting rivers of light? It flows slowly from one to another. Sometimes I watch until the sun goes down."

"Maxfield Parrish does skies like that" contributes Joe, "Did you know, in the art world, there's a shade of blue named after Max."

"Amazing. Say Teddy, are we going to hear the rest of the story tonight?

"Nope, it is an evil and grisly tale and has no place being told after dark. Better left for the light of day, we'll finish it tomorrow. Night time is better for Rom Com."

"Rom Com?"

"Romantic Comedy. Something that will make you laugh and feel good. You'll sleep much better."

"A funny successful love story is called for, do you have one written?"

"Of course I do, just not with me, we can watch one on Video."

"What would you suggest?"

"Shakespeare in Love. I brought a copy on DVD. Let's set it up."

13

When Feathers motored down the bay the next morning Joe was at the helm and Roxy was on deck. Breakfast was also underway. Teddy was making waffles.

Their trip was 10 miles to the south and passing a few points of interest. They made it to New Suffolk by 11am.

They poked around, found a spot, broke out the headsets and were at anchor by 12. When they dropped anchor, Teddy declared,

"That's her parent's place over there."

The crew went about their tasks and Teddy continued the tale.

"You see, her parents were symbiotic, they were mates in the truest sense. When her father's mind went, Beth's mother was lost, so lost that she had trouble tending herself. After Ivan's death, Beth felt that her mother would not live long. And when her Mother died, the entire estate would be executed by her older sister, Gloria, a useless wet brain drunk. Beth was afraid that Gloria would fuck up the family fortunes, just as she had fucked up her own life."

They all muttered.

"One night, in a fit of drunken rage, Elisabeth demanded that someone had to get rid Gloria, and her dog. She just spit it out through her wailing and weeping, and it just hung there in the air between us. I asked why, and the weeping began again, pleading for me to understand. She looked at me with giant tears welling in her eyes and rolling down her cheeks, yearning for help."

Teddy rises and paces while telling the tale.

"I was confused, and concerned, so I asked if she knew the terms of her mother's will. She left the room and returned with a copy of the last will and testament of Willhamena Gibner Hirsch. She said Gloria was so impaired during those days that her mother had asked

Elisabeth for help in the drafting the document. Elisabeth took her to the family lawyer to make it legal."

"The document specifically named the Gloria to be primary recipient and executor of the family estate. And, in the event of her sister's demise, the entire estate would be passed on to Elisabeth."

"There was a substantial inheritance involved. Between the Bedford Falls home and property, the Nassau Point summer home, and various other holdings in stocks and bonds, all listed, the total came to a little over fourteen million."

Roxy asks, "Jesus Teddy, did this really happen?"

"As Bubastis is my witness."

Joe asks, "Who's Bubastis?"

Roxy says "The feline 'Cat' goddess of the Pharaohs, if memory serves."

Angel says, "It does, and She was. Go on."

"Thanks, So, I had to think, went for a walk and ended up on the beach, right over there." Teddy pointed to a big house on a knoll with a boat dock below.

"Beth and I had bought a catamaran, an 18 footer with a racing jib. We were both sailors. For her birthday, I bought her a windsurfer, I wasn't into it but she was good . . . . . " He trailed off as if in a deep memory from long ago.

"Anyway, I stayed out all night, roaming the beach all the way out to the point and back. I ended up on the boat dock watching the sunrise. I imagined several scenarios."

"One, I did the sister and got busted, probably because

Beth turned me in. Two, I did the sister and framed Beth for it. Three, we did the sister together, Beth and I married, and lived out the inheritance."

"Or, I could just walk away from it all. And that's the one I chose."

Angel said, "Smart boy. Sometimes the best way to fight I with your hat. You pick it up and leave."

"I walked up to the house and found the three of them where they had each collapsed the night before. Willy was in her bed room, half in and half out of the covers. Gloria was passed out on the floor beside her bed. And sweet murderous Elisabeth was asleep on the porch laying on the swing, exactly where I left her."

"I wrote a note saying I had to get back to the city and for her to call me. Packing took no time. I drove the family car into Cutchogue and hopped on the jitney bus. I was back in Brooklyn before they were awake. I spoke with Beth a couple of times after that, but I never saw her again."

Angel asks, "Did she ever mention the proposition?"

"Never."

Roxy asks, "How did she take the break up?"

"I told her it wasn't working for me, I said I only wanted to be friends. She seemed okay with that, and eventually stopped calling."

Cap' Joe asks, "How long ago was this?"

"Let's see, almost 10 years I guess"

Angel is interested, "What happened to the family?"

"Willy died of natural causes soon after I left. Beth

left me a message on my service, but I didn't return the call."

Roxy queries, "Did anything happen between the sisters?"

"Dunno, I kind of figured while we're here, I'd try to find out."

Joe is aghast, "You walked away from 14 million bucks?"

"No, I walked away from homicide, from killing someone over money."

"Wow." Angel rose from the bench. "Good tale Teddy boy. You hungry?"

"Not really, The memory gives me, I don't know. I'm going swimming."

He peels off his shirt and jumps off the stern. Angel went below to make lunch. Joe stood and said to Roxy.

"Let's drop the Dinghy. We'll need it to go ashore."

14

Teddy swam most of the afternoon. Joe and Roxy took the dinghy into the public dock at New Suffolk to look for fresh produce. Angel started up her lap top and began a search program. She found Elisabeth Hirsch listed as a local nurse practitioner. She found the obituaries of Ivan and Willy Hirsch. Both obits mentioned that two daughters, Gloria and Elisabeth, remained.

When Teddy returned he found lunch leftovers on a cold plate. He took the sandwich and a cold beer up on deck. After he ate he rigged a hammock between the shrouds and took a nap. Angel awoke him,

"Yo lover boy, Captain Joe and Roxy called to say they had some luck. Said they would be back for dinner in a couple of hours."

"Hmm, okay. What are you doin'?"

"I've been down there on the computer, but I was thinkin' about you."

"Thinkin' what about me?"

"I was thinkin' about you swimming, wet, and naked."

"Are we gonna do something here?"

"I was thinkin' more like down below."

"Well, okay. Let's go." He rises and follows her. As they pass the consol Angel picks up a remote and keys on some music. Nina Simone plays soft and low as they go forward into Teddy's quarters.

15

We see Captain Joe motoring up beside Feathers and shout, "Ahoy."

Teddy appears in the companionway and takes quick strides toward the stern. As Joe brings the dinghy along the starboard side, Teddy catches the line and pulls the dinghy forward. Angel steps to the top of the swim ladder to receive the bags Roxy has for her. Joe holds the stern of the dinghy against the free board for Roxy to climb aboard, with Teddy taking a kiss as she passes.

After the Captain is aboard, Teddy leads the dinghy

aft, and ties her to a stern cleat. Capt. Joe sniffs the air and smiles. He receives plates from below.

"I knew it felt like a red meat day ", said Teddy as he surveyed the plate.

Joe growled, "Steak, Good, Uhmph!"

We see bowls of fresh vegetables placed on the table.

Roxy asks, "How was your swim babe?"

"Good, worked out some knots."

"Where'd you go?"

Teddy is pleased, "Where would you think?"

"Over there?"

Joe asks, "Did you go ashore ?"

"Yep."

Joe is curious, "Really."

Roxy is fixed, "What did you find?"

"I found the T-Bird we bought from her Dad, in the garage under a tarp."

Joe perks up, "Yeah? An old T-Bird, what tear?"

Teddy smiles, "1960."

"Wo. Over fifty years old? Was it in good condition?"

"Yeah, I guess, that's how I left it, so maybe, it was under a tarp."

They look at each other, nod at one another, and do a guy shrug.

Angel dings the bell and says, "Soup's on."

They all begin to dine but the conversation continues.

Roxy asks, "What else did you find?"

"Someone is using the sunroom as a clinic, and maybe an office."

Angel says, "That would be Elisabeth as well. She is listed as a nurse practitioner at a Nassau Point location."

Joe says, "We found a missing person report on Gloria filed by Elizabeth in 2010. It seems she went out one evening in January and didn't come back."

"Where did you find that?", asks Angel.

"Cutchogue PD." Roxy answers for Joe as he chews, and continues,

"They found her Volvo parked in the Long Island bus transit lot. Apparently she went into the city on a Friday evening and never returned."

Teddy asks, "Do we know that for sure?"

"We talked to a deputy who said she bought a ticket online with her Visa."

"Did they confirm that she went into the city."

Joe says, "They found out the ticket was printed, picked up, and used."

"Any visual confirmation?"

"No, they couldn't say.", said Roxy

"Hmmm." mused Teddy.

Roxy asks, "What does that mean?"

"To quote Bogart, it means, Hmmm."

Angel says, "To Have and Have Not?"

"Nope, another Bogart and Bacall."

"'The Big Sleep'."

Teddy says, "Ding Ding Ding. Correct."

"You think Gloria took 'The Big Sleep'?"

"All we know for now is that she disappeared. The rest is assumption."

Angel asks, "Are we, considering investigating this ?"

Roxy says, "It looks like we already are. It'll be fun, right?"

"Ok then, we investigate. But first we clean up, and do after dinner drinks."

They all fall to and soon enough all is done, they continue the conversation.

Angel says, "Let's do the list for tomorrow's fun."

"Let me get the pad." Roxy dashes and returns. "Shoot."

"When did Elisabeth move out here?" asks Teddy, "When did she apply for licenses to practice in Suffolk County?"

Joe speaks up, "What is the statue of limitations to declare someone legally dead in New York State?"

"Good question." says Teddy.

Roxy asks, "What happened to the New Bedford house?"

Angel asks, "Can we examine Gloria's banking activity?"

Teddy asks, "Has Beth been paying the annual taxes on the beach house?"

That made them think, and thinking only brought about more questions.

Angel asks, "Does Elisabeth have another car? Or a boat?"

"I forgot to tell you, guess what else was in the garage?"

Roxy exacts, "Spill"

"The Hobie Cat she and I bought together. We shared the cost of the car and the boat"

Cap'n Joe asks, "Okay who wants what assignment?"

Roxy says, "I'll take the legal death question."

Angel says, "I'll take the relocation and license."

Joe says, "I think I should make an appointment at the clinic for my aches and pains. Meet the girl and look the place over. Do some location research."

Teddy says, "Okay I'll take the New Bedford property information."

Angel says, "Do you have any photographs of Gloria?"

Teddy admits, "No, why do you ask?"

"It may come in handy to know what she looked like, how she dressed."

Roxy says, "She was a kind of a slob, I mean her clothes were unkempt. They were expensive, but poorly kept."

Teddy says, "Yes, how do you know this?"

"I told you I used to lived out here. I was a teller in the North Fork bank."

"You knew the family?"

"Kind of, I mean they sometimes used the branch where I worked in Cutchogue. But, then I got transferred to Southold."

"There's got to be family pictures in the house."

16

Teddy spent the morning on the phone finding the contractors who had worked on the New Bedford house years before. He chatted them up with the prospect of another renovation job. He got bits and pieces of information from each contractor he propositioned. The best lead was getting the name of the real estate agent who ended up trying to sell the house.

Angel did a records search from the boat computer because it was registered to an NYU professor; Captain Joseph Sposetta. After trying several different paths she got what she wanted.

Roxy went after the easiest on her I Pad. She was done so quickly that she assumed lunch duty.

Joe had the most fun. He had an appointment with Nurse Elisabeth Hirsch which he attended by dinghy. He phoned her and pretended to be a victim of nausea. During the conversation he asked for her location and if he could get there by water. She seemed delighted and gave him the location of her dock.

The late lunch was a repeat of Day 1 with cold cuts, sliced French bread, cheeses, and crudités. Ice cold sassafras tea was on hand with sprigs of mint. As they ate, information from the morning's endeavors was revealed. Roxy went first.

"The filing procedures differ by state, but it's pretty simple. Most states require seven years, 'in abstentia', to obtain a death certificate. It starts from the date the missing persons report was made to the police. Each state requires other proof as well, like no banking or financial activity, no record of having voted, and proof that all personal assets have been frozen for the term of absence."

Angel began her report with a compliment. "Very good iced tea Roxy, just like my granny used to make with the mint sprig. Okay, Elisabeth Marigold Hirsch acquired her local licenses while she worked out of Suffolk County Hospital in Brookhaven. And then, she started practicing out of the Nassau Point just before big sister Gloria's disappearance. How did it go for you Joe?"

"I had so many aches and pains I couldn't describe them all. And I'm allergic to practically every type medication and pain reliever on the market. So, no medications are involved.

But, having arrived by dinghy I got a firsthand tour of the grounds and the house. The house was built by the Audubon family before indoor plumbing. There was a woodshed and an outhouse which were torn down and filled in years ago. She said the house was left to her by her family.

She's not married; lives alone, happy to show me around. There were plenty of family photos. I saw Gloria in a lot of group shots. So I snapped a copy or two. Couldn't find a close up, there were no photos of Gloria alone."

Teddy took Joes phone and mused, "Hmmm, . . . am I wishing?"

"She was most impressed when I told her about Feathers. We went up to the widows walk and had a look at our girl through a telescope. Said she was a lifelong sailor and would love to come aboard."

Joe blushes, "Oh, and I think she was hitting on me."

Roxy looks at Angel and says, "Well who wouldn't, ya big ol' goat."

Angel comments, "Did you have any time for your medical appointment?"

"She gave me a shoulder and back massage and made me promise to come back tomorrow."

"What did she charge you?" asked Angel.

"A first time fee of $50.00, but tomorrow's appointment is only $25."

Roxy says, "At least you kept it professional."

Angel asks, " Teddy, are you gonna tell us about your morning of three and a half hours on the mobile, or make us wait until suppertime?"

"Untwist your knickers Angel, you'll rest easier. It seems that I have not quit the business. I just moved up to a better class of clientele. Services to the rich and famous only, you know."

"The carpenters, plumbers, and roofing contractors were all helpful. I was just 'Teddy Boy' who asked for a couple of bids over the coming months. They all admitted to doing work on the place on spec until the sale went through."

"Sale?" asked Joe.

"The real estate broker almost shit his Gay self when I started name dropping, Gates, Coppola, Ford. He told me Papa Ivan left that house to Elisabeth because Gloria was getting the beach house."

"Oooohh, juicy gossip that explains soo much," crowed Angel

"Right? Well, it just so happens I have a client interested in an 'upstate getaway place'. I asked if he could find out if the house was currently for sale."

He said it was not, but he would make an inquiry. He told me quite smugly that he almost sold the house twice in the past seven years. He also 'let it slip' that he could have got the price up to 3.7 mill if it sold.

Roxy asks, "What do you mean 'if' it sold."

Teddy hesitates, "Neither deal went through, it seems the place is haunted."

"Wowzer Teddy Boy, I feel like a piker next to all that," said Joe.

Angel says, "She couldn't touch any of Gloria's money, it was frozen, and she didn't take in borders to pay the taxes. Joe did you see what she was driving?"

Joe says, "There was an old Volvo in the turnaround."

"Probably Gloria's, she couldn't sell it, might as well use it for appearance"

"And with all that money, she's a cheap bitch to boot." said Roxy.

Teddy paced and thought and muttered to himself. Finally he said,

"Let's do tomorrow's questions and then do some fishing for dinner."

Angel queried, "I'd like to know the taxes on a place that old."

Joe says, "Yup. that's a good one to find out her annual nut."

Angel asks, "Was the death certificate issued? Did she inherit it all?"

"Another good one, along your BS Teddy. Any repairs done to the place?"

"BS ? Pearls of wisdom, if you please, along the line of inquiry."

Joe asks, "Do I let her aboard Feathers?"

Angel snorts, "You do and she'll want to go sailing."

Roxy's turn, "Do we let her see Teddy?"

Teddy says, "No, not yet" He stops and asks, "Is it time for Gloria to visit?"

17

Dinner that evening was of blue fish and striped bass on the barby. Roxy made a green bean casserole and there were baked Yams. It started with Boat drinks and progressed with ice cold Pouilly-Fuisse.

Random discussion of the investigation occurred throughout the meal.

"Here's a question, "asks, Angel, "Does she play golf?"

Teddy says, "She didn't back then, but her parents did."

"I ask because the North Fork Country Club is very close to New Suffolk.'

Roxy says, "That's true."

"And she's a lifelong sailor, she owns a catamaran, but it sits in her garage. Is she a member of a local yacht club?'

Teddy says, "The Old Cove boat club is in New

Suffolk, just over there, or is it over there? I can't see the shore from here. Why do you ask?"

"Well, we know a few things that add questions. Golf clubs and Yacht clubs are expensive and both are a big part of social life here on the island."

Joe says, "True Dat."

Roxy says, "We know that she was infuriated with Gloria for putting the moves on you. Enough, that she caused a family upset that resulted in her Father's, and eventually her Mother's, demise."

Teddy says, "For which Elisabeth blamed Gloria."

Angel says, "Speaking of whom, we need a bad natty wig."

Joe asks, " Natty', Like, like ratty looking?"

"Did you see a wig place on shore?"

Roxy says, "There are plenty of hair salons. Probably find a wig or two."

Angel asks, "Right, She lives alone so, how, or where does she get laid?"

Joe says, "She probably keeps paying memberships to 'socialize'."

Roxy considers Teddy and asks, "How would you know?"

"Seen it happen too many times to count."

Joe asks Angel, "Could you play dead for me?"

Teddy says, "Not a chance of that mate. She's too lively that one."

Angel is curious, "What did you have in mind?"

"Could you stand on a dock in the moonlight, maybe moan and scream?"

Angel grins, "Sure, like this ? "

We see Feathers from across the water and then hear a very loud and eerie scream. Back on deck all have covered their ears except Angel who coughs a bit.

"Here's to the departed. 'Vade en Deum'. Go with God."

All toast and drink.

17A

A mist rises over the harbor as the toast happens on deck. A shape forms within the thick condensation that gathers around Feathers. The air begins to circle. It swirls a time or two and moves off toward the Hirsch hold.

The mist rolls off the water and up the hill toward the house. It hovers around the flower trellis and travels up to the second floor windows.

18

Day 4 started with the blast of a boat horn alongside Feathers.

"Ahoy! Anybody awake in there? Harbor Patrol, safety inspection! Ahoy."

Captain Joe rises from the companionway with a cup of coffee in hand.

"Hold it down mate. The missus isn't up yet." From the rear port we hear,

"I'm awake. Who's here at 8am?" queried Angel.

"You the Captain?' asked the officer, Joe nods. "Permission to board?"

"Granted, use the ladder on starboard."

The small craft pulls near, an officer scrambles up with a hand from Joe.

"Officer Estrella Ibanez," she holds his hand, "And you would be?"

"Captain Joseph Sposetta; co-owner. Welcome aboard, safety inspection? Don't the Coasties usually take care of that?"

"They do, unless we do it first. May I see your papers Captain?"

"Yes, please call me Joe".

"Okay, then you can call me Stella."

"Certainly," Angel appears in a robe, "Ah, here is my partner. Officer Ibanez, Captain Angelina Domingo." Angel bows and extends a hand.

"Encontada Senorita. Mind your step."

Angel reaches below the console and pulls out the required documents. Joe stands by and watches Stella peruse the papers. He offers, "Coffee, Officer?"

"No thank you, These seem to be in order," and hands them back to Angel.

"Seem to be? They are in perfect order. What's going on here?"

"Perdon Senora, One of our residents reported a

suspicious vessel at anchor, with, uh, suspicious people aboard," states Ibanez.

Joe says, "Officer, as of noon today, we will have been anchored here for 3 days. We have been ashore several times, and I am being treated by a nurse on Nassau Point. In what way are we suspicious?"

Stella raises her eyebrows. "Would that be nurse practitioner Hirsch?"

"As a matter of fact, yes. Why do you ask?"

Ibanez almost smiles, "Because she was the one who made the report."

"Now isn't that interesting?" Joe pours a cup, "Espresso? It's Bustello."

"In that case, Gracias, I will share. Is there anyone else aboard?"

"Yes, we have two boat mates. Hey Teddy Boy, Roxy, Cops!"

The forward cabin opens and Teddy steps aft wearing pajama pants,

"Morning, is it coffee yet? Yes? Morning Officer. Hey Rox, coffee."

Roxy comes out wearing the pajama top. "God's breath, coffee, thanks."

She crosses to Joe and Angel with her hands out. "Yes please," she casts a quick glance at Stela. "What have we done now?"

Joe says, "Apparently we are suspicious to nurse Hirsch."

Roxy says, "The one you were telling us about? With the missing sister?"

This gets Ibanez' attention. She turns to Teddy and asks,

"You know about that?", she asks. Teddy shrugs and goes for coffee.

"Well, it's more like we heard about it. I dated Elisabeth before her parents died. I heard about the sister through friends. What's for breakfast?"

"I'm thinkin' French Toast," says Angel, "Can you stay a bit officer?"

"Yes, let me send my boat to guarantee our resident we have checked on her suspicious characters," she goes to the side deck and speaks to her driver.

Teddy looks at Roxy "You continue to amaze and delight, She is the perfect source," and kisses her.

Joe yells, "Breakfast in twenty!"

Angel asks, "What time is your appointment Joe?"

Coming from below. "Not 'til eleven. That is one nice house. She has the clinic. It looks newer than the rest." He looks at Ibanez.

"Her parents had the sunroom added on about 20 years ago."

Angel smiles, "Oh? Are you from around here officer?"

"My parents moved here from the Bronx when I was 5. My father was a cop in the city, NYPD. I grew up in Southold, just up the road a bit."

Teddy offered, "Lovely little town. Always seemed like old money. So officer, The Hirsch house, we heard it was built by the Audubon family. It must be some kind of historic site, am I correct?"

Stela replies, "Yes, it is, The house is listed in the national registry of historic homes, It's not quite a National Landmark, but the tax breaks are good."

Joe offers, "I would imagine so. Landmarks are practically tax free, and the property stays in the family for generations."

Teddy asks, "Officer, the missing sister, Gloria, did she ever turn up?"

Officer Ibanez answers, "No, she never did, why do you ask?"

"Just curious, I knew the family, must be 9 or 10 years."

"Gloria Hirsch was declared legally dead about a year ago."

Roxy exclaims, "Really?"

"Yeah, statute of limitations."

Angel says, "So the nurse got everything. I'd call that suspicious."

Stela confirms, "I always have." Radio crackles, "That's my boat on its way back. Looks like I can't stay for chow. Captain Joe, Captain Angelina, my thanks for your hospitality, " she rises and shakes hands all around.

"Cops are always welcome aboard Feathers. We even enjoy feeding them."

Joe says, "I've got an appointment soon, gotta use the dinghy. Teddy, you and Roxy want a lift to town first."

Teddy turns to Ibanez. "May we get to shore with you

officer? Is there a car rental in town? I promised Roxy I would show her Greenport and Orient Point."

"No, but there is one in Mattituck by the airport, I can get you there if we forget about breakfast."

"Shake a leg Roxy we're off. I'll just grab my wallet. Angel see you for lunch, okay.' Joe, can you pick us up on shore in Cutchogue after your treatment?"

"Yup should be there about 1:30 or 2."

"Two would be better, we'll have more time to shoot some pictures!

19

We see Elisabeth in town. She is being stalked and photographed. Angel is disguised as a tourist with her wide brimmed hat and camera. She is visible as Elizabeth moves along main street. Angel is shooting pictures at the florist, she is also there at the pharmacy, and the French market.

As Elisabeth becomes aware of Angel she becomes increasingly suspicions. She is concerned but more curious than anything.

20

The late lunch was grilled ham and cheese with cold potato soup.

"So what did you rent?"

"A Ford Explorer. It's a four door in case you and Joe want to come."

"Could be we do. How was your treatment Joe?"

"She gave me another massage, this one was a little more interesting. She asked a lot of boat questions, and who my passengers were."

"What did you say?"

"Well, I was short on passenger details and long on boat details."

"Did you mention our visit from the Harbor Patrol?"

"I did, she feigned ignorance. She asked if she could come aboard."

"I said I would have to check with my partner."

"Good man."

"Hey, if a husband is alone in the forest and he makes a decision, is he still wrong?"

"Funny. True but funny. The question is, 'Did he call the wife ?'"

"Okay let's sum up. We know the house has a tax break, right?"

Angel speaks, "I checked on line Homes in the Historic Registry are taxed according to the income of the owner. For seven years the owner was absent, so no taxes. After that the taxes were based on a part time nurses salary, so zippo."

Teddy speaks "We know a death certificate was issued and that Beth has come into the inheritance. I spoke with a landscaper, Smithe and sons, who said Beth had an old woodshed and outhouse torn down and filled in. They built her a small garden and a flower trellis which is doing quite well."

Roxy says, "I spoke with the Country club and faked a golf date but wanted to make sure I had the right place and that Beth was a member. They thought it was odd because Beth is a social member but rarely played golf. Old Cove Yacht club told me the opposite. She is a member and sails a lot, especially with the more 'well established' senior instructors."

"Oh, she is SO getting laid." said Roxy, "Don't you think Angel?"

"Oh Yeah, right? Now, do we let her aboard? Do we reveal Teddy?"

"First things first, Let's have some fun and see what happens."

21

The moonlight illuminates a solitary figure out on the end of the dock. A side light reveals the figure is dressed as a female with a frumpy dress and natty hair full of twigs, grass, and leaves. Her feet are bare and filthy.

She moans and holds herself. She looks up and screams at the moon as she extends her arms. " NOOOOOOO, . . . Please NOoooo. NOooo Elisabeth"

Through a pair of binoculars we see a faint light in an upper window. The window curtains part for someone to look out and watch.

The water around the end of the dock begins to mist over.

The ghost figure turns and screams again. "NOoooooo." And then runs toward the house as she screams, "NOoo, Please!" and then disappears in the dark.

The mist follows her onto land. It stops and begins to increase in size and rise up the side of the house.

From far across the water we hear the faint opening lyric of a old song, "Gloorriiiaaaa...... Gloorriiiaaaa.", over and over again.

The upper story window slams shut and the light goes out.

The mist turns a countenance toward the music and moves out over the water and back to the Feathers. A boombox is playing and repeating, ' Gloriiaaa.'

Angel is still in costume with twigs in her hair as she peers through a set of binox toward the house. The lowers the set and says, " Pleasant dreams."

A light wind swirls the mist up the mast and out toward the hailing bell. It rocks bell slightly enough to create a small single, ' Ding'.

22

At breakfast Joe asks, "Are we out to solve this? Or do we just put a scare into her, like someone may be taking a closer look at Gloria's disappearance?"

"Aren't they the same?" says Angel

Teddy says, "I say yes to both."

"Why?" asks Roxy.

Teddy paces, "Because Ibanez confirmed that local PD has its own suspicions. I put my money on one of two possibilities. One, she chucked Gloria's body over the fence of a pig farm and it was digested years ago."

Angel erupts, "Bleowuuu. Disgusting image, thanks for that Teddy."

"Hey, it's a fact. Your average pig sty can go through 7-8 pounds of uncooked flesh a minute. Throw a body in a pig sty and it'll be gone by morning."

"Enough. Eaten by pigs is disgusting." says Angel

"Millions concur. My second thought is that the body is about eight feet under the garden trellis. She could have dumped Gloria down the outhouse shit pit and added plenty of raw lime. Then a few wheel barrels of dirt on top. She had the shack torn down and filled in the hole."

Roxy asks, "What about the smell?"

"It was an out house. What smell could be worse."

They all look at each other and try to stop from laughing.

"And then she planted flowers?" asks Roxy

They all shudder. Joe shakes it off with, "Naw, she paid to have that done."

"Can we prove it?" asks Angel

Joe asks, "Do we want to?"

Roxy asks, " Do we have to?"

Teddy says, "Maybe, Maybe not."

"So, you figure poison?" Angel asks.

Joe says, "Dunno, according to popular fiction, poison is quick and easy."

Teddy asks, "Where did she get poison?"

Roxy answers, "Hello? She's a nurse."

Angel says, "Ya think? I figured something more painful."

Teddy retorts, "Just goes to show ya. I ask again, can we prove she did it?"

Joe adds, "Not without a body, she'd have to admit it, and she'll never."

Angel says, "Here's a thought. Suppose she sees officer Ibanez standing and talking with someone by the trellis. She comes out to see what's up and realizes it you. That should shake her good."

"I can work with that, maybe go one further," Teddy adds, "Let's talk to Ibanez."

23

Roxy drops Teddy off and as the Explorer pulls away Teddy walks into the Harbor Patrol shack by the docks. We hear Teddy's voice say,

"I'd like to ask a favor."

Within minutes a Cutchogue patrol car pulls up and a cop enters the shack.

Inside the shack we see officer Ibanez introducing,

"Miguel, this is Teddy, he used to date Elisabeth Hirsch. Teddy this is Lt. Miguel Ibanez, he's my brother." The two shake hands.

Teddy looks back and forth and then again before he asks, "Fraternal?"

The Ibanez sibs smile, then face each other, and nod to "Twins, cool."

Miguel says, "Yep. Yeah, I remember you. You and Beth used to sail off Nassau point some years back right?"

Teddy says, "Wow, impressive memory you got there. Have we ever met?"

"No, but you two bought a catamaran from 'ol Freddy Bart when his beach washed away. And I heard the two of you bought her daddy's T-Bird when he got too sick to drive."

"She's still got 'em both in that big assed garage out on the point."

"I was kind of waiting for Ivan to put that car up for sale when you two bought it. She doesn't drive it. You think she'd sell it?"

Teddy muses, "Good eye there, She might, you never know."

Miguel backs and fills, "Unless you still want it."

"Technically, I still own half of the boat and half of the car. She never liked that car. It was too powerful for her, and had too many memories. Ivan smoked cigars, the smell stays, ya know?"

"Yeah, you two were dating for what, a couple of years? When you bought that car, some folks here about figured you were gonna become family."

"Some folks did?"

"Well, yeah, I mean who could have blamed ya. Some

serious bucks out there on the point. Do you mind if I ask, why'd you walk away?"

"I walked because I believed Elisabeth Hirsch wanted me to kill her sister."

The Ibanez siblings stiffen and glance toward one another.

24

Teddy and Stela Ibanez arrive at the Nassau Point home in an official vehicle. Miguel pulls in behind them in his POS. Teddy has on a gangster hoodie and mirrored shades. Ibanez is wearing her harbor uniform. Miguel is dressed in PD blues and hat.

The three of them get out and walk to the garage door and look in the window. They chat for a while and look in again. Teddy points as something.

The three of them walk over to the flowering trellis, they stop and talk until they hear the front door open.

Elisabeth Hirsch walks over to the three. They have their backs to her. She asks, "Can I help you Officers?" Miguel turns first.

"Afternoon Elisabeth, how are you?"

"Miguel how nice to see you."

"You too, you remember my sister, Estrella?" Carmen turns.

"Afternoon, Ms Hirsch. Nice Flowers." Teddy still has his back to her.

Miguel takes her arm and walks her back toward the garage.

"Elisabeth I wanted to ask you about buying your Dad's old Thunderbird,"

She stops and looks at him perplexed. "You know it's not for sale."

"Yes, so you've said before … But this fella claims he owns half of it."

Elizabeth turns quickly to see the person now facing her. She jerks as if she has been slapped.

"TEDDY?" She cries out, " What are you? Why are you? Uh it's been . . ."

"It's been years hasn't it Elisabeth? I was passing through and thought I'd stop and say hi to Mike and Stela. One memory led to another and Miguel asked about the T-Bird. I had no idea, no clue, but he said it was still out here with you."

Elisabeth is still sputtering and a little wide eyed glancing back and forth between the twins and Teddy.

"I uh, I, it's just such as surprise to see you, in a good way, really,. . . good"

Teddy says, "Good to see you too," he gestures toward the garage, "You and the boat, and the car. Sorry to hear about Gloria. No word in years? God's pity."

"Thank you Teddy. It's been tough . . . . and well, tough, alone."

They hug.

"Well, the old place looks good. Not much change here, except, I was just telling the twins, there used to be an old style Outhouse where this fabulous trellis stands now." Elisabeth is thrown off again, but tries to join in,

"Um, Yeah. It has lots of climbers and some bloomers, uh, Hydrangas, Trumpet Flowers, and Vines."

"Is that Boston Ivy mixed in with Honey Suckle?

"I uh, Jesus Teddy, I, uh planted those over, time, for Gloria. She, uh, hated that stinky old thing, you know, the, uh, the Ivy, I planted for Gloria!"

"I see. Listen, I'm sorry to bring it up. But I have an offer for you about the car. Please step aside over here and speak. Officers, excuse us for a moment."

He guides her to the trellis, but she resists and starts for the front porch. He follows and stops her.

"Here's the idea I had for you. I'll give you my half of the Hobie for your half of the T-Bird. We paid about the same for them. What do you say? Sound like a good deal? I know you don't drive the car. I thought you might want the boat."

"I don't know, I have to think about it all. Please ?" She reaches out,

"Miguel, I'm sorry, I would like to think about it, alright?"

Miguel waves. Teddy says,

"You do that, I'll be around for a few days. I still have the same number, is yours the same?"

"What? Yes it is, if you will excuse me. It's is quite a shock, to see you, here. The last time I saw you here, was, yes, it was a different time."

She turns to go inside as he holds the door for her. As she enters he lifts the mail box flap, slips in an envelope, and leaves the flap up.

Teddy walks back to the police cars and says,

"She's going to think about it and call me. Let's look at the flowers again before we leave. I know she's watching."

Miguel says, "You have a bit of a cop side, don't you Teddy. Let's point at beach and the boat house too, just to mix it up."

Stella says, "Sin should be that guilty. You smell the fear coming off her?"

"Let me point at something here." He jabs his finger again and again.

"Okay that should do it, Let's go. I'll ride back with Miguel."

25

As the cars drive away Elisabeth cannot help but wonder what Teddy was pointing at in the garage. She goes to the garage to look but see's nothing of interest.

As she returns to the house she notices an envelope sticking out of the mail box. She opens the envelope and finds a folded paper with a hand drawn picture. The drawing is of a graveyard head stone. Elisabeth's hands tremble as she looks at the tombstone which reads:

RIP
Under this earth
lay the mortal remains
of Gloria Hirsch

Elisabeth can barely believe what she is reading. She tears her eyes away and breathes, only to look at the page again. A mist rises from the water and blows toward her as she starts to shake. She stumbles into the kitchen, rips the drawing to pieces, puts them on the stove, and burns them.

Her mind is racing. Who suspects? Who could know? Who drew and wrote this? What was she doing burning clues? She started to swat at the ashes but it was too late. Good god, what if …. No Teddy was the only one near the mail box. But she hadn't seen an envelope, Shit, the envelope, had she dropped it outside? She ran and found it blowing across the yard. She ran to retrieve it but stopped at the sight of the flowers moving in the soft breeze of mist.

She thought she heard a voice saying her name and closed her eyes only to relive the memory of helping the sick and stumbling Gloria to the boathouse. The horrid vision of her dying sister's distorted face repeating,

"Elisabeth No, Elisabeth NOooo…"

26

Aboard the Feathers Teddy reports the afternoon's excitement to the others,

"It looked like she couldn't believe what she was hearing. The Ibanez twins are convinced. Estrella said the stink of fear was rolling off of her."

"I've heard good cops often know guilt before they have proof" said Roxy.

Stela says, "Thanks, that would make me good cop, I know she's guilty."

Joe says, "If we can get her to show up, she's going to be in bad shape."

Teddy says, "I only wish I could have seen her read the note."

"You can watch her later."

"Show time is about 11. Don't be late."

27

We see the front of the Hirsch house. The yard and drive are empty. However, the big assed garage is showing some signs of life. The T-Bird has been started and its lights are flashing. The engine races and the horn begins to blow again and again.

The lights upstairs begin to come on and a curtain is drawn. The drive and yard are illuminated. A figure dances in front of the flower trellis. Elisabeth is at the window watching her Sister's ghost as the lights flash and the engine races.

The ghost stops in the middle of the small garden and faces the trellis. As both hands reach out, the flower trellis begins to explode in front of their eyes. The petals and buds are severed and sent flying every which way. The leaves are shredded and pieces were drifting among the severed quivering vines.

Elisabeth shrieks and flies through the house toward the front door. When she yanks the door open, the T Bird goes silent. The Ghost girl is gone. The flowers are destroyed.

There is a fake headstone standing at the trellis and it reads,

RIP
Under this earth
lay the mortal remains
of Gloria Hirsch
$50,000.00
Or we dig her up.

27A

Angel and Teddy are aboard the dinghy returning to Feathers. They are motoring without lights, as silently as possible.

Angel is stripping the ghostly attire. She looks back toward the shore at a sound. The sound comes again and she hears, "NOOooooo, NOOooooo,"

They listen and then look at one another, Angel says, " Nice one Roxy."

Joe and Roxy are making their way back to the rental car when they hear,' "NOOooooo, NOOooooo," They turn and Joe says, " Nice final touch Angel."

28

We see Elisabeth on a video screen in the salon of the good ship Feathers. She appears frantic, wild eyed, and determined to get rid of the grave marker. She runs to the garage and stops at the door, looks in, enters, and quickly extracts a wheelbarrow.

The guilty parties watch Elizabeth on video as she attempts to get the headstone into the wheelbarrow. And after a while it gets comical. They break and discuss what they have done.

Angel is drying her hair, "So what did she do with it?"

Roxy says, "She threw it off the end of the dock."

"What, like nobody would think to look there?"

Joe says, "She's spooked. Let's bust her."

Teddy points out, "Too soon, no confession yet."

Stela says, "She's a wuss. Shouldn't be long."

Roxy asks, "You think she's dangerous?"

Teddy says, "She is starting to show crazy around the edges."

"She can only suspect who else knows," says Stela.

"Records show she has a permit to carry. She may be armed." says Miguel.

Angel says, " If she is, the gun will be in her purse. You think she'll come?"

"I invited her for dinner. Told her we'd be drinking at seven." says Joe.

"So, can we have fish for dinner?" asked Teddy

They hear from the video, "NOOooooo"

Joe says, "That sounded just like the final chant you did as we left."

Teddy says, "We heard that, we thought it was you."

Angel asks, "Then where is this one coming from?"

28a

We see the petal covered earth around the trellis begin to swell slightly. It moves about a bit and begins to release steam. A fresh breeze pushes the steam up into a vague shape. The shape spreads over the decapitated flowers littering the ground. The rose petals and buds begin to grow forward, then leave the ground and fly to the trellis reattaching themselves.

Another, smaller, issue of steam rises from the earth. We hear a distant bark.

In the center of the mist, the apparitions walk down the lawn to the dock. Elizabeth watches from an upper story window. She is captivated by fear. The spirit forms in the mist stops on the dock, turn toward the house, then drift away like fog into the night air.

Elizabeth looks out the side window at the trellis restored with flowers. Her eyes roll up in her head and she faints dead away.

28b

A dinghy motors in the mist. Angel is at the helm. She is dressed like the ghost again. Her motor sputters and dies. She turns to assess the trouble when she hears someone say,

"Thank You ". She turns forward to see a misty shape resembling Gloria Hirsch sitting on the bow. Angel opened her mouth to speak but nothing came out.

"Thank You for caring what happened to me," said the shape. Angel reached out to touch the visage as the form swirls. She drew back a wet hand.

She inhaled a filling breath, blew it out, and said,

"You're welcome. May I ask, what happened to you?"

29

We see the mist vaporize as we hear Angel and see her telling the tale,

"And then, as it went away, my motor started by itself, which almost made me jump overboard."

"Wo, no shit? She appeared to you? Gloria spoke to you?"

"She wanted to thank us."

Roxy says, " Wait, did you get to do the frightening thing with Elizabeth ?"

"No. I was too blown out. I turned back to see you guys first."

Joe is amazed, "You actually said 'You're Welcome' to ghost?"

"Yep. That's not all, I don't think she's under the trellis."

30

The skiff sounded a horn and coasted to a stop in the light of a fast approaching sunset. Joe went to starboard and caught Elizabeth's line. He drew the boat alongside as Angel offers a hand up. Elizabeth looks a little worse for wear, almost unkempt.

"Welcome aboard The Good Ship Feathers, Ms Hirsch. I am Captain Angelina, Joe's partner. I have heard many wondrous things about you."

Elisabeth stepped aboard and said, "Thank you, 'Wondrous' is an unusual word. I'm happy to be aboard. She is quite lovely."

Joe returns from securing the whaler to a stern cleat.

"Thanks for arriving promptly. Cuba libre?"

He holds out a pitcher and fills a tall glass. Elisabeth looks a little worn, she drops her bag which clunks softly, takes the glass, and drinks it clean.

"Thanks for that. I feel better already."

"Want a tour? Our cook is putting the finishing touches on dinner." He leads her below. "This is Roxy, our cook d'jour, as well as many other things."

Roxy turns and says, 'Welcome aboard Ms Hirsch, we're having fresh sea Bass and legumes in few minutes. Toasted almonds okay with you?"

Elizabeth responds, "Perfect. What a fine ship, so clean and well cared for"

Captain Joe shows her below with pride, "She's 85 feet and in good shape,"

Topside Angel examines her bag and finds a hand gun. She opens the chamber, dumps the ammunition over board, and replaces the gun.

Roxy hands Elizabeth and Joe another drink. Joe continues,

"Two state rooms with baths, and two that share."

He opens cabin doors making a show of each, "And of course, the Captain's quarters are aft. 'RHIP, you know the term?"

She confirms, "Rank Hath Its Privilege, I was raised on such a vessel,"

"Really, here, in these waters ?"

"Yes indeedy. A custom ketch much like this one ."

"Let's go topside and salute the setting sun."

Angel turns from the magnificent sunset, winks, smiles, and hoists a glass.

"To the day behind, and the night coming on." All toast and drink.

Teddy emerges with plates. Elisabeth gasps, but he just smiles,

"Hello, Beth."

She exhales, "You, how can you be here?

"I get around, these are my friends I told you about. In fact I referred you."

"Teddy told us about you," says Angel, "You've been good for Joe's aches."

Joe chimes in, "Yes indeedy. That's why she's here, right Elisabeth ?"

Roxy stings her with, "Did you think about the car?"

Elizabeth turns to Angel, "No, I didn't have . . . "

She turns to Teddy, "I didn't think we would meet again so soon,"

Teddy hands out plates. Roxy emerges with a vase of multi colored flowers. Elizabeth jolts and stiffens

"Ms Angelina, we thought these might brighten your table." She places the vase in front of Elizabeth and then sits.

"Teddy told us all about your trellis. It has been years since I've seen your place." Elisabeth jerks and looks at Roxy.

"Did you, . . . Do I know you?"

"We met years ago, I was a teller at the North Fork Bank here in Cutchogue. I don't suppose you would remember some teller, from years ago."

"No, I can't stay, . . . uh, I couldn't say."

"But I remembered you, and your sister. My condolences, Miss Hirsch. Teddy told us all about your fortune."

Teddy brings more drinks and sits. Everyone has a glass except Elisabeth,

"My what? What did you say?"

"Your Mis-fortune, the disappearance of your sister. I was offering my sympathies. I saw you together quite often, back when you cared for her."

"Roxy, this bass is fantastic, why won't tell us your secret?" Joe laughs

Teddy says, "She has so many secrets, it's hard to tell what she knows,"

"How, do you, did you all get together, get to know one another?"

Roxy says, "It was Teddy really, He's a sailor, we're all sailors. We wanted to take a week off and take a trip together, He said he knew the perfect place, Said he had some friends on the water in New Suffolk, so here we are."

Teddy chimes in, "We all belonged to the old Manhattan Yacht club before it capsized. One day Roxy walked in wearing an Old Cove boat club tee shirt and we started comparing notes. We found we had you in common."

Elizabeth repeats, "Me? In common?"

"Well, you and Miss Gloria. We had a laugh about how smashed she would get, and your parents too, and how you took care of them all." says Roxy.

Teddy is not laughing when he demands, "You took care of her, didn't you!"

"I, what do you, ... What do you mean? I have no reason to answer that!"

Angel shouts "We could give you lots of reasons to tell us what happened!"

Elisabeth shakes her head and clutches at her purse. Angel stamps twice.

Joe shouts, "We could give you 50,000 reasons to tell us what happened!"

Elisabeth gapes mouth open. "You? It was You?"

Roxy says, "I saw you, I saw how you took care of her."

"I didn't, . . . You couldn't have . . . I don't understand."

Teddy says, "I want an answer about the car and boat. They are half mine."

Roxy smashes the vase and says, "You put her down, didn't you."

Joe and Angel sing

"And her name was GLO - RIA,"

Elizabeth is screaming, "Stop it! You assholes are so wrong and so stupid. I can have you arrested, locked up for extortion."

Singing and spelling, "G. L.O.R.I.A. GLO----RIA ."

"You're blackmailing me. 50,000 and you'll keep quiet? Over what ?"

"Over your sister. Did you kill her before you shoved her down the shitter?"

Angel adds, "You buried her alive. While she died, did she call to you?"

Teddy taunts, "You can't even say her name. I can"

He pushed the button on a music player. A older version of the name plays

Roxy sings along, "GLO-RI-A."

The entire group sings, "GLORIA."

"STOP IT!", Elisabeth screams,. She pulls out her gun and aims it at Roxy.

The group sings and dances shaking their fingers, "**G. L. O. R. I I I I I A**."

"STOP SAYING HER NAME!"

They all chant, "GLORIA, GLORIA."

She pulls back the hammer, "STOP IT OR I'LL KILL YOU ALL!"

"Over a car and a boat? " asks Teddy. "Really Beth? Over an old car?"

She turns on him,

"SHUT UP ABOUT THE CAR. I'LL GIVE YOU THE FUCKING CAR."

And she tries to fire the empty gun twice, 'click, click'.

Elizabeth anguishes as she throws the gun away. But she laughs as she pulls out another hand gun from the back of her jacket.

Officer Ibanez rushes up the companionway with her gun drawn.

"Drop it lady! Put the gun down now!"

Elisabeth shifts the gun to the officer and fires. The round goes wide and splinters the companionway.

We see the fog swirl around her. We hear a dog bark.

Elizabeth stumbles and recovers her balance just as she is struck in the head by the ships bell. She shrieks, dropping the gun and holding her bleeding head, she and the bell and fall to the deck. Stela rolls her over and cuffs her. She speaks to her com link.

"You get all that Miguel?"

He replies into his link, "Yep, every word, including her giving Teddy the car just before she tried to shoot him."

"Shoot him, that bitch tried to shoot me!"

Elisabeth writhes, "You've got nothing, You've got nothing on me."

Teddy states, "They have taken my sworn testimony."

Stela says, "And with that, Miguel will send a team

over to your place with a high intensity scanner. We'll see what it shows."

Elisabeth writhes, weeps, and laughs heavily.

Officer Estrella Ibanez holsters her gun. "Elisabeth Hirsch I remand you for suspicion of murder. You have the right to remain silent . . . ."

31

Miguel and Teddy are motoring the 1960 T Bird. They come to a stop on the Hirsch property. Miguel tosses the keys. Teddy catches and pockets. They walk to the trellis.

Joe turns and says, " Say, uh, the uh, flowers are back up, you know . ."

Teddy says, "Interesting, eh?"

Angel says, "Very."

Stela approaches with a technician and a lap top.

"You're gonna love this. The remains of Gloria Hirsch are not there."

"No remains there ?" said Teddy

"Nope, the scan only shows the remains of a couple of animals."

"Lemmee see that." Miguel takes the lap top.

Joe says, "Damn, missed that by a meter didn't we ?"

Angel is smug, " Told Ya So, Told Ya So, Nah- nah, Nah-nah."

Stela asks, "So, what do you think? Did she say anything else?"

"We didn't really get a chance to talk okay? She was, dripping, ya know?"

Joe says, "What are we missing?"

"Duh, a body?"

Miguel shows, " Hey look at this. There, it's something like a circle."

Everyone crowds in to take a glimpse of a skeleton enlarged on the screen. Teddy zooms in again on the circle and a dog tag.

Teddy says, "Mugsy".

32

Late in the 5th day of their week afloat, the fearsome foursome are entertaining the Ibanez twins on board the Feathers with boat drinks.

"The exhumation team found a dog skeleton, decomposed with lime. It was Gloria's dog, Mugsy, the tag also matched with the vet in Greenport."

Stela says, "That bitch whacked her sister's dog."

"What is happening with Elisabeth?" asks Teddy.

Miguel answers, "She's being held for evaluation. Due to the fact that she attempted to shoot Stela. We'll be able to hold her a good bit longer."

Everyone around the table in the HPD station ponders one question.

Roxy asks, "So where's the body ?"

Joe asks, "Anybody ask Elisabeth ?"

Angel says, " I just had a thought."

"Yours usually turn out pretty good," says, Joe.

"Share please," says, Roxy

"Every time we have seen her, ya know, she's been wet. I think Elizabeth put the body somewhere in the water."

Joe asks, "Does that sensor thingee do, ya know, work, on water?"

Stela and Miguel look at each other and say, "Dunno, let's see."

32A

We see Elizabeth in her cell. She is crouching in the corner of the bed. The space over the toilet is filled with a swirling frog. The fog moves to cover her head and shoulders. She gasps and claws at her throat. She waves her arms through the mist trying to get a breath of air. She feels a dog at biting her ankle as she hears it bark and growl.

The combination of the two sensations disturbs her so much she cries for help. A guard comes to the cell but cannot see anything out of the ordinary. He shrugs and leaves.

The dog barks, and the fog wraps her head again. As she gasps for air she hears Gloria's voice,

"You killed my dog, You murdered me! "

Elizabeth recoils from the image saying, " NOoo More Please."

We see a flashback of Elisabeth whacking the dog

with a shovel. She scoops it up and throws it in the outhouse door.

Her head is soaked with water, running down her face and from her mouth.

"You left me to drown !"

We see Elizabeth swimming away from Gloria's body, just below the surface, eyes open, mouth gagged, arms and legs restrained with cinder blocks in shallow water.

"You Murdered Me !"

We see Elizabeth climb out onto the boathouse dock. She stands and takes her gun from a shelf. She kneels and aims, the fires a round into Gloria's head. The water around is filled with red froth and obscures her face.

A red froth chokes Elizabeth in her cell. She feels her head surrounded and believes she is getting no air. The guard outside her cell can only see her moving as if possessed. He sees no water, and sees no misty fog. He watches her writhe.

"You Murdered Me !"

"Guard! Guard! Help Me, please, Please. Help."

33

Angel and Teddy are fishing off the stern while Joe and Roxy sunbathe. The radio cackles and we hear Stela's voice,

"Harbor patrol to the sailing vessel Feathers."

No one moves but Joe raises his mobile and speaks, "Officer Ibanez."

Stela answers her link, " You might want to see what I see." and hangs up. She turns toward the anchored vessel and sees the dinghy already departed.

We watch Stela as she catches the dinghy's painter line and ties it off as the four climb out.

Angel kisses her and says, " My beautiful cop, what have you found?"

"Skeletal remains in the crab pond, under the boat house."

Teddy asks, " Any possibility of identification?"."

"No need, Elizabeth cracked up. Confessed to the whole thing. Told us where to look. The lower arm and leg bones, just above the ankles and wrists have blocks chained to them. The examiner says the rest was picked clean years ago."

The examiner hands Stela a human skull and says, "You were right, you'd like to see this. Looks like all the crabs left."

The skull is dripping water as Stela turns it and looks closer. A piece of metal falls from one side to another. She turns the skull upside down and catches a spent and dented bullet falling out of an eye socket.

Ship mates and cops are back aboard Feathers and spread around the galley table as she throws down the spent round for all to see..

"So, what happens to her?" asks Angel.

"Not sure, there is no surviving family, her assets will be turned over to Suffolk County, with the exception of the T-Bird, which we all know, she gave you, before she tried to shoot you."

Roxy asks, "Can I have the catamaran ?"

Stela informs, "Ballistics matched the bullet to Elisabeth's gun. My guess is that she's toast, guilty of the crime. Therefore her holdings are forfeit. "

Miguel adds, "When the property becomes available, the coroner thinks it would make a fine site for outpatient treatment. Most local medicals think this is a pretty good idea, due to the fact that it already has a clinic."

Angel suggests, "Be sure they seize the Bedford Falls house too. If they get market value it would provide a good endowment for many years to come."

"I know the car's got to stay here until after the trial," says Teddy,

"After that, keep it."

"So, are we free to go back to the city?" asks Joe.

"Yes, as long as you come back for the trial."

Angel answers for them all, "We are so willing to assist your case."

Teddy stands for a toast,

"Here's to Gloria, She was a mean drunk, but she didn't deserve to die over her family's money."

Their glasses and touch,

"Descansa en Paz, Rest in Peace, Gloria."

"Salute"

Estrella's link rings, she answers, "Yo., what?" she shushes the others.

"Come on, really? No shit? Okay thanks. Yep, we'll be in soon. Thanks."

Officer Ibanez looks at the people around her in mild astonishment.

"What's up pup?" asks Angel.

Stela says, "There won't be a trial. Elizabeth Hirsch was found dead in her cell about an hour ago."

Roxy gasps, "Found dead from what, in her cell? How is she dead?"

"The coroner says she drowned."

eos

The Piers of Pearl Isle

by

T K Wallace

The Piers of Pearl Isle
or
The 250 dollar Stroll, Shuffle, Stumble, and Crawl

Dr. John would sing that it was,

> *Such a night,*
> *Sweet confusion under the moonlight*

I drove my Shelby across the north bridge onto Pearl Isle a little before sunset. Cruising down the windward side I saw the western pier. On this Saturday evening there was a big crowd for Geechee Bingo.

Rumor was a special guest band would play out on the far end that night. I parked along the beach road, walked back to the pier, and took the long way around the bingo perimeter.

The sun was going down in such a manner as inspired by the Gods. The blazing orb was just past the horizon and the clouds were lit from below. Only Maxfield Parish could match these ever shifting rivers of light.

The clouds had round pink bottoms and golden crispy tops in front of a blue sky igniting everything in my imagination. I had come to meet a girl with eyes of that sky blue color, the one and only Christina Mathews.

She had texted earlier that day inviting me to the island for fun and games. I knew it would be a chancy meeting because a member of the band, Jim, was seeing more in Christie, than Christie was seeing in him.

So I strolled while looking around, and then saw her

standing beside Jim watching the sunset. I also noticed they were standing about a foot apart. Christie spoke sharply and turned away to leave. Jim didn't stop her. I heard the music in my brain and had seduction on my mind.

> *Oh, but if I don't do it, you know somebody else will If I don't do it, you know somebody else will*

She turned with her head down and started walking the other way, away from me. Shit. So I hustled back across Bingo-land and through the side door to the sound of the bingo caller saying, 'B 8'.

I exited the north side and came to a casual pose at the railing as Christie came around the far end. She looked up, for as much as seeing each other, we felt one another's presence. I smiled when she came into my arms. I thanked her for the invite, hugged her, and whispered in her ear.

> *'Cause it's, such a night.*

As we walked arm in arm back to the Shelby, Christie suggested we go for a drive around the Island. I stopped, waited for her to stop and said,

'How big is the island?'

She smiled, and replied, 'Big enough.'

'Can we walk or should we ride?'

'What are we talking about?'

'This beautiful sunset, the rest of the night, and our mutual attraction.'

'Let's ride.'

Christie grew up on Pearl Isle and knows every branch from every tree. Her folks owned a house mid island which they left to her as a graduation present before they moved to St. Barths. As we drove she described the reputations of several establishments.

She knew the owners of the two bars, Lucy's and Dick's. Dick was an ex sea captain who had been lured ashore in order to marry. Lucy had been in the bar business in Boston before she fell for a southern boy and followed him down to Dixie.

During high school and college breaks Christie had worked at both bars and the two restaurants, Lu Lu's and Toni's. All four places allowed same sex social gatherings and therefore, according to Christie had hosted some wild ass parties. One could say, Easy Come, Easy Go, if one would dare to say.

The 'Oh Yeah' was also part of the south island smile. It was just another bi-sex bordello, like anywhere else. Christie had never worked there, but admitted to being curious about trying the place out.

We crossed the island to the east side or the Sunrise pier which, according to Christie, is usually filled with every conservative person left on the Island. The Straights, as she called them, were still stuck somewhere in the 1950's. Tonight the eastern pier of Pearl Isle was filled with a square dance in full swing.

'Lets head north, and then go west again before we drop the car.'

'Gotcha, you tell me where and when, okay?'

'Turn left here and right up there. Then on past the street lights a bit.'

I found a good spot to stop well down the street from any light. We parked and strayed a bit. She let me know I was welcome.

'Whoa there girl, you are hot.'

'Me ? I thought it was you. How hot can it get?'

'Can't see out the windows. Come on let's go.'

Exiting the car I saw an official vehicle parked behind me with the lights off. As we walked toward the PIPD vehicle, the window came down.

'Hey Christie, you ought to know better than to park out here with some stranger.'

'Howdy Clyde, this is my friend JD. He ain't no stranger to me. How's Marie doing?'

'Mean and biggin' up with our third. You sure this guy's okay?'

Not to be left out, or talked over, I said, 'I'm okay unless you're Clyde Barrow, In which case I might have to call the law.'

The policeman replied, 'Not that Clyde, not this week. Okay, See you Chrissie Baby. Watch yourself around her Mr.'

As Clyde drove away, Christie took my arm, laid her head on my shoulder and we strolled along the Island road.

She said, 'Let's start over. I had a plan to show you the island, the way it should be shown.'

I said, 'Which island are we talking about? The one we stroll along, or your own little paradise?'

She half sings, 'This is now, and that maybe then, Let's stroll on back and start again.'

A distant saxophone was leading the soulful lyric,

Come, let's stro-oh-oh-oll
Stroll across the floor

We strolled along the island toward the Windward Pier. She took my arm and led me toward LuLu's.

'I'm hungry JD, how about you? Care for an Oyster Po Boy?'

I was trying for suave, 'I'll be your oyster If you'll be my pearl.'

'Whatever that means.'

'Or, were we talking about food ?'

'You all twisted up JD. LuLu's should straighten you out.'

LuLu's is a raucous affair decked out with misappropriated traffic lights. Reds for Stop, Yellows for caution, and Greens for Go, all surround the dance floor as music swells from the juke box. The kitchen is just across from the front entrance, the aromas of fine southern cooking enticing patrons to dine.

LuLu is a large black man dressed in a pink rayon waitress outfit complete with a white collar and his name stitched into the left breast. He beams at Christie and bellows,

'Clear number Five.'

The bus boys, dressed about the same as LuLu, shuffle over to table 5 and clear it in front of the couple sitting there. As the couple start to object the bus boys take each under the arm and lead them to the cashier. LuLu follows brandishing a wooden stirring spoon. Somewhat frightened, they pay the bill and offer a tip to the cashier.

Lulu says, 'I'll see the waiter gets it. Hey Chrissie baby!'

'Hey LuLu, My friend JD here likes to stroll, That still on the juke?'

LuLu chuckles as he stops at the juke box on his way back to the bar.

Feel so good
Take me by my hand

As I sit, Christie whistles through her front teeth and yells

'2 Oyster Po Boy's on 5. Make 'em Fat'

The waiter backs off, LuLu just smiles and moves in to kiss a cheek. I stand and offer my hand. Ms. Chris takes my hand and leads me to the dance floor. We Stroll.

Strollin', Strollin' aah-huh-uh
Well rock my so-oul
How I love to stroll

The food comes and as we return, we look before we sit to eat

She presents with pride, 'These are LuLu's specials !'

'They look good, what's the best way to go at 'em?'
Several hundred calories later,
'JD? Just what does JD stand for?'
'John David? Long John David.'
She laughs, 'We'll see about that.'
'You ordered these with a snap and a whistle.'
'I'm a regular who has also worked here. Why should I wait?'
'R.H.I.P.'
She asks, 'Again?'
'Rank Hath It's Privilege.'
'Exactly. I paid my dues, what's it to you?'
LuLu's Po Boys are good as they look and then some.
'JD could be for Just Devine.'
I admitted, 'Jack Daniels.'
'Juvenile Delinquent.'
'Say what? Never until now.'
LuLu arrives with three double shots and a can of Coke
'I heard you across the room, 3 double Jacks and a Coke. I'm in too.'
'Across this room? You must be reading lips these days LuLu.'
'Naw just rememberin' your favorites. This is the least of them.'
He winks at JD.
'So what ya'll after tonight?'
I raised my glass in a toast.
'Good Times?'
She raises hers, 'Let the Good Times Roll.'

We toast and drink, slam the glasses down as Lulu shouts, **'G2'**

Uncle Ray Charles sings,

> *You only live but once*
> *And when you're dead you're done*

LuLu returns with three more shooters and a take out bag,

We all slam the shots, slam down the glasses and I shout it out.

'WO! Uncle Ray is the Man !'

> *But don't let no female, play me cheap,*
> *I got Fifty cents more than I'm gonna keep.*

Chris stands and weaves in time to the music. She steadies, looks at me, LuLu laughs and leaves. She extends her hand and I get up to dance.

> *If you want to have a ball, you got*
> *to get yourself together,*
> *Oh, get yourself under control, woah,*
> *and let the good times roll.*

As the song ends I hold her and breathe her delicious aroma. My conscious mind is focused on her big blue eyes. I glance down to her lips, and I see them smile. We kiss, and the night's promise is fulfilled.

*

We stroll back to sit and LuLu drops back by,

'So what ya'll after tonight?

Christina says, 'Hey Lou, So far so good. We started with a beautiful sunset we could not see'

I say, 'Steamy windows.'

'The best kind if you're in a parked car.'

She adds, 'Then we came here for some nourishment.'

I follow, 'And tha's plenty for now.'

She says, 'So, You Say.'

'What's next? You making your way towards Sunrise out east?'

Christie says, 'That's the plan. Got to get there before church starts.'

Lulu laughs, 'Thought so. Here take this batch of your faves, sweet potato fries and cole slaw.'

Christie howls and throws her arms around LuLu.

'You're the best. What's the tab?'

'Gimmee twenty.'

I offer, 'I got it, let's say twenty five, for luck?'

'Ya'll have a good time, And if you're out late, I'm open early.'

*

As we stroll out, we look at the sky to determine what's what.

She says, 'I need to walk on the beach and eat some food to soak up all that whiskey. Let's sit by the water and eat.'

The beach is public from Windward Pier to Leeward

Pier. The south side of Pearl Isle between the piers, the smile, is all beachfront. Each of the five businesses have their own frontage with pathways to the water through the dunes. There is one inlet which fills and drains a lower island pond through twice a day.

Chris and I do the sand dune shuffle and find a swing overlooking the beach. We sit and eat and laugh and swing. She asks,

'You still hungry?'

As I am hungry for her, I say, 'Yep.'

She teases, 'Ohh my, I got some cole slaw on my shirt.'

'Let me get that off for you. Oh dear, I smeared it all over.'

I swipe my thumb back and forth across an erect nipple.

'Mmmm, slower lover, Do that again but slower n slower to get the nip just right.'

'Slow hand is what I do best.'

'Mmmmmm.'

'We should move this along. The car again?'

'Down Boy, we're moving forward for dancing and drinks.'

Smiling as I look forward to the rest of the evening, I say,

'Andiamo. On we go.'

We leave the beach through the dunes and come out just across from Lucy's. Lucy's is an old Surfer Bar built across the entrance to a Billabong, or a tidal pond. The bar rests on pilings and bridges None Such Creek.

The inlet fills and empties the back pond from shallow to a couple feet deep. It has provided many generations of blue crabs. So, Lucy's is also a crab farm providing a fresh daily harvest for herself and many locals.

As we cross the road I can tell that Lucy's is a three part deal. The entrance and bar is center and tables are to the left. The bar starts center, becomes a dance floor, and the band stand is on the right.

From the top steps we hear,

'Ms. Chris Tina? I heard you were comin' along.'

Lucy hugs Christie.

'Oh lawd girl, I been thinking and wondering about you? And sending out our wishes to you jus' like always. And now this man? What do I know of this man. What's he doin' here?'

'This man is a friend of mine. Ms. Lucy, Mr. JD; Mr. JD, Ms. Lucy.'

I bow in honor without knowing what else to do. As I rise Ms. Lucy takes my face in her hands and kisses me completely. Kissing her is a very satisfying interaction from start to finish with Lucy leading the way.

Ms Christina breaks the spell, 'Hey Lucy, You still got crabs?'

My eyes widen as the others laugh, so I laugh too.

'How many miles ya'll got out of that one?'

'A few more than yesterday, with many more to come.'

Lucy points to a sign which reads.

We've Got Lucy's Crabs. You Should Get Some Too!

I just smile as Christina answers her pocket link.

'JD, the band's all there, You want to warm up or what?'

She pockets her phone, collars JD, and they head out the back toward the Shelby.

'No need to warm up, I'm hot to trot.

They stop at the car, open the trunk, pick up a guitar case, and meander toward the Windward pier. Ms Tina takes an arm and escorts him. They take the entrance stairs up onto the main stage. JD surveys the scene while he counts time.

JD slings his guitar and starts playing a fast rhythm before he steps onto the stage. He plays all the way to the mic. He plays a fast strum repeat for several more bars before he stops, and says,

'I dedicate this show to the late, great, Richie Havens. Freedom ! MUSIC !'

The MC says, 'Ladies and Gentlemen, I give you JD, the Jolly Dude'

JD steps toward the guitar mic, hits four musical notes, and sings.

Just let me hear some of that Rock and Roll Music
Any ol' way you can choose it
It's got a back beat You can't loose it
Any ol' way you use it

JD loves his job. He lights up like a beacon as he sings. The rest of the band plays behind him, Jim on bass,

Sister on the keys and Olaf on the drums. Miss Tina Christina is in the back of the audience on the sound control platform swinging and clapping to the end.

> *It's gotta be Rock and Roll Music*
> *If you wanna dance with me.*
> *If you wanna dance with me.*

Three notes get them out. ' ***Da Da Dum*** 'The crowd loves the energy.

'Well thanks folks. I'm JD and just one part of this great cover band. We got Olaf back there drummin' and Sister on the keyboard. Playin' Bass we have fabulous Jim. Who is gonna help me out with Waylon and Willie's duet, Pick up The Tempo '

JD takes the first verse.

> *Some people are saying that time will*
> *take care of people like me,*
> *That I'm living too fast, they say*
> *I can't last much longer.*

Jim takes the second one.

> *But little they see that their thoughts of me as a savior*
> *And little they know I really don't give a damn*

It goes back and forth until they end the song playing at the same mic while facing each other and singing.

Time will take care of it's self So
we'll leave time alone.
Just pick up the tempo a little and bring it on home.
Just pick up the tempo a little
and bring it on hoooome.

JD and Jim bow to each other and then to the crowd. JD gestures Jim forward. Jim shrugs and starts to sing this song slower than usual.

My Baby,

He gestures to his right. Sister preens and hits the note. She glares, rips her shirt open to the navel and pushes the girls up. 'Let me have it here', and takes the lead.

My baby when He walks by
All the Sisters go 'mmmm', and I know why

The crowd starts hootin' and hollerin'
'Go Sister ! Go Sister!'
Sister continues through the song

Everybody in the neighborhood
Will testify my Lover, he looks so good

All together now

And I know that he knocks me off my feet,
Have mercy on me.

JD and Jim gesture to Sister

Cause We Knock You off Your Feet !

They all stop in time and with a very sexy exhale; they say,

Oh Yeah!

The crowd loves them and stands to prove it. JD waves to the band,
'Sister !'
Cheers follow the intro
'Olaf !'
Cheers follow
'Fabulous Jim !'
Big cheer
'And I'm JD. We're happy to be playin' the Windward, But, we wouldn't be here if it weren't for the invitation of Ms Christina Mathews. Chrissie, you still here?'
'I'm Here and I ain't leavin' without a steak dinner at Toni's. You promised !'
Cat calls erupt, 'Do Her Right!'
'Cheapskate.'
'Turn him loose Crissie, I'll feed him'
'Well, that settles it folks, I gotta go see to a previous commitment. Ya'll cover me'
Sister takes the Mic and Olaf takes the guitar as JD steps down to depart.

One, two, three, four
Can I have a little more?
Five, six, seven, eight, nine, ten, I love you

Black, white, green, red
Can I take my friend to bed?
Pink, brown, yellow, orange, blue, I love you

All together now

The music fades as the couple leave arm in arm.
Christie says, 'That turned out well, thanks to you.'
'Seemed like the roight thing to do'
'They're good together.'
JD turns to her, 'You knew it too?'
'Felt it, thought of it, then saw the proof. Look.'
Sister and Jim are embracing on stage center
'So, Are you free to sup and dine with me?'
Chrissie smiles sweetly, 'I'm never free, but you know
I'm available.'

*

A near full moon rose over Pearl Isle from the east.
During these magical moments of moon rise, the world
can change. We left the pier and headed for the beach, I
felt the spirit of a song, and felt the need to sing.

The shadows sway and seem to say
Tonight we pray for water.... cool, clear water

And way up there He'll hear our
prayer and show us where
there's water... cool, clear water.

Miss Chris asks, 'Joni?'

'Sam Cooke and many others, actually written as a cowboy song by Bob Nolan.'

'I think JD stands for James Dean

'Nope, Jack Doff'

She chokes and stumbles, 'Sorry'

'Gag reflex?'

She stares him down with one hand on the hip

JD says, 'This seems to be an evening of back and fill.'

'How so?'

'Well we started at the Pier and then moved forward, then went back and stopped at LuLu's and Lucy's and then back to the Pier for the show.'

She confirms, 'True Dat'

'And now we are off to somewhere else.'

'How about, We go get laid?'

My turn to choke'

'Gag Reflex?'

He chokes through, 'I resemble that remark. You mean the bordello?'

'We call it, the 'Oh Yeah'.

'Oh Yeah ?'

'Oh Yeah.'

She looks wide eyed and serious

'You've never been to one? You've never done that?'

'Let's say, Been that; Done there.'

'Not like here.'

The two of them ask. 'Oh Yeah?' and break each other up.

JD laughs and then stops to ask,

'What do you know that I don't know?'

'That's a long list, ask me again, way on down the road.'

*

The 'Oh Yeah' is down island center. It has two entrances and two exits and stands two stories tall. The main entrance is center and a generous staircase leads upstairs. To the left is a music room with a live pianist. There is a decadent lounge to the right. Both sides have a Madam and one is in drag.

Ms Chris whispers to JD, 'Comfy?'

JD says, 'Working on it.'

'Give it chance.'

'Have you? Do you, um come here often? Get it ?'

'JD this is about being seduced, and not about doin' the seducin'.'

'That would be new music for me. I mean, I've tuned up to it, but I've never played that song.'

She starts, 'I will if you will,'

'I will if you will.'

She sticks out her tongue.

'Don't you point that thing at me unless you intend to use it.'

'You don't know if it's loaded.'

JD laughs, 'I do so know'

'I'm goin' this way, where you gonna go'

'I'm gonna go take a look. Said I would didn't I?'

'Good, see ya then.'

JD walks over to the piano player who is picking out a familiar tune. He looks and then looks again.

'Joe Bananas?'

'Ya never know, with Big Joe.'

'I got that tune now.'

You can get anything you want at Alice's restaurant

Walk right in it's around the back,
Just a half a mile from the railroad track
You can get anything you want at Alice's restaurant

JD and the piano man sing along,

X-cepting Alice

Big Joe says, 'Hey JD, nice tunes out on the Pier earlier. I had to see Sister play, but, uh, booty called.' He looks at JD and says, 'Wha'choo doin' here boy? You blow through Chrissie already?'

'Naw we're taking a quick break. I'm on my own.'

A small woman approaches from the side. She asks,

'See anything you want stranger? We've got plenty to choose from.'

She takes his arm and leads him into the room.

'Your friend said I would find you here, probably hiding by the piano.'

'Joe's sister plays with me.'

'Is she any good?'

'She's great.'

'So what do you like about the way she plays with you?'

'Well, everything, uh.....'

'Is she a tease or a flirt? How does she play with you JD?'

His eyes widen and he stammers...

'I'm talking music here, right? Sister plays my organ in the band. I mean she plays the organ in my band.'

'Ah, so, you want someone like her?'

'Maybe.'

'You don't know? Mister, why are you here if you don't know what you want?'

JD looks around and says, 'Well, there's got to be plenty of folks who come in here not knowing what they want, Am I right?'

'Absolutely, but we try not to let our clients go away unsatisfied. Take your pick.'

She gestures to three girls and a boy standing at the bar.

'And Sugah? The first one is free. I'm LeeLee, in case you want me.'

JD scans the girls and waves the boy away. He smiles and licks his lips as he hears Big Joe play and sing,

But I'm just a soul whose intentions are good
Oh Lord, please don't let me be misunderstood

'I TOLD YOU, NO !'

Ms Chris stomps in a doorway with two half dressed Asian boys behind.

One boy says, 'So Sorry miss we thought you wanted Fun and Games, that's what you said.'

The other says, 'I'm fun, and he's game.'

'Maybe I did, Maybe with one of you and a little fore play, but you brought another and assumed too much. That's not my thing, sorry bud. I'm done with you two.'

'Lee Lee !'

She appears behind the Buds.

'Go on back boys. As for you two. I think I have what you want but they are both occupied right now. Come back later, and we will see what see shall see.'

Christy says, 'Come on Stud, you owe me dinner.'

'Let's roll chicka'

'Toni's has the best steaks on the waterfront.'

On hearing singing, they look back at the front of the Oh Yeah. The staff is singing to them, with LeeLee leading the choir.

But I'm just a soul whose intentions are good
Oh Lord, please don't let me be misunderstood

The Oh Yeah choir all laugh and we hear the madam yell, 'You come back soon, yeh?'

An older couple stroll by arm in arm smiling and wave at the choir.

The woman says, 'What a charming musical send off. LeeLee only does that for her favorites. Remember Harold?'

'Only when you remind me Cupcake. The rest of the time it's all about you.'

He winks at JD and Christie as he pinches his beloved's butt.

'Ow, Oh You just wait til I get you home . . . .'

Slapping at him, as they depart she says,

'I'll bite you . . .'

JD shouts, 'The best ones always do!'

Ms Tina punches his shoulder.

'Did I tell you I saw Joe Bananas in there?'

'As in Sister's big brother?'

'Joe is the house piano player. Who knew?'

'That explains the send off. I take it LeeLee found you hiding behind the piano.'

'Well, yeah, more off to the side really. You certainly got to it quick enough.'

'Too quick evidently. You saw how it turned out. Sorry if I rushed things JD.'

'Sorry to be dragging my feet. I was just stalling, looking over the merchandise.

JD sings,

But I'm just a soul whose intentions are good
Oh Lord, please don't let me be misunderstood

'Good Lady. You make me hungry.'

'Let's feed like there's no tomorrow.'

'You said that Toni's has the best steaks on the waterfront. Let's go there.'

*

As we walked the waterfront we came within listening distance of Dick's deck. Season of the Witch floated toward us.

When I look over my shoulder
What do you think I see?

Chris and I smile and sing the rest to the distant music.

Beatniks are out to make it rich
Oh no, must be the season of the witch

Toni's is mostly an all girl affair until you get a closer look and find that all are welcome. The hostess opens the door for us and almost squeals, but subdues her voice.

'CHRISSIE ! UH, Ms Mathews. . . Welcome.'

'Thanks Jen, is Toni here about?'

'Somewhere. She's all over South End to keep things moving. Ya'll dining?'

They pass a big aquarium filled with Tiger fish and are led to a table.

*

The scene changes to the stage at the 'Oh Yeah'.

We see Big Joe hit a key and turn to the suit on stage who sings,

> *I used to be a big skanky*
> *Yep, A Big Ol' Skanky Ho!*
> *Butt ?*
> *I ainna gonna be No Ho No Mo*
> *No I ainna gonna be No Ho.*

Toni points the mic at the audience and they sing along.

> *I ainna gonna be No Ho No Mo*
> *No I ainna gonna be No Ho.*

She laughs with the audience as Big Joe begins to sing,

> *De Policemans said, "You Got to Let Her Go,*
> *She ain't turn no tricks in a Month or so,*
> *She sho' ain't been, No, Not No Mo"*

Toni laughs and follows the musical lead.

> *Never had no Pimp, Never did no Dope*
> *Now my life, has got some Hope*
> *So, I Ainna gonna be No Ho No Mo*
> *No, I Ainna gonna be No Ho !*

The crowd goes crazy as Toni bows center and then to Big Joe.

'Oh Yeah is saying good evening to tonight's guest artist, Mz. Toni.'

Toni takes a bow. LeeLee takes the mic.

'We want to thank you all for visiting Pearl Isle. Ya'll feel free to linger here some more. Let's have another hand for Ms. Toni.'

Toni waves at the cheering crowd and throws kisses as she departs.

*

Back to Toni's with J.D. and Christie.

He asks, 'So what makes Toni's steaks the best on the waterfront?

'They way they are cooked. Toni's chef collects the steak drippings under the grill and then saturates and marinates the meat in it's own sauce.'

'Sounds good.'

She only smiles, 'You'll see.'

'Hey there sugar bumps'

'Toniiiii !'

Chris jumps up and hugs a smarmy looking gent in a zoot suit. Toni pushes her back and takes a better look.

'You look good, not too much wear, you home for a visit or you staying ?'

'A visit for now. Thinkin' about stayin' if I can get the road out of my head.'

Toni asks, 'Is this one from the road?', and JD speaks,

I say, 'Yep, and this one is here for a couple of steaks for she and I; if that's okay?'

'Don't jump salty on me Breeder, you're a guest in my place, behave yourself.'

'You shouldn't be tellin' a paying guest what to do Tranny Girl.'

Christie gets between them, 'Ya'll get your back fur down and stop spitting at each other. JD! On Pearl Isle it is not polite to deride sexual, uh explorations or differences.'

JD defends himself, 'She started it, called me 'Breeder', I only returned the compliment.'

'My fault Chrissie girl, I assumed he was baggage and showed no respect.'

Christie settles it, 'Down and Dirty, and done is done. No harm no foul. I'm still hungry for Toni meat.'

'I'll tell 'em out back.'

Toni winks and leaves as we hear

A Weem a Wep A Weem a Wep

JD asks, 'Don't we get to see a menu'

Chris replies, 'No need they only serve one thing in bigger and smaller portions. Tiger meat.'

'Really'

'Really and truly'

JD recalls, 'I know that song, You know it ?'

'I don't know it, but she sings and hums it all the time.'

He shifts his voice Imitating Yoda,

'Too young you are'

He shifts his voice to sing

In the Jungle,
the mighty jungle,
the lions sleep tonight.

The wait staff looks up Toni re-enters, smiles, and says,

'My favorite song'
JD says, 'One of my Daddy's too'
'You know the rest?'
'That I do,' he sings,

Near the village,
the peaceful village,
the lions sleeps tonight.

'Lawd, Lawd, Lawdy.'
'They're playin' our tune JD. You wanna dance?'
'Only with you Ms Chris.'
'Your loss.'
'My gain.'
Toni calls, 'Steaks are up where do they go?'
'Roight Here.'
'The secret's in the drippings. Bon appetite.'
The juke continues playin'

I've flown around the world in a plane,
I've settled revolutions in Spain,
The North Pole I have charted, but I can't get
started with you

JD sets back and sighs,

'This is great'

Chris adds, 'Better than good Toni, what is that fabulous new taste?'

Toni responds, 'Tiger Fish, It's a little known aphrodisiac. Not that you two would need it tonight.'

'But they're so little'

'Yep. And they breed like crazy, even the rabbits are amazed.'

JD asks, 'Got any Barry Whites?'

Christy snorts, 'Funny.'

Toni fills in, 'Not kidding, the sperm count is off the charts. We move the fish and drain the tank every week. Then we test the water .'

Toni grins and arches her eyebrows a couple of times.

'Don't tell me'

'You wouldn't'

Toni asks, 'Wanna taste?'

He and Chris do a Gag reflex

'Hey, It keeps the staff in tune, horny as goats. We've found that mixed with a little Pomy juice it reduces diarrhea and improves eyesight.'

Chris says, 'TMI'

JD adds, 'We'll take a double'

Toni signals

JD says, 'Over Ice'

'Not permitted. Take out is straight juice only. Pure take out may cause PDA's, Public Displays of Affection, which are not our scene.'

The shots arrive. JD says,

'They look perfectly normal. I expected steam or something'

Toni explains, 'No not at all, It's an elixir. Don't expect anything right away. It comes on later after the heart passes it further on down.'

'Come on lover, let's not do that here.'

Christie says, 'I know a perfect place. Toni I need to borrow a blanket'

Toni pours the shots into a go cup and passes them to JD. Christy returns with a blanket.

The full Moon rose over the dunes. As they tramped out the dunes to find a private place, they were accompanied by some other couples. They found a place near the water.

'Is that a horse blanket? It's kind of small, I'll get sand in my hair.'

'You and me both. You have a problem with getting sandy all over?'

'JD, Hold me here and kiss me .'

They both moan.

'So you say. So say it again.'

And so again.

'No more sand, let's go swimming'

From onshore we hear the voice of truth

You send me

We see both taking off their shoes stripping off their pants and dropping shirts. With his back to us JD drops his boxers and Chris smiles big. With her back to us Chris drops her bra and JD smiles reaches out, takes her hand and they walk into the moon lit surf.

Ohh, you thrill me,
Honest you do

They walk into the water until it comes up past their waists. Chris turns and puts her arms around JD's neck and kisses him with a thirsty need. JD enjoys and returns the kiss with hands in her hair as they sink beneath the surface.

They rise above the surface again still lip locked, but quickly break for air. JD moves further out into deeper water. Christie moves in closer and tighter and they kiss again. His hands move through water as she rises. His eyes sparkle and hers go wide.

'Oh Yes. Don't stop. Yeah Baby. Oh YES, oh sweet Jesus'
Janis Joplin pours through the air

So come on, Come on, Come on,
Come on, and take it,

'Your turn Sir', and She sings to him

Take another little piece of my heart now Baby,
You know you've got it and it makes me feel good

'Oh baby, Oh Chrissie, don't now, you better stop, don't do now, stop that now, I can't hold it much longer. Don't. Stop.. Don't Stop, Arwooow !'

Oh Yes indeed.

They move slowly resting their heads on one another's shoulders and kissing one another's necks, brushing hair out of the way, they look into one another's eyes kiss again and eventually stumble naked into shallow water.

From the shore they hear again the end of

Ohh, you, you, you,
you send me

Christie says, 'I thought that song finished and Joplin got started.'

JD says, 'Me too.'

'Then how?'

'Maybe it was the Tiger Fish.'

Christy rebuffs, 'Naw that's probably just a story she tells the tourists and then sells 'em, like ginger beer for $10 a shot.'

'You're no tourist. Would she do that to you?'

'Hmm, don't know. JD? She never asked to be paid,'

'Chrissie? We never did those shots, they're still in the go cup up by the blanket.'

'Wow, right?'

'I know, right?'

'Wanna try 'em now?'

'Let's save 'em for later.'

'Or we could return them.'

'Tru Dat, and we didn' pay for the steaks'

'And those were some damn good steaks'

'And the marinade was all that was on the meat?'

'So, where did Janis came from, you heard her too right?'

'Yeah, weird, but up on the beach Sam Cooke is still playing.'

They stumble from the surf and pick up the trail of clothes.

As they make it to the dunes they look at the horse blanket. It is covered with seagulls flapping and squawking.

One takes off with the go cup of Tiger Juice and others follow.

'If we heard Janis, I wonder what the gulls hear?'

'Spoken like a musician. We'll never know.'

As they start to dress, they stop and kiss again, and it builds.

'There's more where that came from.'

As they look into one another's eyes.

'Water or sand?'

'Sand gets everywhere'

'Race ya.'

They race down into the water and run diving into the surf.

But when you hold me in your
arms, I'll sing it once again
Have another little piece of my heart now, baby
Well you know you got it, child,
if it makes you feel good

JD and Ms Chris climb the few steps of Toni's past a female punk rocker leaning against a porch light pole. Chris stops to look.

'Nice look Toni'

JD stops to look and grins at the sight.

Toni takes a drag on her cigarette and blows out smoke.

'Weirdest thing, some gulls have been swooping on other birds.'

'Birds don't usually mix Ms Toni.'

I say, 'They might if they had some Tiger juice.'

Toni gasps, 'You didn't.'

Christy says, 'Nope. They took the go cups while we were, uh, busy.'

Toni says, 'Well, shit, never tried that. Let's get inside before they figure out I got a tank full.'

'Either that or we get a camera and shoot another ending for The Birds.'

'Not funny.' She starts to shutter up.

JD offers, 'Anyway, we came back to pay for the meal.'

Chrissie says, 'And the drinks, for the gulls anyway.'

Toni admits, 'I didn't collect because you left in a hurry, but I knew you'd be back Miss Chris.'

JD asks, 'What's the tab?'

'Well, let's go in and figure it up, before them seagulls come callin''

They check the skies as they go inside. Toni shuts the doors tightly.

'Okay, two Tiger steaks with all the trimmings and a couple of shots to go, $75?'

Christy adds, 'You include a half dozen double Tiger shots and we'll make an even $100.'

'Singles.'

Christie chides, 'Toni I know where you get that shit. There's an organic shelf life, is there not?'

JD hands her a single $100 bill. 'Six Doubles? In a cold jug?'

Toni holds up her palms, 'Done and Done.'

JD adds, 'May I apologize for jumping on you, for jumping on me?'

'You may do so.'

'I do so Toni, I was salty and regret not understanding you protecting your turf.'

'Let's sit a spell. Chrissie ya'll forgot your trimmings. I saved 'em for you. Go see Rick in the kitchen. We'll be right here.'

Toni turns to look at JD face to face.

'On Pearl Isle we learned long ago that tolerant people are happier people. And well, tolerant people are kinder than most folks who look down on things they don't understand or behaviors that challenge their beliefs.'

'Yeah, I get that. Like music, Like the beginning of Rock and Roll'

'Exactly. Same goes for cross dressing or same sex relations. It's all mostly just for fun.'

JD admits, 'So?'

'So we have come to believe that these past 2 or 3

generations have the ability to enjoy anyone and everyone else. That is until society or religion forces them to choose sides exclusively.'

'I see, or I'm beginning to think I do.'

JD hands Toni a C note. She bra tucks it.

'We believe in kindness and consideration. We believe that our common belief should be 'To Each Their Own', but 'Hurting No One'.'

'Your point of view is both kind and considerate. It obviously works here.'

Chrissie returns with two bags of food and a cold jug slung on her back. She says,

'We're all set for the night, and some more fun. Everything all right here?'

'I Love Him and He Loves Me, We're gonna take on Society.'

'How about you JD?'

JD stands, 'We're all good here.'

'Paid Up?'

'Let's Rock.'

Chrissie says, 'Let's go for some Dicks.'

JD chokes, 'It may take a while'

Toni asks, 'What if, never mind, Moving on. . .'

As they emerge into the moonlight we see a cluster of street singers under a lamp pole. Two are snapping fingers and one is starting the song.

Soothe me baby, soothe me
Soothe me with your kindness

JD stops and snaps in time. Christie asks, 'Sam and Dave?'

JD replies, 'Sure thing, but written by Sam Cooke'

The singers look over and wave them in 'One More Time'

JD sings to the group

> *I used to have a lot of girls*
> *Had 'em big and small*

Laughing and high fives all around as the vocals fade away smoothly

> *Come on y'all, Come on and soothe me*
> *You got to please, please soothe me*

The Five singers take off their hats and extend them toward JD. They alternate singing

> *Sooth Me, Sooth Me.*

'I hope tens are okay.'

JD peels off one per hat. The street singers speak,

'Yeh man,'

'We're cool wit dat,'

'Good tunes,'

'Let the good times roll.'

'Thanks for dat sexy babe version of Mercy Mercy out western pier.'

JD smiles, 'Tanks fo de music bak atcha. Oh, you

saw that, Glad you caught the act. The babe - sex part was all Sister.'

'Figures, we know her brother, Big Joe, from the Oh Yeah.'

'You should see him in a prom gown'

'You know who wrote that tune?'

'What song, "Big Joe in a Prom Gown"?'

'Naw you fool, "Mercy Mercy Mercy"'

'Cannon Ball Adderly.'

'A brit-pop group, I heard Lennon & McCartney added the lyrics. The Buckinghams recorded the first rock & roll version.'

Chrissie gapes and shakes her head.

*

As we walk away we hear the music coming from Dick's deck.

> *Where are you going now my love?*
> *Where will you be tomorrow?*
> *The questions of a thousand dreams.*
> *What you do and what you see,*
> *Lover, can you talk to me ?*

Dick's bar is a cowboy / cowgirl place for shit kickers with chicken wire to protect the band. There is a large Asian sumo man dressed like Dale Evans in her cowgirl garb guarding the door. He asks,

'Password?'

Chrissie answers, 'Dick sent me.'

'Entre'

She asks, 'Where's Dick?'

'Behind the bar, or maybe out back with the band.'

'Gotcha. I'm Christie. You?'

'Lola'

JD asks, 'L O L A, Lola?'

'Yeh, Like the song.'

'I've played that tune.'

They walk through the bar and out the back door to find the band and Dick passing a joint. The band is flicking bottle caps at an empty bucket.

'Yo Big Dick !'

They all look up and the wrangler smiles

'Hey there Little Slitch,'

They embrace and JD takes Dick's place in the circle to get a hit.

'Who's this hippie they say you draggin' round town?'

Christie makes intro's, 'JD . Dick . Dick . JD.'

Dick asks, 'JD. What's that for ?'

'Jemimah Duckbar'

No one laugh

'Jasmine Douche?'

All laugh, Christie punches him, takes the joint, takes a hit and says,

'JD stands for good music, good times, and . . .'

She draws, holds, exhales, and passes

'Just like ya'll, it stands fo' Juvenile Delinquency.'

One musician says, 'We heard some of your stuff as we drove in.'

Another comments, 'Cept it sounded like a girl.'

Dick asks Christie, 'You?'

JD answers, 'Nope, Sister.'

A third musician speaks, 'As in Big Joe's Sister?'

'Yep'

Mus #1, 'Lucky Man'

Mus #2, 'How is she on yer organ?'

JD chokes

Mus #3, 'That good?'

Chrissie pounds him on the back 'She's better than Joe.'

'How would you know?'

Mus #1, 'It's an Island 'ting Mon'

Mus #2, 'You mean on the organ.'

Dick returns, 'Whose organ?'

Mus #3, 'JD's'

Dick speaks, 'Well, good shooting there cowboy.'

Christie punches Dick, 'I'm not finished with him yet.'

Mus #1, 'Come on, We promised the door man he could dance.'

We see the band head for the stage, and as Dick says, 'You gotta see this to believe it.'

The door person, Lola, strolls to the dance floor to cheers and jeers.

I met her in a club down in North Soho
Where you drink champagne and

it tastes just like cherry cola
C-O-L-A cola.

Lola starts to strip with her cowgirl hat first, then her rawhide gloves.

Well, I'm not dumb but I can't understand
Why she walks like a woman and talks like a man

The cowgirl shirt is undone to mid body. He starts to loosen the skirt.

Lola has taken two bus boys on stage, they dance and spin with her. She stops and stares at the crowd with a mixture of lust and joy. She gets help from the bus boys to remove her shirt to reveal a leather fringe bra. We see a cattle brand on each breast cup. Both are a circle L brand.

As she moves from side to side they peel off her skirt and reveal a leather fringe thong. Lola begins a slow bump and grind.

Well I'm not the world's most masculine man,
But I know what I am, and I'm glad I'm a man,
And so is Lola!

The crowd is mesmerized, and terrified that she may go further.

Shouts from some Women
TAKE IT OFF!
GET RAW.
ALL THE WAY DUDE!

Shouts from some Men.

Put It On !

EEUUUWWW !

No More, Please, No More.

A shout from someone.

YEAAHH, You Go Girl, you go. You go girl, you go!

Lola stops with the last chord of the band and rips away the bra. The crowd stops and stares. We see the crowd read one, then the other and scream in Laughter. Tattooed on each pectoral muscle are the words,

EAT   **ME**

*   *

JD stares in disbelief as Lola flees the floor with the bus boys following gathering her discarded clothing. Dick is watching the crowd and laughing. Christina is holding her eyes and saying,

'Scarred for Life ! I will never be able to remove those images.'

Dick is laughing as the band starts a little Sly.

Sometimes I'm right then I can be wrong
My own beliefs are in my songs.

We hear further applause as the crowd moves to the dance floor.

JD hands the go bag and the cold jug to Dick.

'Guard this with your life. We'll be back.'

They hit the dance floor

> *I am no better and neither are you*
> *We're all the same whatever we do*

'Ain't it the truth.'
'Sing it again.'

> *You love me you hate me, You know me and then*
> *Still can't figure out the bag I'm*
> *in, I am everyday people*

They return to the table where Dick is holding the bag out of reach of a small dog who is circling and yipping and panting at Dick's knees.

'What the hell is in here? I ain't seen Sherman so agitated since we tried to raise squirrels.'

'Take outs from Toni's'

'Oh. Down Boy. Down, DOWN! Stay.'

Sherman drops into a sit quivering, never taking his eyes off the bag.

'He gets like that over my take outs too. I have to lock him up.'

'Better do it now. That's concentrated Tiger Juice in the cold jug.'

Dick hands JD the bag and takes Sherman away. Lola enters in full drag and sniffing the air.

'Mmm, Mumph. Yeah. Got any?'

JD clutches the cold jug bag to his chest.

'Nope just enough for us.'

Christie says, 'Nice dance Lola, and great tattoos.'

'Arrrrrr, thanks.'

He returns to the door with a wig hair flick in full Dale Evans drag.

Dick returns, accompanied by a beautiful young girl with a tray of three beer mugs.

'That there is some potent shit. Just don't open it in here, okay? Lola wouldn't be able to hold it together. I'm pretty sure He gave Toni the extraction process.'

Christie says, 'Then he can get his own.'

They all hoist a mug.

Dick says, 'I think he gets some on his way every night.'

JD asks, 'Where does he go.'

'Straight to the, Oh Yeah. Funny thing? Lee Lee says he never pays.'

Christie says, 'They probably pay him.'

'Lee Lee has banned him a couple of times, just to let the girls and boys rest up. But the kids usually have their way and he's back in there the next night or two.'

Christie says, 'We had a taste on our steaks and then we went swimming for a while . . .'

JD says, 'Probably scared most of the fish away.'

Christie admits, 'The gulls on the beach raided our go cup, so we stopped and got some more.'

Dick comments, 'For fun and games?'

'Why Uncle Richard, what would make you say such a thing?'

'Yer folks fer one. That stuff will make you howl at the moon.'

JD says, 'That it does.'

Dick asks, 'And did You?'

Chris contributes, 'He did.'

'Good Boy, let it out'

JD says, 'That I did, long and loud, with a few nips and yips'

Chris adds, 'And he bit Me, here and . . . . '

'The best ones always do. Salute.'

They all hoist a mug.

'So. You're in Love.'

The two lovers gag, cough, and spit as they look embarrassed.

'Uncle Dicky!'

'Okay, Too soon to tell. You're still young, that's your fault. Answer me in a year.'

Chrissie stands and salutes.

'Will do Sir Dick.'

'Poorly said, but well enough, and you?'

JD says, 'Yes sir.'

Dick pauses with Christina watching.

JD rephrases, 'Yes Sir, and Yes Mam, I will report within a year.'

'Good enough, and you?'

Christy says, 'I'll let it pass. Good enough for now'

Dick says, 'Equal is best'

The band interrupts with an a cappella beginning,

There are stars in the southern
sky, southward as you go.
There is moonlight and moss in the trees,
down the seven bridges road

The three of them move outside to watch the moon to her apex in the evening sky. They all watch and breathe from a quiet part of Dick's deck.

'So what kind of mischief ya'll up to with that Tiger juice?'

Chris considers, 'Dunno know quite yet. You got a plant sprayer?'

'Yep, big one for the outdoors, or a little one for the indoors.'

'As little as possible.'

'Jamie! Go get that atomizer from my office.' Jamie takes a detour.

'Not usually your style'

'Different strokes for different folks'

Jamie returns, 'Here you go boss.'

'Yeh yeh, so on and so on, and scooby smoked a doobie'

He hands the device to JD

Chris says, 'We could dose a bunch of Puritans and then sell tickets.'

Uncle Dick thinks, 'That would be both unkind and illegal, I like it,'

They all nod and smile

JD says, 'Incredible images, but no, I cannot do that.'

'Yeh, especially since yo' Grandma might be there.'

Christie says, 'No No No visual of that please, not so soon after these Lola images in my head.'

JD offers, 'We could learn from the experiences we have had so far.'

Dick is curious, 'Meaning?'

'The Seagulls had a good go of it and-'

Christie responds 'Then they had a good go at each other,'

'I thought we had some sauce on our steaks. But, I spoke with Toni and she assured me that our sauce was the natural drippings as normal.'

'So we weren't,' comments Chrissie.

'No we weren't', responds JD.

They embrace

She asks, 'And the go cup?'

'The Gulls had the best of it'

They kiss passionately.

Dick says, 'Well, that explains the Gull droppings all over the island.'

He looks at the couple, coupling, and coughs expectantly.

Christie thinks aloud, 'Mmmm, Sorry Unc, I lost my train of thought.'

'Glad it was that good'

She says, 'Wheww, it SO was.'

'Loud Cheers, welcome home. What's up for the rest of the evening?'

JD adds, 'We'll let you know.'

Christie kisses Dick on the cheek and waves as they walk the road.

'Ya know, we never had any of Lucy's crabs.'

JD considers, 'Now there's a thought'

'Where's a thought?'

Christie finishes, 'Lucy's Crabs and Toni's Tiger Juice.'

'Race Ya.'

They take off skipping and trotting playfully.

*

Lucy stands in her hip waders with a pair or tongs in one hand and a catch basket under her other arm. She snags a crab from the None Such Creek and pokes it into the basket. She sings as she gathers her prey.

Honey, get it while you can, yeah,
Don't you turn your back on love, no, no, no.

JD and Miss Christie stop at Lucy's front steps panting and laughing from the run. Sherman the dog bounces up just behind them nipping and yipping at the Thermos slung across JD's back. Lola runs behind holding an empty leash and trying to coax the dog away.

'Sherman Heel, Bad Dog. Down Bad Dog, Down.'

Sherman sits and awaits the leash.

Christie hands Lola the go bag

'Here. You two share these leftovers.'

'From Toni's?'

'Hush puppies and some steak bits.'

'That'll work, Come on Dog.'

And if anybody comes along,
He gonna give me love and affection,

Get it while you can, yeah!
Honey, get it while you can, yeah!
Honey, get it while you can,

JD asks, 'You hearing Joplin ?'
'Yeah, you didn't open that thing did you?'
'Nope, but, we didn't do any before, remember ?'
'Yep. That was all us.' Christie asks, 'Kiss me? Please ?'
'Only if you kiss me back'
We embrace, and the kiss moves forward
Lucy says, 'Ya'll should get a room'
JD says, 'That's good, comin' from a woman with crabs.'
'Ha. Good on you mate.'
Christy asks, 'Lucy was that you singing Janis?'
'Get It While You Can. I like to sing it while I'm picking out some new ones for tomorrow. These ones have their own tank for now. They got to go one way or all the other as stews, salads, sammys, and such.'
Lucy continues down into the creek along the other side.
JD says, 'Interesting, try some blue grass. They're blue crabs right?'
Christy says, 'You do it.'
From the railing JD sings.

I'll lay around this shack
'Til the mail train comes back
An' I'll roll in my sweet baby's arms

Lucy exclaims, 'Holy Guacamole! Look here, they's dancin''

Christy says, 'JD quick, go inside.'

He does.

Lucy says, 'Dey stopped'

Christy says, 'Afraid of that. Sing it again'

Lucy does so,

My daddy owned an interest in an old gin mill
Just-a watchin' that money rollin' in

Lucy says, 'No dancin', time to poke'

She grabs crabs with a quick dance as she sings

I'll lay around this shack
'Til the mail train comes back
An' I'll roll in my sweet baby's arms

'My basket is full o crabs Honey, Let's go in.'

Christy says, 'Lucy, JD has a jug full of concentrated Tiger Juice.'

'Oh no girl, Choo say Tiger juice? No mam. You got to get that stuff outta here quick.'

'Why?'

'Cause the crabs were dancin' They go a little Woo Woo over it.'

'JD? We got to go, honey!'

He comes back out and Lucy's basket starts to shake.

Lucy says, 'Off to the kitchen wit all o' you,' and smacks the basket with her tongs as she leaves.

Christy explains, 'She says the crabs go a little nuts for that stuff.'

'No shit?'

JD muses, 'Probably a salt water thing.'

'Ya think? Maybe it was a blue grass thing.'

> *And I loaned him two or three dollars*
> *And he gave me the latest news.*

Christy says, 'Look down there, They're dancing again.'

> *The grass is all synthetic*
> *And we don't know for sure about the food*

'That's so cute. Look at 'em dance back and forth', says JD

'There's some more of them coming out of the Billabong'

JD says, 'Looks like a lot more.'

> *I'll tear off down the river some*
> *day before I'm through,*
> *With the steamboat whistle blues*

'JD I'd stop singing that song if I were you.'

'Okay, . . . but they ain't stopped dancin''

Christy fears the truth, 'They're climbing the creek sides.'

'I think we better get.'

Christy exclaims, 'Okay let's go.'

JD asks, 'You think they're after Lucy?'

'I think they're after You and the Tiger Juice. Is that all we have?'

'Almost all, I dropped some off for savings.'

'Shit, let's go'

They jump down off of the front steps and skip across the road.

Scuttling noises are heard behind them, over the bridge when and we see a wall of crabs burst forth from the dry creek.

JD says, 'Yikes. You want this thing'

'Hell no, You got to get rid of it, Now.'

'Where? No where is safe from a wall of hungry horny crabs.'

Christy exclaims, 'There sure is, the water. Let's run.'

As they stumble into the surf at the mouth of None Such creek, JD un-slings the cold jug and launches it out over the coastal waterway.

The wave of crabs passes outward and into the water following the Tiger Juice. A few stand guard between the lovers and the beach.

Christie shrieks as we see a crab start up each of JD' legs. He knocks them off and Christy knocks one off his back while she says,

'It's your shirt, it's all wet with juice.'

JD rips it off and throws it toward the water.

At that time we hear a muffled "FaVoomph" from behind them and see a small fountain come out of the water.

'Yip! I guess they got it open'

The other crabs all chase into the surf.

Christy says, 'One thing for sure.'

JD asks, 'What's that?'

'I'm damn glad it's low tide'

'You mean they're not comin back'

'No time soon anyway. The ocean has 6 hours to dilute that shit.'

'Let's go warn Lucy.'

We see Lucy stirring the crab boil as our musical background plays

Please, please, please,
(Baby please don't go.)
Please Please

She says, 'May Allah Have Mercy, what happened to you ?'

Christy says, 'Crab Fest'

JD laughs, 'More like Crab Stock'

Lucy laughs, 'Maybe ya'll were listening to the Crush Station.'

'Ha'

'Stop.'

Lucy asks, 'What did you do with the you know what?'

JD answers, 'The Atlantic took it and all those that followed after it'

'I felt them come by and said a quick prayer.'

Christy says, 'It worked, thanks.'

'Glad I could help.'

JD explains, 'Maybe a couple of Hundred followed the cold jug out and I think they got it open'

'Hmmm. It'll prob'ly be alright, The tide's out, the creek's dry'

Christy confirms, 'Yep'

'First time Lola came by with that Tiger stuff, the pond emptied out and chased him up the street 'fore he figured out what was what.'

JD understands, 'Good to know, my time ain't the first time.'

Lucy asks, 'So where is your shirt ?'

'It sleeps with the fishes.'

Christy genuflects, 'Dosvedanya, Don't get none on Ya'

'Blue grass is gonna give me nightmares. I'm sticking with Gospel.'

JD laughs, 'Or maybe Soul,'

'Ha'

'Stop'

Lucy says, 'Holy Mackerel,'

JD laughs, 'You're giving me a Haddock'

Christy says, 'Fish puns. That's a new low.'

JD says, 'Hey these are the 4am jokes ok? You want fresh? Come in for the early show.'

Lucy speaks 'I got a tee shirt you can use but it's got . . .'

She turns the shirt around to reveal a big crab with extended claws in fighting stance.

'Ah . . . no thanks once a night is enough. I got another in the car.'

Lucy holds up the atomizer, 'Hey I found this thing on the counter and figured it was yours, and figuring what might be in it I stuck it in the fridge.'

She hands Chrissie the spritzer from Dicks

Christy says to JD, 'You didn't'

'I did, that's probably how I got some on me.'

Lucy says, 'We better seal that in a cold sack. I got some for frozen shipping.'

JD comments, 'Speaking of which, can I send some frozen to my Mama in the Ozarks?'

'Why not? How many you want to cold ship.'

'Let's say about $50 worth. Birthday gift.'

Lucy pulls out her link, 'Let's bump'

JD pulls out his link, taps a few times and bumps with Lucy's phone.

Lucy says, 'Done and Done any message to go with?'

'Yep, just write, 'Who Loves Ya'.'

Christy says, 'Let's go get you dressed.'

*

Walking outside they hear the street singers a distance away.

But since I met you baby you're mine
All I want to do is stay home and say

Christy says, 'That was so sweet to send your Mama some crabs.'

JD says, 'She'll eat 'em up. How many you think Lucy will send?'

'Nothing small about Lucy. Yo Mama will feed some others too.'

'Good. Glad about that.'

As they walk to the car Christy says, 'I think it's sweet that you sign your notes to me the same way.'

'Who Loves Ya?'

'Of course I do, and evidently so do you.'

JD says, 'I got another shirt in my guitar case.'

'I'm not sure I want you dressed just yet.'

She puts her arms around him from behind and bites his neck as she scratches his torso. She runs her hands down his chest and one enters his belt line.

JD says, 'I give you exactly 30 minutes to stop that.'

He turns to her and undoes a few buttons as they kiss, he pushes the shirt off and starts to tease her in return. He undoes the top button of her jeans and then slowly slides down the zipper.

Christy pushes him away and says, 'Start the car.'

She walks away from him towards the front. He follows while pressing his key chain. The Shelby rumbles to life. She spread her hands over the hood and purrs. He comes from behind and runs his hands up her half naked back and starts to run her jeans down.

We see the jeans going down and we see her smooth -

'Hold It right there.'

JD pants, 'I am, oh I am holding . . . on. We stopped? Why?'

'You think I'm some tramp you can do from behind over the hood of a running car?'

'But, you asked me to . . . I only did . . .'

Christy explains, 'I just got you started, you said you needed help, I was just helping. Put this on.'

She tosses him a shirt. And dances into the darkness laughing and carrying the cold pack, she yells over her shoulder,

'See ya round JD!'

He struggles with his composure as well as his zipper.

'Damn that girl, she makes me walk like a penguin.'

We see JD waddling while trying to dress around an erection.

Christy is dancing along Southern Cross rd. As she comes to the 'Oh Yeah' she stops, giggles, and then enters.

*

JD is cruising the bars and restaurants they have visited so far tonight and she is nowhere to be found. The restaurants are closed. He checks the beach swing. He looks at the only place he has not checked, 'Oh Yeah'.'

He bursts through the main entrance to hear,

You better change your way of livin'
And if that ain't enough
You better change the way you strut your stuff

Big Joe is playin' and singing as a fan dancer in mask is doing her thing on stage. The fans are ample to cover some parts of her nude body.

Lee Lee approaches and takes JD by the arm and leads him to a corner. She asks,

'Would that be more of what you want?'

JD stares and asks, 'Is that Sister?'

Lee Lee says, 'No, while she is working she is known as Sissy. So far all I can get out of her is fan dancin'. You like to give her a try?'

JD exclaims, 'Thanks but no thanks. I'm looking for Ms Chris, uhh, wow, have you seen her?'

'She came in and asked for sanctuary. I put her back in room on 2.'

'Thanks.' He races up the stairs as LeeLee finishes,

'But I think she left already.'

JD opens the door of 2E to find an empty messed up bed.

'Damn that Girl is making me work too hard'

He sees a note left on the pillow.

'Glad you got this far. I'll be on the leeward pier at sunrise. Hope to see you Thor'

JD rushes out and tries to go down the stairs only to be blocked by Lola taking up the second floor landing to the stair case.

'Jeez Lola ! Sorry, uh How's it hanging?'

'To da left. Same as always 'til I get me a whiff of a girl. Ha!'

'Right – Oh could we move down?'

He knees Lola in the butt to keep him moving. JD thinks of the note and knees Lola again. When Lola steps off the stairs the staff quietly moan.

JD yells 'Who's THOR?'

'WE ALL ARE !'

Everybody has a laugh, including Lola as he leaves. As LeeLee greets JD, she drops her character attitude.

'Well, that's a relief for tonight anyway. Sometime he doesn't leave til dawn.'

JD asks, 'Anybody seen my girl Chrissie?'

'Yes. She left out about 5 minutes before you came in. Did you find the note?'.

JD reads, 'Glad you got this far. I'll be on the Leeward pier at sunrise. Hope to see you Thor.'

Sister says, 'Fuckin spell check, It's supposed to read "Hope to see you There"'

'You think?'

'I know. She asked me to write and print it. Hope to see you There?'

Big Joe says, 'Well it was a good laugh anyway,'

JD says, 'See Ya Sister, See Ya Joe. LeeLee . . .'

She says, ' Just go, don't make her wait anymore.

JD stumbles out of the Oh Yeah and looks up at the stars. He extends his arms to the compass points. 'East,' and he runs.

*

As he runs, he looks to his right where the sun begins to rise.

JD races toward the Leeward pier passing an early morning coffee cart. He runs the length of the pier. He sees no one. But, at the end of the pier is a small tent. He looks inside only to see some empty sleeping bags.

He runs back to the cart.

'Hey there mister. Have you seen a girl come through here?'

The coffee guy turns and we see Ms Chris in disguised as Chico Marx wearing a curly wig and a beat up hat.

'Naw, nobody like that around here sonny.'

JD blinks and looks again. Chico speaks again,

'Well maybe I did see a pretty young thing pitch that tent out there. But she left a while ago.'

'And which way did she go. You think she's still around?'

'Mmmm Maybe. Who knows with women these days. Maybe she's still there.'

'Nope I looked.'

'Did you look close? You didn't even go inside. She could have been hiding.'

'In a tent that small? Doubt it.'

'Yeh, you're right. Besides, what do you care.'

'Oh I care. I care a lot, more than enough to chase that girl, all through high and low waters. How about her starting by giving me a set of blue balls in my car?'

Chico muses, 'Oh that's nothing around here, We getta them all the time. Happens all over. Nope, not quite enough.'

'Enough to brave a sumo waitress? How about no touching on the dance floor? How about enough to risk salt water sex, twice, while the air is teeming with crazed seagulls.'

'That does go some . . . .'

'How about being abused and lectured by a retired hooker? And, How about feeding and watering that girl only to be told she needs to find a whore house.'

Chico considers, 'Well that maybe comes under a different category.'

'How about a 350 pound drag queen, a crazed dog, and a hoard of ravenous horny crustaceans while fearing for our lives. How about that?'

'All that huh? What's your real name anyway?'

'There's more ! Another set of blue balls over the hood of a running car, me running across town with my pants down and an erection that made me waddle like a Penguin.'

'Ha ! Could I use a picture of that. We could put in the newspaper,'

'Not on your life! I've had all I can stand, and I and I can't stands no more!'

Chico takes off her hat and puts on Groucho glasses with eyebrows and a moustache. She pulls out a cigar and says,

'What about the decent god fearing people from this community who get victimized by you tourists who come over here looking for fun and games.'

JD snorts, 'Some join the fun by running the outsiders ragged.'

'And some of them stay at home and wonder,'

JD asks, 'They ever wonder what they're missing?'

'Okay, mister no name. This girl, did you tell her that you love her?'

JD admits, 'Nope, started to a couple of times but things kept happening so fast. Plus she gave me a year to think about it.'

'She did?'

'Well, it was actually she, and her Uncle Dick.'

'Sounds like something a Dick would say.'

'I wanna tell her, I just don't want to scare her off by, for being so . . .'

'Did you look all the way out on the dock? Maybe She's fishing . . . for breakfast.'

'Think it's worth my while?'

'Could be. Stranger things have happened. Question is, of course, are you worth waiting for ?'

'Hmph, Duh ?'

He turns and walks the pier while watching the sun rise. At the end there is no one on the dock, there is no one fishing.

He turns and sees Christina walking toward him carrying two cups of coffee. They meet in front of the tent.

She says, 'Hi ya stranger, long time since I've seen you.'

JD kneels, 'Too long not to say what needs to be said. I love you.'

She laughs and kneels and sings as she pulls him into the tent.

'Have I told you lately that I love you?'

Have I told you lately that I love you
Have I told you there's no one else above you

We see the two lovers facing each other. A close kiss turns into a more passionate one filling the next lyrics.

For the morning sun and all its glory
Meets the day with hope and comfort too
You fill my life with laughter,
somehow you make it better
Ease my troubles, that's what you do

*

They rest in each other's arms gently stroking one another while falling asleep.

We see the back of a person looking under the edge of the tent. We see the cooler bag along the side of the tent. The edge rises beside the bag as a hand snatches the bag from the tent.

Outside we see hands remove the atomizer from the bag. We see the same hands pouring the Tiger Juice from atomizer into another container.

*

We hear music. We see JD sit up quickly and Christie just after him.

We hear a hymn being sung by a crowd.

When the trumpet of the Lord shall
sound, and time shall be no more
And the morning breaks eternal bright and fair.
When the roll is called up yonder I'll be there.

They look at each other and then peek out of the tent and see the rear of a church service with people standing and singing.

When the roll (when the roll) is called up yonder
When the roll is called up yonder, I'll be there

They look down and notice their state of undress. A hand comes in the back flap of the tent with the atomizer. It does not spritz and withdraws.

They blink and smile. JD glances at the tent flap, then draws it tight.

'I want you.'

'Are you sure?'

'Very'

These kids have no qualms about submitting to temptation, they do so in style. As they embrace we see them making love again. They romp home with the break of day. Somewhere a rooster crows.

They lay back and fan themselves as the sun continues to rise.

*

Christie and JD hear a bass drum go,

Boom !

The chorus follows,

We shall come rejoicing, bringing in the sheaves

They see a chorus line marching behind the big drummer who resembles Lola. The others following resemble characters we have seen before. Taking up the rear is small man in a somber suit.

He is singing from a hymnal.

The Drummer stops at the back of the assembly. The troop divides and starts down the center aisle and both side aisles.

Sowing in the morning sowing seeds of kindness
Sowing in the noontide and the dewy eve
Bringing in the sheaves...

*

We see the troop turn and every few steps a slow mist emanates from them. Their leader steps to the podium and speaks,

'Dear friends, I am reverend Anthony and this is my flock of sinners. We've come to join with ya'll in worship.

BOOM !

Please sing along with me.

Jesus loves the little children

The troop circles behind the choir at the pulpit as a slow mist rises.

Several of the congregation are nodding, tappin', and snapping.

The two groups merge and some dancing breaks out. Some of the parishioners break away with staff from the 'Oh Yeah' while Madam LeeLee is arm in arm with the Reverend Lady singing along.

> ***All the children of the world***
> ***Red or Yellow, Black or White,***
> ***They are precious in his sight.***
> ***Ahhh Mennnn.***

'Yes dear Friends we're up early to bring about a new day on Pearl Isle, we are here to commune, to absorb the rising mists of the sunrise, and to pray,

The Lady Reverend is looking down but her hands are palm up.

'Yes. We Pray with all of you for guidance and understanding. And we wanna pray a little harder for forgiveness, Yes, dear friends, forgive the sins of others so they can forgive the sins in you'

The Reverend Lady asks, 'Can I have an Amen?'

'AMEN.'

'Reverend Lady, May we begin the tithe by passing the hat?'

'We use baskets.'

'Even better, and let me start.'

Toni throws in a thick stack of bills, starting the baskets around,

'Let me tell you my own story.'

> *I ainna gonna be No Ho No Mo,*
> *No I ainna gonna be No Ho.*
> *Got to give that up, Got to let it Go,*

'So that's my story. Sad but true. For me to tell, from me to You.'

The Reverend Lady asks, 'Can I have an Amen?'

Everybody shouts, 'AMEN!'

'I want you to turn to the person next to you. Tell them your story of sin and redemption, Go on, do it now, and then offer them a warm and friendly hug.'

Toni is pulled aside and embraced by the Reverend and whispered to. She returns a smiling reaction. The crowd is doing the same with many a giggle and a couple of shrieks.

The Lady Reverend steps to the pulpit and shouts.

'Friends let us be generous by welcoming these Sinners into our flock, because . . .'

> *She used to be a big skanky*
> *Yep, A Big Ol' Skanky Ho!*
> *But ?*
> *She ain't turned no tricks in a month or so,*
> *Cause, She ainna gonna be No Ho No Mo*
> *No, She ainna gonna be No Ho.*

The crowd gets into the spirit of song and chimes along.

Time ta grow up, Gotta let that Go,
No I Ainna gonna Be No Ho No MO !

BOOM !

On the big drum beat the congregation is filled with a light mist. JD and Chrissie walk up from behind.

He says, 'Stay Upwind darling.'

She says, 'Look at 'em Go'

'We gotta get in on this.'

Chrissie and JD dash to the front and JD yells,

'I Wanna Confess !

Christina yells, 'YES !'

Christina yells,'I Wanna Confess !

JD yells, 'YES !'

Someone yells, 'TELL IT ALL GIRL !'

And she does,

I saw the light, I saw the light
No more darkness, no more night.

The crowd is high on forgiveness, acceptance, and a little Tiger mist.

They all sing

Just like the blind man, I wandered along,worries
and fears, I claimed for my own.

JD steps forward and throws money into a passing basket.

An older woman and her boy toy step up to sing.

I saw the light, I saw the light

Christie gasps, 'Granny Mathews?'

Barking with fun, 'You kids don't to get to have all the fun. By the way, Pass the basket and the microphone.'

Granny sings in a strong healthy voice

I was a fool to wander and stray
For straight is the gate and narrow the way

JD yells, 'Everybody now!'

Praise the Lord, I saw the light.

All the clapping and yips and yells follow the end of the song.

Reverend Anthony takes the pulpit once again.

'Now that we're getting' to know each other, I would like to ask ya'll to get to know one another a little better.'

The Reverend Lady speaks,

'Most of Ya'll have a Sunday luncheon planned at home or somewhere else, and if you have enough for a guest or two, I'm sure they'd be glad to come along.'

Lee Lee adds, 'And, those who wish to commune with any of us down south? We welcome you.'

The crowd disperses with strains of I Saw the Light in the distances.

Toni appears with the Lady Reverend and Lee Lee arm in arm.

'We're walking back, she needs some air and an explanation, or three.'

JD says, 'Good luck with that.'

'I'll need it, thanks'

As they depart, Christy calls after, 'Go for it Toni.'

BOOM !

JD and Chrissie cringe a bit.

Lola stands with the bass drum and four baskets full of money.

He says, 'The Reverend Lady should get this'

JD asks, 'Should we take it to the 'Oh Yeah' ?'

Christy says, 'No.'

'Dick's ?'

'Nope'

'LuLu's ?'

'Uh Uh, they'll be at Toni's having red meat. Then maybe a little pink.'

Lola laughs, 'For desert, ya?'

JD turns the drum up, throws the baskets in. Lola marches away.

BOOM ! (rattle rattle rattle)

'You are one generous guy JD. I thought you were gonna take a basket or two.'

'Thought crossed my mind.'

She takes his arm and they face the morning sun.

'You could have taken back what you laid out last night.'

'As the Reverends would say' 'Tis better to give ... than to receive'

'How much ? '

'Bout 250 so far.'

'Nobody said Love was cheap'

'Hey ! I know the goods when I see 'em'

They speak in unison, 'And I'm looking at 'em right now'

They kiss passionately.

'Are we gonna do this right out here in front of everybody?'

They look around to see nobody and a bunch of empty chairs

'Nope.'

JD opens the tent flap and they both dive in.

*

We see a Crab and a Seagull watching from the top of two pilings. The seagull holds out a wing and the crab raises a claw to do a Claw to Wing bump. The gull flies and the crab dives. We see sunlight reflected off the water as we hear . . . . .

I see skies of blue, And clouds of white.
The bright blessed day, The dark sacred night.
And I think to myself,
What a wonderful world.

I hear babies cry, I watch them grow,
They'll learn much more, Than I'll ever know.
And I think to myself,
What a wonderful world, yeah?

eos

'The Piers of Pearl Isle' Song Titles List

Such A Night	Dr. John
The Stroll	The Diamonds
Let the Good Times Roll	Ray Charles
Freedom	Richie havens
Rock And Roll Music	The Beatles
Pick Up the Tempo	Waylon Jennings & Willie Nelson
Mercy Mercy Mercy	The Buckinghams
Lawd Have Mercy	T. K. Wallace
All Together Now	The Beatles
Cool, Clear Water	Bonnie Raitt
Alice's Restaurant Massacre	Arlo Guthrie
Don't Let Me Be Misunderstood	Eric Burden
Season Of The Witch	Donovan
Ho No Mo	T. K. Wallace
The Lion Sleeps Tonight	The Tokens
Can't Get Started With You	Ella Fitzgerald
You Send Me	Sam Cooke
Piece Of My Heart	Janis Joplin
Soothe Me	Sam & Dave
Carry On	Crosby, Stills, Nash & Young

POPI song list cont.

Lola	The Kinks
Everyday People	Sly & The Family Stone
Southern Cross	The Eagles
Get It While You Can	Janis Joplin
Rollin' In My Sweet baby's arms	Leon Russell
Steamboat Whistle Blues	John Hatrford
Please Please Please	Stevie Wonder
Soothe Me reprise	Sam & Dave
Ya Better Change Your Ways	Bob Fosse
Have I Told You Lately	Van Morison
When The Roll Is Called	James A. Black 1893
Bringing In The Sheaves	Knowles Shaw 1874
Jesus Loves the Little Children	
Hon No Mo reprise	T. K. Wallace
I Saw The Light	Hank Williams 1949
What A Wonderful World	Thiel & Weiss

Water Songs 5

Gambling with
Darn Old Grump

Maritime Dreams

Somethin' from Nothin'

Gambling with Darn Old Grump

by

T K Wallace

I never had much of an interest in gambling. I live in New York City and for many years I rode a bicycle all over Manhattan and Brooklyn. I worked as a free lance non union carpenter, electrician, and rigger within the entertainment industries. I figure those are enough of a gamble.

My father and his cronies had a Monday night poker game running for many years. It seemed like fun and they certainly had a good time. When I got old enough, about 12, and had saved the minimum required five dollars, I asked to sit in. They plucked me dry and sent me packing in about ten minutes.

It did encourage me to study and learn the odds on many types of games. And, I found that the house is the big winner in almost all cases. After all, when you own the game, the tables, the cards, the wheel, and sell the chips, let's just say it's no wonder the house comes out on top.

I went to Las Vegas once to see the scene, check out the strip, and catch a show. Tom Jones was playing the Sands. I was amazed to hear he had imitators. It was a gas, women were throwing underwear at him during the set. He seemed as amused as we were.

Vegas in August is like living in a blow dryer. Where Atlantic City in January is like living in a snow globe. I come from the south and we rarely have cold weather. Naturally I was curious as to how the beach and boardwalk look when covered with snow.

The show I was running had just closed, so I had

some time off. And, the NY / NJ area to had a blizzard coming on, so I suggested to my lovely bride that we take a few days out of town. The weather predictions were poor and I knew the beaches in AC would be covered.

I called Susan and asked her to upgrade the car rental to the biggest and heaviest car she could find. We left around 11 pm in a large black sedan DeVille. Blowing down to NJT to AC we passed many sidelined cars and a few trucks. The rest stops were packed with vehicles waiting out the storm.

After a couple of hours and too much coffee we got punchy from driving through the oncoming swirl. The constancy of the big caddy ripping through the night snow was hypnotic. I suggested that we play games to keep us alert and entertained. We tried a game called, 'Spot Em First', a game designed to spot potential traffic threats, like way out of state cars and trucks, cops, etc.

I wondered aloud how we could assure our rooms to be, were on an upper floor with a really good view of the beach. Susan suggested that if we were VIPs this would not be a problem. I proposed that if we had a record of any previous crappy service it could also work toward our upgrade.

We were booked into the Grump Hotel as Mr and Mrs Gordon Clark. We had reservations rooms for two days and nights. And we really wanted to see the entire city, beach, and boardwalk under a beautiful white blanket.

With about 50 miles to go we stopped for another cup of coffee. I asked Susan to help me start another game. I called it Miss-representation. It was to be a two stage game. The first ploy was that Susan would pose as a consultant to Grump Corp and had worked on the tax deal concerning the Grump Towers re-development of the Bon Wit Teller towers.

Darn Old Grump had purchased Bon Wit Teller tower on 5th avenue to re-develop the property into high end shops and ultra expensive residential units. It seems that a very bright lawyer found a law on the New York State books granting a tax waiver for any property which had not been 70% occupied at the time it was purchased for re-development.

As part two of the ploy. A complaint from the last time Mr. and Mrs. Clark had stayed at the Grump hotel. Our rental vehicle had been scratched due to careless valet parking. But, as we were guests, as a courtesy, we had chosen not to report the damage to the hotel. We only wished to make sure that no such incident would occur again.

Through the wonders of cellular technology, Susan called the hotel and gave it her best. In an apologetic and concerned voice she announced her title and association with GC. She spoke of her concerns and informed them that we would be arriving shortly.

So, when we arrived, we received the best of everything we had requested including an upgrade to an upper floor suite facing the ocean, and executive valet parking as well.

The next morning, in search of a good local restaurant, I suggested that we drive around and see the city other than the beach front properties. As we did this, I realized that many of the streets were named the same as the properties on the game of Monopoly.

Close to the AC airport is a very good restaurant. Pilots and crew could dine there, and even hang out there while waiting for their passengers. We drove to the airport and had a late brunch. The food was quite good and cost a fraction of the same meal at the hotel.

While dining, I looked out the restaurant window at the Cadillac. The car was totally clean and gleaming in the light of day. I had driven this vehicle through a snow storm for several hours the night before. It should have been covered with all sorts of road filth.

On the way back Susan spotted a toy store. We stopped and she went in to buy a game. She had decided that rather than gamble any money in the casino, we would play Monopoly for the entire city. We decided the best place to play our game was the pool deck, which had a great view of the boardwalk.

When back in our suite, I called the garage manager to ask who had washed our car. When she asked what kind of car we had driven, I was told that all luxury cars parked in Mr. Grumps section of the garage were washed daily. I informed the manager of the garage that I wished to give a gratuity to the person involved. Shortly afterward a steward arrived at our door.

I assured him that everything was good and only wished to thank the person responsible and gave him a 5 dollar tip. In response he gave me a baggie with a partially smoked joint someone had left in the car's ash tray. So I gave him 5 more for the effort.

After swimming and basking in the enclosed sunshine we set up our game by moving several tables together and proceeded to play. I ordered drinks and snacks to be delivered to the pool deck so we could continue to play for several hours.

When I was a child we would have these marathon games of Monopoly which took forever. I liked the game but it was too slow. With three or four players the game, they would eventually take sides with one another. Secondly, we were not given enough money to continue quickly toward the winning goal and title of the game, i.e. Monopoly.

I invented some ways to quicken the game. We always gave out twice the opening amount of cash. And we instituted a cash bonus of $500 when landing on Free Parking, which also included the monies from Chance and Community Chest. I allowed each player to have multiple characters.

We ran into a safety problem of catering being unable to deliver drinks and dinner to the pool deck. It seems that glass ware and dinner ware, all of which are prime quality at Grumps, were not permitted in a wet and slippery area, i.e. the pool deck.

So I had everything delivered to our suite. I did not allow the table to be set in our rooms, but rather left in the hallway. I called the garage and spoke with Roger, our car washer and newest best friend. He helped me deliver the carts to the pool deck and then departed with another tip. Susan and I brought the carts inside the pool deck and we set out our dinner and drinks.

We played and got rather drunk, and as will happen, got a little louder with each game. We stopped to eat and then played some more. We had to resort to some chicanery and obtain more drinks but did not involve Roger. By the time we quit after sundown it was 2 games each. We stopped with a vow to break the tie over brunch.

The beach and boardwalk were indeed beautiful but we started too late in the day for the full effect. Atlantic City faces east, the sun was already going down behind us. We decided to return earlier the next day.

Susan wanted to visit the casino but didn't want to bore me. So I suggested that we visit several casinos with a $100 limit per stop. The decor was amusingly similar. Loud colors with too many bright and shinning surfaces seemed to be the norm. All of the casinos had security surveillance devices, unconcealed, barley concealed, and more I'm sure I did not see.

We won at most places and lost at others. I think we came out about $400 ahead for the evening. Susan was playing slots and roulette and I stuck with black jack. Yawn and snore.

*

'Early to bed and early to rise, makes us all healthy, wealthy, and wise.' Well, at least we had the disposition for good times and an interesting agenda. This time we ate in our suite and took only the coffee service to the pool deck.

Mid morning was very bright as some of the snow and ice had melted and reflecting off the boardwalk and pier. The water was very active with the waves crashing the beach. No one was in the water, but several couples were walking briskly along the boardwalk shivering in the cold.

I was standing in the sunlight and wearing a pair of flip flops, Birdwell surf baggies, a loud Hawaiian shirt, and a pair of Oakley sunglasses. Susan was dressed for the beach as well, with the shirt opened. Underneath was a provocative bikini exposing the impressive physique of her finely tuned body.

As we set the tables and the board, several casino types came in to get pumped up for their day of gambling. More than one asked how much we were playing for. We replied that we were playing for the entire city.

For some reason, this seemed to interest them. One by one as they finished their swim or steam or sauna, they would stop by the board and check on our progress. Some of the gamblers noticed the accelerated system we were using to jump start the game.

We had set the tie breaker today at 5 more games making a total of 9. At the count of 3 and 3 we began to gather spectators, or rather speculators, as they were starting to make side bets with one another on the outcome.

The pool deck attendants had ignored the catering transgression of the previous day, but did take notice that gambling was happening on the pool deck and reported such to management.

A manager from the casino showed up and asked what we thought we were doing. "Duh, playing Monopoly?" Susan replied.

He snorted, "You are not permitted to interfere with the gambling practices of the hotel by starting your own games". He crossed his arms across his unimpressive chest and rested them on top of his impressive belly.

"We are not gambling, they are gambling" I pointed out.

He declared, "Well, it is simply not done this way at Grumps. You must stop all of this and leave the pool deck immediately."

"Why?" I inquired, "We aren't doing anything wrong, just playing a simple and popular board game on this lovely pool deck." He sneered at me and was interrupted by Susan saying, "We are playing for your entire city chubbie."

At this insult he pulled out a radio and barked, "Get the manager and tell him to bring security with him to the pool deck." To us he barked, "We'll see about you two malcontents."

One of the gamblers stated loudly, "You're just pissed because the house isn't getting a cut." Another said, "He's just pissed that the house gets nothing from any gaming that goes on here on the pool deck. None, nada, zero."

I said, "Perhaps you'd like to get in and play like a normal customer for a change." He frowned; indecision being apparent, the casino manager, his name badge read, Hightower, started to answer as the doors to the pool deck opened. A well dressed man entered with a security guard.

"Good morning, I am Mr. Van Pufflen, the concierge here at Grumps. Is there a problem?" he said as he surveyed the tables.

"I asked for the manager, this is beyond your scope of responsibility or interest", replied Hightower.

"Mr. Grant was busy with a special guest. I was in his presence when you attempted to summon him. He asked me to come and assist you in any way possible. And he was curious why you were swimming on duty."

"Do I look like I am swimming? I was apprised that there was gambling going on here on the pool deck. These two are conducting a private game-"

"Of Monopoly" inserted Susan

"And these people are making wagers"; Hightower pointed. "My department is responsible for gambling here at Grumps"

"And mine is responsible for guest services. This is an interesting situation. Are you playing for money?" Van Pufflen asked.

"No. We are playing for the entire city." Susan pointed outside. "There is the Boardwalk, and we are just next to Park Place."

Mr. Van Pufflen smiled as the doors opened again and a stately man entered followed by a man with the waddle of an emperor penguin. The penguin man was

Mr. Grant the manager, and Darn Old Grump was in the house.

Hightower gasped, "Mr. Grump! Welcome, Mr Grump sir, welcome.

"Welcome to the pool deck Hightower? What are you doing here instead of minding the Casino?"

"Trying to eliminate a case of unauthorized gaming in your establishment sir", Hightower babbled lamely.

Mr Van Pufflen followed, " It seems that Mr Hightower was informed of a bit of gambling going on outside the casino, sir."

Darn Old Grump smiled. "Monopoly, love the game, played it all my life, on and off the board. Looks like quite a bit money on the board, not many properties left; who's winning?"

"I am" we both replied. He laughed.

"What are the stakes?" He asked, "Can I get in?"

"You can get in with them," I pointed to the gamblers. "This is the tie breaker, we're tied 4 and 4, out of 9 games."

"We are playing for the entirety of Atlantic City." Susan added with a smile as she was getting a lot of mileage out of it.

"You can get in with us," stated a gambler, "This stuffed shirt was trying to break up the game before it was over."

While taking off his top coat and loosening the tie, he looked at Hightower and changed from the amused Grump to the scary Grump, he said,

"I am sure that you have more important things to

do in the casino. Or would you rather work here on the pool deck?"

"Yes, Ah No, I mean, by all means Sir, thanks you sir, I'll leave this situation in your hands Sir" and he escaped.

Grump turned to the gamblers and asked, "Okay I'm in. How much to cover the action so far."

"We were at 2k on each player, so it will cost you Two thousand on whoever you choose."

"Okay", he pulled a wallet from the breast pocket of his coat. He counted out four $1,000.00 bills, "I'll buy an equal interest." He laid down the cash and pulled out more. "And I'll raise another $2,000 on each of them."

Susan offered, "Making you the majority investor over all. And therefore You will make money no matter who wins, right?"

"House privilege", and he smiled. The other gamblers matched his wager.

I shrugged in acceptance and rolled the dice. I moved my eight and landed in Jail. Grump examined the board and asked, "I see four players on the board. What gives?"

I said, "We like to play two characters each so when the time comes to combine forces, either of us can do so with total control."

Grump smiled, "Like match racing."

One gambler offered, "They also start with twice the capital for each player at the beginning." Grump smiled even bigger.

We all surveyed the board as Susan shook the dice in

her hand. She rolled and came up seven. She moved a piece onto a railroad she owned.

Mr. Van Pufflen stated to the manager, "Mr Grant, I would love to stay for the outcome but cannot. Hopefully, I will hear of it." He turned to us all, "By your leave then Mr. Grump, Gentlemen, M'Lady". He bowed to us all and left.

I paid my way out of Jail, rolled the dice, came up with a two and pounced on the only remaining utility. "I'll buy it!" the gamblers conferred.

The Grump said, "Grant? Would you order coffee and a variety of tea for us, say for 7 people?"

Susan put in, "Sorry, you can't do that. Not you darling, you may buy the Water Works. Mr. Grant would certainly know that catered food and drinks are not allowed in the wet areas of the pool deck."

"What's this?" Grump asked. Susan rolled a five and whooped, landing on Free Parking. She scooped up the cash and started counting. I counted with her until I saw at least a thousand.

"I'm afraid she is quite correct sir, a safety hazard in slippery areas, not that it stopped them yesterday, or so I've heard." replied Mr. Grant.

"Grant . . . . ", he asked with his palms up. "Coffee ?"

"Very good sir, and well said." He waddled away while talking to his sleeve.

"What did he mean by that? You got around the rules? How did you get around the rules?" Grump asked.

So we explained as we played, leaving out Roger the

car attendant. Then I rolled a seven which rounded the board and landed in my ghetto hotel on Baltic Ave. "It's mine." I exclaimed and took the $200 for passing Go, and bought a hotel for Tennessee.

Susan rolled and got her 6. Atlantic Ave was the last property unsold and she took it, completing her set. She bought two houses for each property.

Coffee arrived with four servers attending. As everyone joined us in a cuppa, I surveyed the board and declared. "You win."

Suze extends a hand, "Thank you darling, for a wonderful match".

"You're not going to finish?" Grump asked.

"They haven't actually finished one yet." said a gambler. He and Darn Old did a high five and then shared the winnings.

"Damn, well I'm out of here," said another, "Thanks for the coffee and the gaming. I'm gonna teach my kids these rules."

"You see," Susan said, "at a certain point in the game, no matter who rolls what, the outcome is obvious, so why waste time and money, even artificial money, although it is real time."

"You're right of course," Grump stood, "Grant, comp their rooms, and all other services, My thanks for the entertainment, I'm going to call whoever owns Parker Brothers these days," and left with his penguin following.

"Amazing," was all I said as we gathered the various cards to sort them. We collected the play money, the dice, and all of the characters back into the box. But before we began to put away the board, Susan said,

"Let's always record the wins and losses on the game board," We asked for a pen and recorded all 9 games with day and date and a star over the circled initials of the winner.

Later that day, we checked out with Mr. Grant and Mr. Van Pufflen at our service. Grant gave us our bill which discounted all charges to zero attributed as "Consultants". It seems that Mr. Grump had been informed.

We departed with the two executive employees wishing us a safe drive home, and inviting us to return anytime.

As Susan drove I asked, "How much was the car rental?"

"A little over two hundred with membership rates and triple A discounts."

I laughed and asked "How much was the Monopoly set?"

"$9.95 before tax." She replied, and I said,

"As far as I figure, after car, gas, food, tips, and the price of the game against the $400 we won, we came out over $150 dollars ahead."

She laughed, "After two days at Grumps all inclusive luxury suite."

We both laughed as the traffic slowed down to a crawl.

"What happened to the rest of that joint?" she asked.

"Gave it Roger." I said

"Too bad,"

It seems that a helicopter crash happened just beside the Jersey turnpike earlier during the day. There were no survivor's. The passengers were all senior executives with Grump Corp.

"Maybe we should turn around and go back to apply for new jobs."

*

But that's another story. And one I'm not ready to tell. Yet .

(eos)

Maritime Dreams

by

T K Wallace

When I sleep on the water the dreams I have are bigger and better than those I normally dream. They are wider of scope and brighter in color when I sleep on a boat. When you are 'OTB' or 'On The Boat' many things are different. Normal regard for land side conditions are altered regarding aquatic conditions to ensure pleasure and safety.

During childhood my family had access to many water activities. I grew up in the foothills of the Ozark Mountains, so we were close to many creeks, streams, ponds and lakes, smaller and larger rivers. We not only swam and fished, we also paddled canoes and rowed small boats, so water safety was important.

My mother used to tease my sister Lorain and I that we knew how to swim before we could walk, and I think she may have been right. I remember my father holding me afloat on my stomach so I could learn to move my arms and kick my legs. They made sure we were given proper swimming lessons at an early age.

I have some very early memories of family picnic outings at a place called Cool Brook Spring. The fresh spring water coming from underground was so cold that if you were too close to the spring body parts went numb. It was a great place to sink mesh bags full of drinks and fruits we wished to keep cold. It was also a great place to throw children who needed motivation in learning how to swim faster. In the summer time the lakeside was dotted with family clusters having a picnic or grilling, while kids and adults passed the time country style.

Being so close to the Gasconade River we also enjoyed float trips. We would drive up river, splash a couple of canoes in the Gasconade and slowly paddle and along with the current as far as Cooper Hill.

Every now and then while camping out close enough to hear the sounds of flowing water. I would see myself popping out of Cool Brook Spring in a small canoe and being swept along all the way to the Missouri.

I am always delighted to remember these dreams upon waking. They were so rich and satisfying I could recall them for, well, through all the years until now.

My father's first cousin, E. H. built a houseboat on the Lake of the Ozarks. It had been conceived and designed by his youngest son Brian. The house was three stories with boat slips integrated into the lower deck. These slips were open on each end in order to make a 'drive through'. It also enabled us to dock smaller craft behind the boats.

There was always at least one ski boat available. The night before my first ski lesson I had a nightmare about the tow boat hitting a rock and flying into the air as they towed me directly into the rock. I did learn to ski the next day but I have never been comfortable with high speeds on lake waters.

That same summer I joined the Boy Scouts of America and attended my first summer camp. I had decided to go for my Mile Swim and Knots merit badges. When I arrived to inspect the portion of the lake where the swimming test was to be held, I found a small dock of sailing boats. I asked the scout running the docks who got to use the boats. He told me they were, 'Sunfish' and were reserved for the scouts attempting the sailing merit badge. So at the end of two weeks of scout camp, I had three merit badges, a Mile Swim, Knots, and Sailing.

*

In 1968, I was 15 when my parents moved us to Savannah Georgia and for the first time I had an ocean within reach. I also had all the extras that went along with the Atlantic. I had beaches and surfing, I had beach games and southern girls, I had seafood and salt water sailing in tides and currents.

Tybee Island was commonly known as Savannah Beach to the penguins who visited from the mainland. These were the large white bellied tourist creatures that waddled the beaches getting sunburned, and quite often littering.

I was fortunate enough to be introduced to the Intracoastal Waterway and beach cat sailing by two brothers, Carl and Charlie Spader. They had a 16 foot catamaran which they sailed from Tybee Island. They sailed for pleasure and sometimes they raced with the local club. They were delighted that I knew how to sail and could crew for them. In exchange, I began to learn as much as I could about coastal weather and navigation. Learning to properly interpret the wind and water for a successful voyage seemed far more intelligent and satisfying than using a throttle.

The Savannah River has a long entryway from Tybee.

The Port of Savannah offices are a good way from the ocean. The river is wide and deep hosting many business concerns along the Georgia side. The Atlantic Ocean at Tybee has two high and two low tides a day. The current flows all the way up the river at about 2 knots.

The Intracoastal Waterway in Thunderbolt is where US 80 crosses the Wilmington River. Some folks regard Thunderbolt as a speed trap on the highway to the islands. The Thunderbolt fishermen knew where to find the best seafood with the greatest variety. There are many separate docks to walk and talk with local mariners. In addition, Thunderbolt had a very good shipyard.

The islands between Thunderbolt and Tybee were residential mixed with the shrimp and fishing industry. US 80 glides through them all like a twisty marsh way to the ocean. At that time Tybee was a little sleepy Georgia beach town. It was primarily residential with many of the better homes elevated 8-10 feet above ground as flooding was common.

South Beach is where the tourist penguins were usually confined and hopefully contained. All of the big tourist shops were there. They could pay to park within ten feet of the beach, waddle another 30 feet, and be wading in the Atlantic.

The very south end of Tybee has a back river which flows with the tide. A loose group of us liked to surf smaller cats using the back river to get us out beyond the swells. As you sail toward the beach, a swell of water will raise the boat and take you surfing. If you turn in correctly you can ride the face of the swell before it curls.

Now don't get me wrong, Surf boarding is great, challenging, fun, and sometimes dangerous. Surfing a catamaran, is twice all of that, but more due to the fact that you are riding between two long V shaped hulls with rudders.

Smart captains had to read the rise and shape of the swells in order to time their exit into the back river current. This would take us back outside the swells for another ride. Dumb captains ended up getting caught in the break, rolling into a curl, and were capsized, or worse, got pounded into the beach.

North Beach is totally residential with only one public parking lot quite a distance from the beach. The 'beach' is rough terrain, rocks and broken shells, as it is the southern inlet of the Savannah River. The off shore water covers a long flat shoal which is pretty good for cat sailing if you watch out for the bottle nosed Dolphins that feed there at low tide. They were really playful and they respond to music and other tonal vibrations.

Mid Beach is the best, the best surfing, the best sailing, and totally residential. The houses sat back from the beach by 100 yards or so. The space in between was all sand dunes and sea oats. The beach was accessed by the walkways built from street to the beach. The T.C.C.; Tybee Cat Club, was afforded a space in the dunes off of 7th street, as it was close to a member's summer home.

The cats were 12 to 18 feet in length and we used two

wheeled trolleys to roll them to and from the beach. Once in shallow water you rig the sails loose, drop the rudders and push through the surf. About waist deep there is clearance for the rudders, so everybody boards, the sheets of the sails are drawn to catch the wind and take the boat and crew for a sail.

I sailed with Carl and Charlie aboard the 'Sea Nymph', and sailed for many other Captains as fill in crew. I was considered good crew and had a great time.

There were two levels at the club; Crew and Captain. Captains were usually boat owners, the crew members were usually learning to sail. My dilemma was that I could join this sailing club as a Captain from prior experience, but I did not own a boat. We could sail one another's boats with the understanding that if any part of the boat were broken, you were obligated to have it repaired or replaced.

There was one other requirement for a Captain's rating. You had to be able to single hand your vessel on a reasonable voyage. Hilton Head was 10 miles by water. You could see it from Tybee on a clear day. Proof of a successful landing was required in the form of any tourist trade trinket emblazoned with the words, Hilton Head Island.

The brothers Spader ragged on me for months to go solo and even offered me the use for the 'Nymph' to do so. I wanted to qualify as Captain and was about to cave in when my mother, Wanda, was informed by their mother, Gloria, that the pressure was on for me to solo.

Mom asked me if I were intending the attempt. I said that I was thinking about it.

She asked me if I were prepared to replace the 'Nymph', in the case of catastrophe. We both knew I was not prepared. I had little in savings and no real employment. I needed a job.

Carl was a senior at Jenkins High and had a job he planned to give up. He worked as the night driver for a local funeral home known as Stipples. Charlie didn't want the job and so I interviewed and was offered the position during the winter of 69.

The job was simple, I was the afterhours hearse driver. I was on DOA call at Stipples from 6pm until 6am week nights. If a local hospital received a dead on arrival they would inspect and then forward the corpse to a funeral home. When a call came in, I would notify the mortician and take the hearse to retrieve the body. By the time I returned he would be there to receive the corpse and begin the process. I could then go back on duty waiting to be called again.

This job did wonders for my grades at school for I had all the study time I could ever need and little to no social life. The pay was good and slowly built into the amounts I needed. I estimated needing $1,000 to cover the boat, a cheap beach heep to get me back and forth, and maybe buy a surf board to keep at the cat club.

My parents knew of my sailing aspirations but didn't like my job. They knew that I wanted my own car but didn't know I had bought a beach buggy and was still parking it at the Spaders. We were careful to keep up the pretense that the boys and I were always together on the way to and from wherever. At other times I would drive my mother's car like always.

By the spring of 1970 I could show my parents a little over $1,400 in savings and informed them that I intended to attempt the solo test in order to earn my Captain's rating with the club. This is when I started studying my charts and comparing observations in earnest.

I would need to plot the best curve within the tide table. I figured leaving about two hours after low tide would keep me along the coast going over and return me with the incoming current. Other considerations involved consulting a weather professional. My 17 year old 'teenage mind' suggested Captain Sandy.

*

Savannah had a local television show called 'The Weather with Captain Sandy'. It was a segment of the local news featuring a shrimp boat captain who drew the weather on a whiteboard outline of the Georgia coast. He had a stuffed seabird that was lowered into the camera shot carrying the forecast in its beak There was a large clam which opened to give up the tide information. And there was, 'Arthur Mometer' to display the daily, nightly, and upcoming temperatures.

A newsman turned meteorologist, Joe Cox, played Captain Sandy. He was known to favor a certain bar in Thunderbolt at about 8pm after the show was over. So, I took my charts and lists to, Teeple's, and waited for the captain to arrive.

I was asked by the bartender what was up with all the stuff and I told him I intended to ask Captain Sandy advice on a sail boat crossing. He scoffed and told me that Joe was not a shrimper, he just played one on TV. The bartender suggested that if I wanted some good advice I should go to the far end of the bar to the Oyster station and buy a round for the old gent sitting there.

The old gent happened to be Willie Teeple, a local shrimp boat captain, and owner of the bar. I asked his permission to buy a round in exchange for some advice. He accepted. I could only have oysters and iced tea as I was 17 at the time.

After the first tastes were over, I started with the words, "Sir, I'm a sailor". He put up a hand and said, "What's yer destination?"

"Hilton Head and back."

"Tybee Cat Club ?"

"Yes Sir."

"So you want to be a sail boat captain? What they call a skipper?"

"Yes Sir, how did you know?"

"'cause that's their solo course."

"Yes Sir, I uh, I have done my homework, if I could ask your opinion . . ."

"Let's see what you got, lay it out here . ."

And so I laid out my chart as a bottom layer, took out the speed, time, and distance equations, and my calculations for hull speed. He examined each and asked questions, his questions prompted questions of my own and back and forth we went. Sometime during the discussion a guy walked over to say hello to Mr. Teeple. I looked up to see and be greeted by Joe Cox out of costume. They exchanged pleasantries and small talk. Mr Cox looked at the prep work, smiled and stated that I was in good hands.

Mr Teeple confirmed all of my homework and asked me what I was missing. I looked down and shook my head. So he asked me how determine when an onshore breeze would be guaranteed at the speed and the duration I needed. I must have looked determined as I considered the best answer. 'Maybe look for a weather front so I could sail the wind forward of the front as it built.'

He smiled, asked, " You like to surf ?" I could only smile, nod yes.

*

I watched Captain Sandy for another week or so before I saw the front I wanted. There was a warm front pushing up from Florida about three days in front of a tropical storm. I decided that a few hours after low tide a day and a half from then was perfect, and started making arrangements.

The night before my departure I had a dream or three.

I dreamed that I was sailing across the Savannah River shipping lane when a dense fog set in and calmed all wind. I sat there with sails luffing when I heard a fog horn blow in the distance. I looked at my watch and waited 60 seconds and heard the horn again only closer. I was in the path of a freighter who could not see my little sail boat. The next time I heard the horn it was right on top of me, as the hull emerged from the fog I dove away from the 'Nymph' as she was crushed.

I clawed awake drenched from fear rather than salt water. It took me some time to get back to sleep. This time I dreamt that I was in high winds and in peril from the seas pushing me onto the rocks of Bloody Point off the south end of Dufuskie Island. Every time I tried to tack and go further out to gain distance from the shoreline the wind would not allow me to steer up high enough to come about. I felt the hull strike something and was thrown from the deck.

I awoke wet again from more fear sweat. I had soaked the sheets and fallen out of bed. As I sat there shaking I remembered that it was all a dream. So I got up and took a shower. As I stood in the shower surrounded by cascading steams of water I began to wonder why I was doing all this, and what desperate need made me pursue this course of action. I stepped from the shower to dry myself and slumped against the headboard of my bed only to dream again.

I was sailing with HHI in sight when the boat was picked up by a swell which began moving me rapidly forward. The swell lifted the stern of the boat and plowed the pontoons into the swell in front of me. The front of the pontoons dug into the water and the boat began pitch over forward. I jumped clear and when I came out of the water I saw the 'Nymph' on her side waiting to be righted. I knew how to do this. I swam under the boat to make sure that all of the sails were released. Then I located the righting line and threw it over the top pontoon. I stood on the bottom pontoon and with the righting line in hand leaned back to pull the top pontoon over toward me. With a big splash the boat was righted. I was swimming to climb aboard when the main sheet assembly hooked around the edge of the tramp frame, the main sail took wind and the 'Nymph' sailed away out of my reach with her deck empty.

This time I woke up yelling, " No. No, No," I shook the vision from my head and slouched back again. I looked out the window and saw faint light. I looked at my watch and found two hours left until departure. It was low tide in more than one way, it was time to get going and I had none of the rest I needed.

I realized that it was a weekday and I could not use my mother's car, she needed it for work. My father's car was never a part of the equation. And hey, let's face it, I might not make it back. So I decided to hitch hike.

I walked away from my parents place in Magnolia Park with a heavy heart. As I got to Skidaway Road I heard the horn of a VW beetle. I stopped and turned only to be closely missed by Charlie driving my buggy. He opened the door and as I got in he hit the gas slamming the door for me. We sped away toward Thunderbolt and Tybee. It was 6:00 am.

*

When we got to Butler St we parked on 8th and walked to the boat lot. We were alone and quiet as we rolled the Nymph into the shallow surf. I rigged the main as Charlie rigged the jib. I took out my wallet and withdrew the check. As I handed it to him, I said, "Hold onto this in case I want it back." He took it and put it in his shirt pocket and said, "Probably bounce anyway," and pushed me off.

I jumped aboard and drew the main sheet to capture the breeze. The warm air was colliding with cool air coming from the land. I steered the cat north and headed directly for Dufuskie Island. As got into the shipping lane the onshore breeze lessened and the cat slowed. I was so focused on defining the wind and water I did not hear the vessel slowly approaching. First I knew of her proximity was the sound of a boat horn close by. I whipped around to see a shrimp boat crossomg my stern. Then I heard one horn meaning the boat was going to pass me on the right, starboard, leaving my vessel to port, or its left side.

I looked closer and saw Mr. Teeple hanging out of the window at the bridge. He waved and laughed as he accelerated sending a good sized wave toward the Nymph. That wave pushed me through the rest of the doldrums and I caught a fresh breeze on the outside of the shipping lane.

As I sailed toward the coast of Dufuskie I could hear the waves crashing the rocks and remembered part of a dream. I tried to tack out to starboard but found too little wind to counter the waves and got pushed back toward the rocks. Instead of trying this again I swung the tiller to starboard and did a 270 degree gibe, turned the stern through the wind and headed back toward the channel. At the channel I felt the current pull me further out to sea.

When I was a safe distance from Dufuskie I tacked over to a starboard run and made my course directly for the channel between the two islands. As I approached the channel narrowed and the depth must have lessened for I felt my boat speed increase. I realized that I was entering a funnel of rapid water known as a 'race'. I felt a swell lift the stern of the cat and point bow down as the cat was pushed forward. As I swung the tiller to port the cat turned 20-25 degrees and I glided along the face of the swell, surfing the boat. After surfing for an eternity, which was probably about 20 or 30 seconds, the Nymph outran the rising build.

I continued on course for the southern end of Hilton Head and the docks at Sea Pines. It was 8:30 am when I docked and tied up. The dock master office was closed with a sign indicating they would open at 9:00am. I sat on the bench and wondered where to get the needed trinket.

Someone was running down the dock yelling that I couldn't dock here unless I lived here. I turned to see Charlie Spader striding toward me with a white sailor's hat in his hand. I stood, hugged him in greeting and he handed me the hat. I turned the hat to read ' I Sailed Hilton Head Island ' stitched into the front face.

I checked my watch and saw it was 8:50. Charlie pointed to the sign for docking fees 'Pick Up and Drop Off, $5.00 per foot' We raised our eyebrows and ran back to the cat. As I jumped to the tramp deck Charlie tossed my lines and I was away by 8:55. I looked back and saw a dock master speaking with Charlie. Charlie looked at his watch and walked away with the guy following while Charlie waved goodbye.

I set a course of thirty degrees, just offshore of Tybee due to the time of tide and the current which was now beginning to run. I knew the current would 'set' the vessel to the east as I was gently pushed that direction despite my course.

As I got to the channel the current pushed me harder and I adjusted my course to further off shore. By the time I was in the middle of the shipping lane the Cat was crab walking at 45 degrees just barely sailing toward the long jetty line of the North Beach. Before I left the shipping lane behind I decided to get further away to clear the jetty, so I let the current push me further out.

My course felt solid. I could let go of the tiller handle and they boat stayed on it's heading. When a cat is in sync with the surrounding conditions, the rigging begins to vibrate and starts to sing. As this was happening I saw a bottle nosed Dolphin emerge beside my starboard pontoon and gave a head bump to port.

I slapped the side of the cat twice and tacked to port,

ran for about two minutes and tacked back to starboard, and took a look at the shore line. I repeated this maneuver twice and brought my vessel far enough out to skirt the jetty line.

I smiled when I thought of Charlie tearing up the buggy miles between Tybee and Hilton Head only to tear it up again on the way back. I smiled hoping I would get there first. I didn't, he and half of the Cat Club were on the beach waiting for me to navigate the beach break and glide the Nymph onto Tybee sand.

As two crew persons rolled the boat into the dunes, Charlie withdrew the check from his pocket and handed it to me. I tore it through three ways and threw it to the wind.

We grabbed our boards and went surfing.

Later, as I sat in the swells waiting for the right rise to form, I thought of the solo journey again and realized that the dreams of the night before were me helping myself, 'see' the correct course of action when needed.

For the first time in my life I felt a balance of wind and water, of sailing and surfing, and understood the need for Maritime Dreams.

Somethin' from Nothin'

by

T K Wallace

You never can tell from which direction opportunity is approaching. It's not like the weather, as if we've mastered prediction there, opportunity is most often, stumbled upon, and sometimes recognized for actual value.

Stan didn't know diamonds from diphthongs the day he and his partner Jamie encountered this particular opportunity. They were cleaning out a basement room for a real estate client. His client wanted to make a play space for her daughter and the space needed to be renovated.

Sunita was a venture capital investor who believed in making every asset pay at least three ways. She had purchased a five story brownstone on the east side and had given Stan and Jamie the renovation contract.

The first thing S & J did was to gut the street level storefront in preparation for Sunita finding a new tenant. The second and third level were to be living quarters for mother and daughter. The forth and fifth floors had 2 apartments each, all four of which were occupied, and covered most costs.`

The previous street level commercial tenant was a travel agent who had no need for the basement space. The tenant before that had been a small time print shop and had used the basement and left quite a lot of printing crap behind when they closed shop some twenty years before. Everything on the main floor had been taken away but the basement remained cluttered.

Sunita and Siri could access the basement from the back yard, but she was not pleased with the condition of the basement and asked S & J to excavate. Being a naturally curious child Siri was interested in what was left down below in the basement. So, her mother allowed her to observe the excavation team.

They found many reams of paper, dozens of front and back hard covers empty of unpublished books. And they found a medium sized printing press which had to be dismantled before removed. They found inks and dyes by the barrel full, and hundreds of letter sets for printing, all of which had to go.

When the project began Stan had evaluated the basement and delayed the beginning work until they could dedicate all hands to the job. But, the day finally came when he and Jamie opened the gate barring the street side entrance. Sunita came along with Siri in hand to gues-timate the amount of work to be done.

Stan led with a flashlight searching for a switch. Jamie followed carrying her own light, and headed all the way through to the back steps. Stan found a switch and one bulb came on. Jamie opened the back doors and more light entered.

The space was large with several rooms and mounds of discarded printing crap everywhere. Stan had a deli shopping bag with several new light bulbs inside. He and Jamie walked about finding empty light sockets and eventually the entire basement was illuminated. Sunita and Siri were eagerly looking beyond the present and laying the place out in their imaginations.

Stan and Jamie were stuck with the present state of things. They would make lists of the work to be done and started imagining the hours to come. They would need at least two dumpsters on the street to off load what they saw. The first one could be filled with all of smaller stuff like paper and bindings. The second dumpster must be larger for things like the printing press, rack sets, inks, and dyes.

There are so many things in New York City that have their own distinctive form. Renting, filling, and removing a street side trash dumpster is one of them. You never have the container delivered before you fill it, or your neighbors and the neighborhood will fill it for you. Sunita didn't believe me when I explained this fact, so she had the dumpster delivered on Saturday, by Monday it was full.

The excavation work down below had started on Monday and the dumpster was replaced early Tuesday morning. At the point of arrival Sunita posted one of my workers outside to turn away would be depositors. We filled the container three quarters full by the middle of the first day, and left the rest to the neighbors.

Which, of course, the neighborhood filled. Then, the whole dumpster got picked over, which left trash all over the sidewalk. But, such is life in the city, someone's trash is someone else's treasure.

Early the following day the dumpster.com had the full one carted away and the empty one left behind. Sunita added some cleaning people to do the sidewalk. Stan added some manpower to cover the heavy hauling of the printing press.

Sunita and Siri would get two rooms each if they left

some of the walls where they were. So it took about two minutes to designate which walls should be removed. And by the end of day two the basement framing was down to a barren state.

Then came the ceiling, and Oy Vey, what a mess, 40 year old asbestos insulation. This took the rest of day three, most of day four, and another large dumpster to be filled on day five. At the end of day five, the sanitizing crew arrived and worked into the night. Sunita's concept of building out began by creating on a blank canvas.

When the crew finished cleaning the floor behind the front steps, they discovered an old wooden hatch door fitted with a lifting ring. The workers didn't open the hatch, but they informed Stan, Jamie, and Sunita of its existence.

The next morning was the beginning of the build out. They put the crew to work at the back steps studding the walls for new sheet rock. Suni, Siri, Jamie, and Stan stood at the front looking at the trap door. Stan asked if Suni knew the place had a sub-basement. Suni did not know and Siri got seriously wide eyed when she asked what Stan thought could be down there.

Stan did not want to open the hatch. He claimed to have opened one before and what they found cost the owner several more weeks of work. The sub basement had been half full of rancid fuel oil. By city codes, it had to be removed and a proper cleanup performed and then inspected, at the owner's cost.

It was Jamie the fearless who bent over and pulled

the hatch door open. Nothing scary or crazy happened, just some musty air on a faint breeze blew out some dust. There were no steps as the lower floor was only a few feet away. It was more of a crawl space that was partially filled with a few large bags and a palette holding some large half printed sheets of paper.

Sunita lowered herself, drew out a sheet and brought it up. Upon inspection they found it resembled money. The sheet had unfinished currency bills that were uncut. The paper / fabric looked perfect. The bills were beautifully engraved with proper coloring. But, they had no president's picture in the middle, the space was blank. Unfortunately, the corners of each uncut bill read $200.00.

They all laughed at the mistake and discussed the IQ of common counterfeiters. Jamie let herself down and threw out the bags. Two were large but light, and one was small but quite heavy. The small one held four printing plates. The larger bags were full of finished bills, each with Ben Franklin's picture and wrapped with a label which read $10,000. The group withdrew the money and stacked them to count 100 wrapped packets per bag. They had found over 2 million dollars in bogus $200 dollar currency.

Siri was delighted and proclaimed their new found wealth. Sunita laughed and explained to her daughter that the bills were useless and worth nothing. Siri had no way of knowing there was no such thing as a $200 bill in US currency and insisted to her mother that the bills must be worth something. Jamie pulled out a $10 dollar bill to show Siri the picture of Alexander Hamilton on the front.

They quickly gathered the counterfeit money and plates back into the bags and took it all upstairs to the family home for further contemplation. They made and shared lunch. Stan or Jamie occasionally disappeared to direct the workers throughout the rest of the day. As the discussion continued they found themselves divided at two points of view.

The conservative point of view was held by Sunita and Stan. They agreed that the entire mess be turned over to the U. S. Treasury. The opportunistic point of view was held by Siri and Jamie. They agreed that the entire mess was a gold mine, waiting for the right miner.

The work down below was progressing too slowly without constant supervision so Stan cut the crew and Jamie scheduled the next day's workers. They decided the work going on up above was more important than the work going on down below. They needed to figure out what to do with the contraband before they were arrested for possession.

The group of four ordered out for there was good Indian food in that neighborhood. Sunita was a good Indian mother who encouraged her daughter in every way she could. So, she asked Siri what she thought should be done with the un finished bills.

Siri acknowledged that the bills should first have a president placed in the middle. Sunita shot a digital photo of the front of the bill and we viewed it from photo shop.

Jamie opened up a lap top and pulled up presidential portraits; starting with Theodore Roosevelt. She copied, pasted, and e-mailed it to Sunita.

Siri liked that one so Sunita posted it on the wall. He looked comical with Teddy's gap toothed grin under that famous mustache. The next one Siri liked was Nixon, but everybody agreed that he looked too sinister. The last one Siri liked was a man she had actually seen in office, President Barak Obama.

Suni thought Obama's photo looked good for cut and paste, but lacked the professionally quality of an engraved image. Comparing the fake and the real, even Siri was forced to admit the fake one would be spotted immediately.

Suni explained the penalties of any attempt to pass counterfeit currency. Siri was distressed at the thought of her mother being arrested and taken away for a long time. She looked at the bills and plates, then she looked at the sheets.

The uncut sheets were only printed on the front. The back was blank.

Stan had been on Jamie's laptop for some time when they heard him whistle long and slow. He turned the screen toward the group to show the webpage of the Department of Treasury.

"It says here that there is a reward for helping stop counterfeiting."

"Is that what we've done?"

"I'd say so, we have 2 million in bogus bills and the printing plates."

"What's the reward?"

"Not sure, it seems to be scalable, but it looks like it starts at $100,000."

That caused high fives all around. "That's not so shabby, who do we call?"

"I'm looking for that."

The following morning the workers arrived to find Suni, Stan, and Jamie speaking with two federal agents. The discussion was taking place in the ground floor storefront. Jamie split off to direct the workers in finishing the stud work around the perimeter of the basement rooms.

The agents and others were standing looking at a finished $200 bill.

Sunita tries the truth, " We didn't know what to think, so we thought we would call you guys."

Agent 1 says," It's obviously a fake, where did you say you found it?"

"The workers found it during our renovation."

"Did they find any more?"

"We understand there is a reward for helping to stop counterfeiting."

"That's true, but finding one bill is hardly a help to stop counterfeiting."

"I suppose that's true."

Agent 2 says, " Okay, let's get down to it, Where's the rest?"

"Safe."

Agent 1 says, " I thought you said they didn't find any more."

"They didn't, we did."

"How many more of these did you find?"

Stan pulled out a smart phone and began to work the key board but, Suni spoke out before he could complete.

Sunita says," 10,000, maybe more."

The agents looked at one another, one whistled, the other pushed his hat back and sat on a vacant desk.

"That would be 2 million dollars of worthless currency. Where is it?"

"Safe."

Agent 2 says, " That would constitute possession."

Stan says, " Not while you're here. We are trying to do the right thing."

Agent 1 asks, " You wish to turn it all in?"

"Yes sir, and also request a reward."

Agent 2 barks, " So where is the rest?"

Jamie says, " You're sitting on it. The bags are under your ass."

Agent 1 drew out a gun, the other agent stood and backed away from the desk as if it were armed. Stan reached under the desk and drew out two bags. He put them on top of the desk and opened one for the agents to see inside.

Agent 1 examines a stack of bogus bills, " Well, take me home to die,"

Stan and Suni looked at each other. " Cause I've seen everything now."

Agent 1 asks, " You know that one?" Stan and Suni laugh as Jamie returns.

"What's so funny?"

"American colloquial wit and wisdom."

Suni says, " We've given it all over. Do we get a reward?"

Agent 2 says, " Maybe, it's a good start,"

Jamie stops, " What guarantees do we have letting you two walk out of here leaving us with no proof that this conversation ever took place."

"Take my card and let me keep this one bill, it's useless, no way to pass it."

Agent 1 asks, " Where did you find this?"

Stan says, " In a subbasement crawl space."

"Can we see the space?"

"Sure but it's empty now."

The three took the two downstairs via the front entrance.

As they all entered the workers stopped to watch. Jamie directed.

"You guys take a break, go out the back and wait outside until I come."

Stan informs, " The hatch is behind the front stairs, right there."

Agent 1 asks, " You the owner?"

Jamie says, " She is,"

"May we see some Identification?"

Sunita rebuffs, " I called you, remember? You're becoming tedious."

"We get that a lot, You two are the renovators, May I see some ID?"

Agent # 2 opened the hatch and pulled out a miniature torch. He bent down and looked around 360 before rising.

"Empty but it goes pretty far in every direction but the street."

Agent # 1 scans the ID's. Agent # 2 closes the hatch.

"We're going to want and search the rest of that space."

Stan asks, " Will it interfere with our work?"

"Not unless you're renovating down there."

Jamie says, " Can we move this outside? I got a team on the clock."

"May we see the rest of the property?"

Suni offers," Yes, we can talk in the garden. Just watch your step, this way."

Stan says to Jamie, " Send 'em in. Pull crew as needed to finish that long wall today. We'll be out back."

They all exited into a landscaping site. The turf was churned and overturned in all directions, although there was a path down the center.

"Is this part of the renovation? Or were you looking for something?"

Sunita states, " It's part of the renovation. The storefront doesn't have this space. Our home is on two and three up there."

Agent 1 says, " okay, you're up there . ."

Jamie says, " When this is done, there will be a

staircase on each side to down come here, which, I can tell, doesn't interest you in the least, does it."

Agent 2 says, " What?"

Suni says " You asked if I were looking for something, what did you mean ?"

Agent 1 explains, " We thought you may have torn up all this to find something. Something else left behind by the printers."

"No, this was only done a few weeks ago, what do you think was here?"

"That's kind of a long answer and classified under order of investigation."

"We'll take the short answer."

Agent 2 says, " You said you threw away a printing press."

Stan says, " Three days ago, in the second haul out.'

"What company?"

"On the printing press?"

"No, on the dumpster."

Suni says, " Oh, Simalchalchi. I have the receipts, they're bonded."

Agent 1 says, " We'll look 'em up. How many loads from here?"

"Three, and a hiccup on the first day, so I guess that's four."

Agent 2 laughs and says to Stan and Jamie.

"Let me guess, you had the dumpster delivered the day before."

"Guilty," says, Jamie, " You know midtown north. The neighbors fill it up for you."

Agent 1 says, " Home turf. So folks, Okay you threw the press away. And you threw away all, reading here, '. . .all the leftover crap from that business."

Stan answers, " Yeah, all of it. She wanted a complete clean out down there, and if she hadn't we would never have discovered the bags."

Agent # 2 nods and paces, he scratches his temples and breathes in and out twice.

"Ms, Kishner-"

"Krishnamurti, Sunita. Krishnamurti. Ms K. will do."

"What we usually find at a scene like this, where currency is recovered and obviously where a printing press has been. Printing usually has test runs, like trials to see if colors are right, or to see if the bills look good; you see?"

Suni says, " Not really but, okay if you say so."

Agent 1 says, " All that is important, but not as important as the plates."

Suni asks, " The plates?"

"Yes Mam, the printing plates for the currency."

Sunita ponders, " Okay, the plates."

"Ms K, have you or any part of your team found any plates?"

She admits, " Well, yes, at least I suppose so, maybe."

He smiles, " I would be able to tell you for sure, if I could see them."

Agent #2 accuses, " Where are they? Have you hidden them?"

Jamie says, " I'm not sure I like your attitude mister. Bad manners don't improve things. Bad manners just speak for themselves. They reflect true character."

Stan adds, " Yeah, behave yourself, Fed boy. Or out with you."

Agent 1 says, " Bruce? Sit down and shut up."

"Yes Sir."

"My apologies Ms. Krishnamurti."

"Well said, I accept; agent Poppadopalus." She smiles and Stan asks.

"Well said, back 'atcha. Say, what's yer Starbucks name?"

"Oh, like when they ask your name? I tell them Jane."

"I use Ted." The three laugh, Bruce looks thoughtful.

"So tell me Jane. Do you have the plates?"

Bruce forces, " What have you done with them?"

"I, well I gave them away." She smiles at Ted

Bruce needs to vent, " Oh, shit, here we go."

"Shut Up Bruce, You know I hate repeating myself."

Jamie adds, " Yeah shut it Mr. Manners."

"Please, young lady? Don't tease him he only gets worse."

Bruce asks, " You gave them away. Why would you do that?"

"Well, they're contraband aren't they? Or some sort of illegal property?"

Ted assures, " They most certainly are."

Jamie says, " Then why would we want them around here?"

Bruce recovers, " Do you know where they are just now?"

Suni asks, " Maybe, would it help with the reward?"

Ted says, " Almost guaranteed to help."

"Okay yes, I probably know where they are." She smiles and waits.

"You are a breath of cool fresh air. Where are the plates?"

"You have them. There are two very well padded in each bag."

The four of them file into the storefront. Agent Bruce digs to the bottom of one bag and hands a small bundle to Agent Ted. He weighs the bundle by raising and lowering it and puts it back in the bag. Bruce pulls the other out, does the same weight test and puts it back.

Suni asks, " Don't you want to see them?"

Ted says, " Yes, but I don't want to touch them. Did you touch them?"

"Yes, we all did, they're quite beautiful. Did you know?"

"I thought the bag was heavy, for money."

"Good, then you were not deceived. When you asked, you got them."

"No worries, we should go report all this. Thanks for your amusing co-operation. You'll hear from us.", and they left.

*

During the next few days a team of investigators came

by to crawl through the space. No one found anything more. The renovation continued for a couple more weeks. The day after the painters finally left, they threw a small party.

Sunita had a new home office with a sleeping couch and entertainment area. She said it felt like a good space since it was close to her daughter's.

Siri had a large play space she could move things around to suit her games. She insisted on choosing the wall and ceiling colors. The ceiling was a blue sky blue which came down three walls and changed into light and darker greens which stopped at the chair rail. From the chair rail down was tan to medium brown. Except for the end wall. That wall had a computer and special wallpaper.

*

On the day Agent 1 returned, Suni received him in the family residence.

Agent Ted said, " Thanks to you, this is an ongoing investigation."

Suni exclaims," Really."

Bruce said, " We found the press and all the gak you had thrown away. It turned up some thirty year old clues, which turned up some more clues. City records gave us names of the print shop owners."

"Amazing."

Ted asks, " Are your renovation people here today?"

"Yes they are, why do you ask?"

"Am I correct that you wished to share any reward with them?"

"Quite right again, they're downstairs installing a ceiling fan."

They all went out the back door of the second floor kitchen, down some stairs into a fresh dirt garden, and then down a ramp and through the rear doors of the basement.

"Stan? Jamie? Stop what you're doing and come on out, The Law is here."

Siri comes running around the edge of her space with a camera. She points it at Ted and shoots an instant photo which rolls out the front.

"Siri, that is impolite without asking, please apologize to agent Ted."

"Sorry agent Ted. I'm being a photographer today, Do you mind?"

Stan and Jamie join them and shake hands. Ted says to Siri,

"May I see that?" She hands it over, " Yep that's me, Here, I don't mind."

"So, what brings you by, anything new or newsworthy?"

"Yeah, some, foot work really, thirty year old footwork. Is this your new space Ms K ? This is nice, nice fan too, always prefer fans to AC."

"Thank you, fans are better, and I like to be on the same level as Siri."

"It's good you were here. I have a thing for you."

He draws an envelope from his breast pocket and gives it to Sunita.

"I hope that's a reward."

"It is. I'm afraid it's little more than minimum, this is a very cold case."

Bruce says, " No useable evidence, those morons, it's no wonder they tried to hide their mistakes, they weren't even smart enough to burn it all."

"Wow, thanks." Suni turns to Stan and hands him the check.

"Wow." Stan hands it to Jamie

Suni asks, " Will you two accept half of that figure?"

Jamie looks at Stan, they nod. " You bet." She hands the check back to Suni.

Ted says, " I hope it will come in handy, just don't forget to pay taxes on it."

They all laugh and more hands are shaken while some hugs are exchanged

Siri rounds the corner with her camera looking for a subject and says,

"You guys look happy."

"Agent T brought us a reward for finding the fake money."

"Actually the reward was given for turning over everything you found to us, so we could follow the investigation through, and maybe find the bad guys."

Siri looks at her mother. Suni folds the check into her shirt pocket.

"Would you like to see Siri's play space? Siri? Is the gallery open?"

"Nope, the paste is drying, come in agent T." She takes his hand.

"Wow, now this a play space, you have project spaces, and computer spaces. Nice screen. What's behind that low curtain?"

"That's the gallery, and you're in it now."

Siri pulled the draw cord and the drapes parted to reveal a wallpaper. There were a dozen sheets of uncut $200.00 bills. Only a few had faces in the face spaces. Agent T was the last face filled. He smiled with amusement as he examined the paper closely.

"Photo Shop?" He asked.

Suni says, "Nope. These are, the unfinished sheets you left behind."

"Huh, The things you learn . . . Well thanks folks, we'll be in touch."

Suni walks agent T to the front steps, shakes his hand, and she hugs him. She walks back and pulls out the check.

"Something from Nothing." She hands the check to Siri who reads a US Treasury Department check for $140,000.00. Siri looks at the others and smiles. Then she asks,

"May I take a picture of this?"

(eos)

About the Author

T K Wallace has written stories, songs, and poetry for most of his life. Creative fiction has always been a passion. He would like to share these seven short sagas with you.

Printed in the United States
By Bookmasters